THE WILD CARD

THE TAROT LEGACIES
BOOK 2

VICTORIA BELUE

For Sheryl Lew Sterrett
and Mother Margaret

CHAPTER 1

Vesta stared at the casket sinking into the ground, a silent spectacle except for the rasping squeak of the crank at every turn. Such a pathetic noise, but at least something felt despair. The assembled group of mourners stood motionless. No tears or anger. Nothing. What a bunch of zombies they must all look like standing there as Uncle Raymond's remains slid into the dirt. He deserved better. Vesta turned her back on the scene and walked toward the row of black limousines and their waiting drivers. She aimed for a handsome and fit young man whose dark skin against his white shirt collar made him even more appealing.

"Do you smoke?" She asked.

"No." He wrinkled his nose.

"What? Is it a crime now to smoke?"

"Here you go lady." An older grizzled gray-haired man standing at the next limo pulled a cigarette from his jacket pocket as he approached. He handed it to her.

"Thanks."

He opened his jacket again releasing the scent of stale smoke and fresh tobacco. Vesta inhaled slowly with appreciation.

Fingers rimmed with pale brown stains pulled out a lighter and lit her cigarette. She took a long drag, exhaled and leaned against the limo, her stiletto heels digging into the loose gravel, her gaze drifting toward the gravesite.

"Your father?" The old man asked.

"No. My uncle. But he was like a father." Vesta took another deep drag and flicked her cigarette. "Better actually."

The throng of black silhouettes gathered by the grave dispersed as the casket disappeared into the earth. Five figures moved further away from Vesta and clustered by a tree, their heads leaning in toward each other. A murder of crows. That's what they looked like hunched together in their long black coats, hats pulled down to keep the chilling wind off their faces. She strained to catch some of the conversation but the wind tore it away.

"When did you start smoking again?" Sandor asked as he walked up beside her. She glanced at him in his tailored black Ralph Lauren suit with his dark hair and eyebrows framing his sky-blue eyes.

"When my life became fucked."

"Whoa," he said looking at the limo drivers who pretended not to hear. "You kiss your uncle with that mouth?"

He took the cigarette from Vesta's hand, took a long drag then ground it into the gravel with the sole of his black leather Italian shoe.

"Where did you come from?"

"I was in one of the cars doing business."

"Picked up a little tart at Uncle Raymond's funeral?" Vesta nodded. "That's classy. Is that part of what they taught you in your fancy Wall Street school?"

"Hey, you're not taking care of me in this life. You're not my wife or girlfriend. What's a rich and powerful hedge fund manager supposed to do to relax?"

"I really don't care. And how I married you in any previous life is far beyond what I could ever hope to understand. You must be the Magician in the tarot cards because it would take some damned good hocus pocus for you to ever get me in bed again."

"You liked the first, second and as I recall, third time we did it that night in Davos."

"I was drunk. Like I wish I was now."

"You didn't really think that first limo driver had a cigarette, with the body he's got. You were trying to do the same thing I did. I just have better skills."

"I don't care about your skills, or what you think you know Sandor."

Pinpoints of drizzle began an assault from the sky. Vesta felt them hit her face.

"You're getting wet out here. Why don't you get in the car?" Sandor opened a door.

Vesta ignored his question and walked toward the grave. The human crows took flight as if they could sense her approach. They headed toward their warm, dry limousines to be whisked away to the Plaza for the after party, or whatever they were calling it. The drizzle increased. Vesta looked down at her black Armani jacket and skirt. Beads of cold rain dotted the lightweight wool. She grabbed an umbrella leaning against a chair and popped it open. Stepping to the edge of the deep rectangular opening in the earth she took in the grim sight. The coffin echoed the color of the postmortem sky. The only movement she could see came from the icy straight pins striking a random pattern in the gaping hole. This was no doubt a done deal.

"Was it my fault?" She whispered to herself.

She felt the sting of a salty tear well up in her eye.

"Did I cause this to happen? I didn't understand. I tried to stop it."

Rage burned inside her. She felt heat blast up her legs and out the top of her head. Raz let his stooge loose with a gun. Sandor, Jared and Amara knew what was going on. They could have prevented it. They could have stopped him, or at least told her what she needed to do. Vesta clenched her fists and lifted her face to the sky so the icy drizzle pelted her. Maybe the frozen shards would prick her skin, bring some physical pain, some relief. She prayed they would but they didn't.

Looking down at the wet earth she told herself she was meant to feel this pain. It was part of the penance for casting the spell to forget who she really was in this life. Uncle Raymond told her the truth in his final breaths. Then it was too late. When the spell was broken, she remembered she was the High Priestess of the ancient tarot cards who reincarnated as the same person life after life. But no concrete memories of her past lives emerged. Just snippets here and there at odd moments.

His death didn't have to happen. The other tarot members, the self-aggrandized trionfi, shouldn't have waited to tell her. Now Uncle Raymond was dead and here she was, standing at his grave without a clue what to do next in her newfound role as a supernaturally imbued protector of humankind, a job she didn't want. All she knew for certain that she did want at the moment was a very cold vodka martini.

VESTA'S HANDS tightened into fists as she entered the Grand Ballroom at the Plaza Hotel. It felt like a rock dropped into the pit of her stomach as she looked around the room. Uncle Raymond loved to stay there while in New York. He adored the old-world atmosphere and had recounted many party memories from the hotel to her over the years. Vesta hung on every word of those stories with his vivid details, humorous sidebars and colorful characters. His wry wit never failed to make her laugh out loud. Being in that room for any length of time would require all her strength.

After a quick scan of the layout she located the closest bar and headed straight for it ignoring the many people who tried to greet her. She smiled at the bartender like he was her oldest and dearest friend.

"Madame, what can I pour for you today?"

"Vodka martini with a twist and very cold. Do you have something Russian?"

"Yes, ma'am. I do."

Moments later a sparkling glass filled with her sanity slid before her. There was no way she could utter another word until she got some grounding back in her body. Her soul was still lost but she would worry about that later. She took a sip and sighed.

Vesta turned from the bar to face the crowd. Amara made eye contact from across the room and began her approach with a well-practiced look of concern stapled on her face. Grabbing her cocktail, Vesta drained the glass in one swallow and set it down on the bar. She could feel the muscle in her jaw relax.

Amara extended her long slender arms for an embrace as she reached the bar. Vesta saw it coming and guided Amara's arms toward the floor, leaning in with a quick air kiss to her cheek instead. A mild disapproving look crossed Amara's face.

"Have you received my phone calls? I've reached out to you so many times. We need to talk," Amara said.

"I got them."

Vesta motioned to the bartender for another drink, pulled a twenty-dollar bill from her black Chanel clutch and slid it under her empty glass.

"You must have a thousand questions and I want to answer

them all." Amara spoke with slow deliberate words like Vesta was a confused six-year-old. She mouthed each word precisely and insisted on shining her bright blue eyes into Vesta's. That expression, smacking of sincerity and authority, helpfulness and superiority, Vesta had known for so long. Sometimes, like right then, she wanted to pinch her just to see if she could rock her from that lofty perch. Maybe cause her to lose that clenched eye connection and smug tone of her voice. Instead Vesta pretended to smile.

"Sandor talked non-stop on the flight home about our little group, the trionfi. I know how we all had to go into hiding or be burned at the stake. So, I'm good."

"Did he explain that Raymond knew that was how his life would end this time, at the castle in Spain?"

Vesta's eye twitched. "Yes. He did."

Amara, with the golden ringlets spilling over her shoulders onto the simple black Calvin Klein dress, was pissing Vesta off. How dare she speak in such a casual way about her beloved uncle. No expression of anger or horror came from her voice even though a gun had been jabbed against Uncle Raymond's ribs by one of Raz's henchmen and fired at point blank range.

"You really shouldn't blame yourself." Amara kept talking. "It was part of Raymond's plan to stop Rasputin from prostituting those young girls. And he did. But without him alive the rest of the trionfi need for you to be aware of your InSight to tell us what's hidden from us and what's to come."

"So you can stop the evil doers?" Vesta smirked. "Well, my InSight, as you call it, isn't working. Since the big reveal of who I really am, my little buzzing spot on my forehead has all but stopped." Vesta rubbed the space between her eyebrows. "I don't know if it works anymore. And I have no idea how to call up the hidden information you're talking about."

"It will take some time. You cast one heck of a spell on yourself. But I can help you remember. Although I'm not sure all of your memories will return. Plus, you need to learn how to control your InSight as it reboots."

"I'm not ready to think about that right now." Vesta looked down at her martini.

"Did Sandor tell you who the rest of us are? How we're represented on the cards?" Amara asked.

"I know you're the Empress, the fertility goddess of nature or whatever. Which means, shouldn't you be running around here barefoot with lambs following you, or something?"

Amara unveiled her beauty queen smile. "I've done that – in the life before this one in fact. Liam credits me with starting the whole hippie generation in the sixties even though I was still a child. He says what followed wouldn't have happened without me."

Vesta raised her martini to her lips but paused a moment before she spoke. "Wait. So you're to blame for tie-dye?"

Amara's smile thinned across her perfect dental work. "This life I was drawn to the chic clothes that the designers like to make today."

She looked down and gave a nod of approval to her dress and shoes.

"I just love them," she continued. "And I know you do. You've created this life around fashion, which is amazing, because I remember lives where you couldn't have cared less about what you were wearing."

Vesta's mouth dropped open and a gasp escaped from her lips. If Amara had grabbed a cocktail toothpick and shoved it in Vesta's eye, she wouldn't have been more stunned or thrown off balance. Was Amara saying that she, Vesta Beauvais, had lives where she didn't care what she wore? That was the most ridiculous statement Vesta had ever heard. Furthermore, she didn't believe a word of it. Amara was only trying to win the verbal volley. Within seconds she regained her balance and rose to the challenge.

"Yes, I know you're all about the labels too. But aren't you betraying your high and mighty trionfi duties by not having a litter of children and staying at home to cook and clean for them since you're the Mother Earth goddess, or whatever?"

The look Amara gave Vesta transmitted loud and clear that she was aware of the sniping game that was in play and that she was more than capable of holding her own.

"Jared, being the Emperor on the cards, and I have had families large and small over our lives together. Sometimes it seemed that we were constantly making babies."

It was a shot across the bow that threatened to sink Vesta's entire fleet. The image Amara shoved in Vesta's mind of her hot former lover, the only man she had lusted for on a routine basis for years, bestowing Amara with giggling beautiful babies was a punch in the gut. Yet Vesta gave her less than one second's worth of satisfaction with her well-placed shot before she recovered. But she was sure that Amara saw the envy that flashed on her face. Vesta never wanted babies with Jared, just mind-blowing sex, and lots of it. Even though he and Amara had been together as long as she had known them in this life, and as it turned out, for at least a dozen lifetimes before this one, they weren't married. And Vesta considered him fair game. Besides, Jared had been more than willing to help out a girl in need on more than one occasion. And Amara had her handsome house manager Gui always on hand. Neither guilt nor regret could be pried from her psyche.

"It sounds like I've always been too busy in my other lives to deal with babies, which suits me just fine." Vesta said with a wink fired straight at Amara's polished gaze. Now she felt her word bullet hit its target. Her smile curled at the corners like

Salvador Dali's mustache as she brought her cocktail up for another sip, then she paused.

"By the way, don't you think this whole secret thing embedded in tarot cards is a bit much?"

Amara stared at her with a stunned look. Vesta sipped her martini as she continued.

"I mean, look at it from my standpoint. In the course of fifteen, maybe twenty minutes my uncle, who was dying after being shot at a party, who was the only person I've ever felt like was family to me since my mother died, tells me that not only have I lived a few dozen lifetimes as the same person until I put a spell on myself to forget who I was in this lifetime, but that I am represented on tarot cards as the High Priestess. And then to top it off, he's on one of the cards as the Hierophant, whatever that is, you are, Jared and Sandor are. Liam and that son of a bitch Raz are too. We're all on these cards and live life after life doing what we were "gifted" to do a thousand years ago."

Vesta drained her glass. Amara's gaze softened relaying that the war games had ended. She reached for Vesta's hand, which she dodged by waving at the bartender for another martini.

"Perhaps you should have some food. It looks wonderful," Amara said.

"I'm not hungry."

"You're overwhelmed by all of this, I know. It's too much at once. Raymond had to tell you before he died. Surely you understand why."

"What I don't understand is why you had to let him die. You and the rest of this pompous group knew what was going on. You could have stopped Raz and his assassin but you didn't."

"Vesta, let me explain."

"And as far as all these super powers go, I don't see any of them from you or the others. I don't think I have any except those hallucinations, or visions, or whatever it was I was seeing.

And those have stopped. So what's the big deal with all of this? I think all you've got are super inflated egos."

The bartender who looked like Al Pacino from his Serpico days slid a third martini across the bar to her. Amara eyed it with knitted brows.

"Our gifts aren't parlor games meant to amuse or astonish with a display. They're subtle but extremely powerful. I can explain mine to you if you like."

Vesta picked up the martini. "I do have more important things to attend to at the moment like speaking to my uncle's attorney so we can settle his estate after his murder."

"I understand, but please slow down on your cocktails. There are better ways to deal with your sadness."

"I don't need a lecture from you. Clearly this is just routine in your world. I realize you're above all this grief stuff."

Vesta tipped her glass toward Amara as she spoke sloshing some of the vodka onto the floor between them. Her eyes looked at the spot then back at Amara. Her pupils narrowed as she tipped the glass to her lips and drained her cocktail dry.

"Forgive me, won't you, if I still exhibit some mundane human emotion."

Vesta placed her glass on the bar and walked away from Amara toward the ladies' powder room. Her legs were moving in a slightly wobbly fashion and her head felt a bit less than screwed on properly. She was instructing herself how to regain control when Jared intercepted her just before she got to the powder room door. Despite wearing a black Savile row jacket and pants he still looked like a lumberjack with his mop of blonde hair scrambled on top of his head, his deep blue eyes sizing up her condition.

"Vesta, how are you? You look upset." He reached his arms out toward her. She shoved them away.

"Really Jared? How perceptive of you. Did it take your super powers to figure that out?"

"Let's talk. I can help you with all of this."

Vesta could feel heat rising up from her neck to envelop her face.

"The time to help is long gone. Move out of my way."

Vesta shoved open the ladies room door almost knocking an elderly woman down who was trying to exit. She apologized and helped her out of the room then disappeared inside.

Bending over a sink Vesta got a good look at her face in the mirror and gasped. The lines on her forehead and around her eyes and mouth looked like they had been drawn on with a Sharpie. She wasn't looking at a High Priestess at that moment but some haggard old witch who had flown in on a broom. Now even her looks were gone. Everything that she loved and cared about had vanished. Vesta turned away from the revolting image and crumpled onto a tufted chair beside the row of sinks. She began to cry heaving sobs that shook her entire body. Everyone and everything else be damned, she had reached her breaking point.

She let the flood of tears pour out like the crescendo of a Beethoven symphony. Tears for Uncle Raymond. Tears for the loss of her job at Sybarite. Tears for the absurdity of the situation she had created. And tears most of all about being beyond confused as to what to do next. Was she supposed to turn loose of the life she had worked so hard for at Sybarite to embrace this new one - that was really her old one? She had no clue about what her duties were as the High Priestess of the tarot cards, let alone how to access her gifts to help humankind. And the entire concept of what she had accepted as a normal life had been turned upside down.

After what felt like an hour the last sob faded away in her throat. Vesta fell silent and dropped her head into her hands.

The room was quiet for a beat until the faint sound of a door being unlatched on one of the toilet stalls echoed in the adjoining room.

"Oh great," she muttered.

Vesta tried to tell herself she didn't care who heard the cacophony of her wails, but she kept her head in her hands as she heard footsteps come in her direction. She had no intention of humoring them, or scaring them, by showing her face, but a slight nudge against her head a moment later sent a jolt through her body. She looked up. Liam stood beside her smiling, holding out a handkerchief.

"What are you doing in here?" Vesta shook her head and glanced around her. "This is the ladies room."

"Thought you could use this." He wiggled the handkerchief.

"But your flight from London wasn't supposed to arrive until tonight. You've been in here the whole time, listening to me?" She snatched the handkerchief.

"I was able to catch a flight with Sir Richard at the last minute. I came here straight away. And what a sad lot of affairs I walked into, I must say. A mortally wounded animal in the forest couldn't have sounded worse."

"How did you know where I was? Wait, you must have come in before I did because I didn't hear anyone come through that door since I've been in here."

"Well, I figured you would be headed this way sooner rather than later considering the state you were in when you arrived."

"Was it bad?"

"Catatonic is the word I believe best describes your demeanor when you arrived at the bar out there. Then you became quite lucid with Amara. That's when I knew you would make a quick exit for the loo next."

"No one had a problem with a man strolling into the ladies room?"

"I was very stealthy Love. No one noticed."

"And you've just been sitting, in there, on a toilet waiting and then listening to me cry hysterically for God knows how long."

"Twelve minutes and forty-one seconds."

"Really? You timed it."

"It's like a total solar eclipse. You don't catch one very often so when it begins, you pay attention."

A half smile flashed on Vesta's face. Liam returned the smile and slid down beside her onto the chair.

"You have the smallest, boniest ass in rock history, don't you?" Vesta said.

"Nope. Mick's is smaller. We measured once."

"I have no doubt you did. What else did you measure?"

"Wouldn't you like to know?"

"I do know. Been there. Twice, actually."

Vesta leaned forward and put her head back into her hands.

"Oh God, Liam. My life is so messed up right now. I don't want to be this ridiculous priestess. Everything I thought I knew has turned out to be complete bullshit. And shit I could have never possibly dreamed up – I'm being told is the truth. I'm barely hanging on right now."

"It was a total mind fuck for me too when I remembered who I was all those years ago. Plus I was still sobering up from that thoughtful combo some fan gave me of Jack black laced with LSD."

"Everybody thought you were dead when you hit the stage."

"I thought I was dead."

"I'm so glad you didn't die."

Vesta gazed at Liam for a long moment, dressed in his usual black attire, his shirt unbuttoned half-way down his chest and his moppy brown hair partially obscuring at least one light brown eye. And always the medallion of the young man in tights in mid-step with his dog following close behind that dangled from the leather cord around his neck. He hugged her and laid his head on her shoulder.

"I woke up in a brand new world where I was immortal. Well, sort of. And I had this amazing ability to entertain people as the Fool."

"You could always do that. But I know what you mean. Suddenly everybody wanted to go see Liam Spencer in concert. You went from sleeping on my nasty old sofa to selling out stadiums around the world."

"It's true. But it was still a mind fuck. The whole being-the-same-person-on-the-same –mission-life-after-life thing; it's a lot to wrap your head around."

"Yeah, I'm not sure I've bought into that completely."

"Oh, it's true. Have no doubts. I'm sure our merry little band of cohorts have filled you in on certain details."

"Them? You should have seen them at the gravesite a couple of hours ago. The statuary on the tombs had more life than that group. They acted like they couldn't have cared less."

"In fairness you must understand that we've seen all of us die, and then return brand new, so many times that I suppose it's just become routine and utterly boring."

"You ass!" Vesta shoved Liam onto the floor. "That was my uncle they put in the ground today. He was murdered by that wretched human being and the only solace I can take is that Raz is rotting in some filthy jail right now."

Liam pressed his lips together for a moment before he spoke. "Hate to spoil your fantasy Love but Rasputin is out."

"What?"

"He's free. He received a pardon or something from someone in your government."

"Be more specific. What happened?"

"I don't know exactly. I'm only repeating what Jared told me."

"Why didn't he tell me?"

"Maybe you didn't give him the chance."

"Shut up! Whose side are you on?"

"Yours, always. Just don't kill the messenger."

"I need to find out the details and get his ass back in there."

Vesta stood up, walked to the sink and began cautiously looking in the mirror.

"Oh my God. I look worse than warmed over shit."

She brushed her short blond hair away from her face then splashed water on it. Out of her clutch she pulled a powder compact and lipstick. Vesta winced as she moved closer to the mirror to touch up what was an unholy mess. She looked at Liam.

"Why are you just standing there? Help me."

"Sandor's the Magician, not me." Liam said as he pushed up his sleeves. "I'm not promising any miracles."

CHAPTER 2

More people had arrived in the Plaza's Grand Ballroom when Vesta and Liam emerged from the ladies' room. A quartet set up on a small stage against one wall was playing Cotton Club era jazz. Despite wanting to stay in a foul mood, Vesta's spirits lightened. Uncle Raymond loved that music. He would have enjoyed everything about the scene. Vesta wove her way toward the bar when she noticed Liam trying to escape her company.

"Where are you going?"

"Just for a little ciggy outside." Liam pulled a Marlboro from his shirt pocket.

"No you're not. You're coming with me to the bar. I need to find Jared but until I do, I don't want to talk to anybody."

"What am I? Some potted plant you found over in the corner that you want to hide behind?"

"Act like we're in deep conversation."

Al Pacino's double was still pouring drinks and smiled at Vesta as she reached the bar. After her hard cry she felt renewed and sober. Time to deaden her misery again. After ordering martinis for both of them Vesta turned around to scan the room.

"There are a lot of people here I don't know. Who are they and who invited them?"

"You're expecting me to know that? He was your uncle, not mine."

"Okay, smart ass. Do you see Jared in here somewhere? You know him, right?"

Bartender Al slid two martinis toward Vesta and Liam. They surveyed the room sipping their drinks. The light from the gigantic chandeliers immersed the space in a sumptuous golden glow. Grand columns supporting the ornately painted and decorated ceiling made the space look like a palace.

Vesta's eyes landed on a group of four standing on one of the balconies overlooking the main floor of the ballroom. One handsome man in particular stood out.

"Who's that?"

Liam followed her gaze.

"Oh, those I do know. You haven't met them yet? No one has told you about Don Francesco Parrino and his family?" Liam said as he turned away from them toward Vesta.

"No. Who are they?" Vesta rubbed the spot between her eyes that began an itchy buzz under her skin. As she spoke, she noticed the man return her gaze. The cool eye contact between them relayed that neither was intimidated by the other staring so intently.

"Well, they are like us for starters." Liam sipped his martini.

Vesta spun to face Liam. "What? You mean tri-phonies? Really?"

Liam almost choked trying to swallow and laugh at the same time. He shot Vesta a wild-eyed look and began laughing.

"You are so irreverent in this life. I adore it."

"God, it sounds like I was such a boring shrew before. No wonder I cast a spell on myself to forget who I was."

Liam was still laughing. It was an infectiously silly sound

that made Vesta laugh too. No wonder he was portrayed as the Fool on the tarot cards. Light-hearted, fun and creative, that was Liam. Plus he was more than a little prone to making poor decisions that always cost him.

"Okay, stop it. Tell me more about the Parrinos."

Liam took another extended sip of his martini then set it on the bar.

"Well, they're not to be fucked with. You must know that first and foremost. They represent the House of Swords on the cards which means they are like us but their gifts are not quite as powerful as ours. They are known for mental manipulation. Persuasion tactics you might say. Francesco runs a huge shipping business. Employs thousands of dockworkers here, in the U.K. and in Italy. Imports and exports all kinds of things, some legal, some not so much."

"Like what?"

"Lovey, you've got my tongue wagging too much all ready. I'm having too much fun in this life to give it up right now. So instead, I will just say that he's a very powerful and private man who knows a lot of people." Liam eyed Vesta for a moment then added. "Like Vatican people."

"The pope?"

"I'm sure."

"So who's the hot man standing next to him?"

Liam still had his back turned to the room.

"You must mean Marco, because I doubt that Giovanni has ever been described as hot."

"I mean the guy with the Mediterranean tan and the black wavy hair in the perfectly tailored Gucci suit who just happens to be staring at me right now."

Vesta's eyelids slid down a notch as she regarded other important details on Marco.

"Checking him out tip to toe, eh? Yes, that's Marco. Interesting story there. Some say that he's not blood to Francesco but you wouldn't know that by the way he's treated within the family. He's the Page of Swords, the golden child. Especially to his mother, Valentina."

"Is that the woman standing with them?"

"It certainly is. Must be very careful with that one. She knows things the rest of us don't. Even you at the height of your skills would have a tough time tangling with her. She's much more powerful than her male family members."

"And why is that?" Vesta asked, her gaze never leaving the foursome on the balcony.

"Because she comes from the oldest blood of our kind."

"What does that mean?"

"That means her kind were created first, before the rest of the trionfi, and they were given abilities that the rest of us weren't."

"Like what?"

"She reads minds like she's reading a restaurant menu."

"Seriously?"

"Quite. The culture she came from is so old that the sands of the Sahara obliterated her village eons ago. Her line is the only one left from that time."

"Is she reading our minds now?"

"Not mine. I've learned how to block her and any others who can do it. I suggest you learn how."

"How do I do that?"

"I'll show you but not while we're drinking. Bad things happen. Trust me. I know from experience."

"Do you think she's reading my mind then?"

"Probably. My guess is that she's aware that you now remember who you are."

Vesta turned to face Liam.

"I must be the laughing stock of the tri-phony group, right? I mean, here I am, almost forty and just now learning who I am."

"I think some of them are a bit dismayed that you now know who you really are. They got away with quite a lot in this life with just dear old Raymond at the helm. He has always been much more thoughtful and forgiving than you."

"It's not like I've been given printed instructions on how to access this gift. And memories of my past lives haven't come flooding back to me."

"Your memories may not fully return. You really wiped your slate clean with that spell. But you can learn how to access your InSight from Amara."

"Yeah, she cornered me earlier volunteering her services. I'm not ready just yet to give her such an ego boost as to teach me that. Maybe there's someone else."

"Well you better get about it because there's still evil afoot in the world from some of our illustrious members."

"Wait a minute. I thought we were all given these specials gifts so we could do good."

"We were but I have just two words for you to explain what I mean. Free will. Rasputin is just one of several others who have chosen to use their gift for not only their own personal gain but to injure others, sometimes mortally, as you now know."

"I won't quit until he is in a prison so deep and dark that he can't see his hand in front of his face."

"Yes, you've worked on that task before. In several previous lifetimes, I mean. He's certainly part of the reason you burned your wick so low that you cast that spell on yourself. I told the others you needed the break. They really didn't understand like I did."

"I must be damn good at spells because I don't remember those things, only bits and pieces, flashes of images in my mind. Maybe more will come back to me later on."

"Maybe. Maybe not. That's why I'm telling you straight up, right now, not to diddle around with our kind who walk on that side of the street until you have gained complete control of your InSight."

"It sounds like you may be including the Parrinos in that group."

Liam raised his eyebrows. "You will find out very soon for yourself. Marco is walking up behind you right now."

Vesta swiveled around to see the approach of what her girlfriends in college would have called a slayer. A devastating smile preceded his voice.

"Hello, I'm Marco Parrino."

"Hello, Vesta Beauvais." As she extended her hand Marco took it and carefully planted a soft kiss on her palm. Vesta's heart beat faster.

"But we've met before," Vesta said as coolly as she could to Marco.

"Ah, yes, I heard that you recently became aware of your great gifts. We were all so happy to hear the news."

"Well, I'm a little embarrassed that it took me so long. I feel like I have a lot of catching up to do."

Liam gave Vesta a sideways glance with a slight eye roll. Marco noticed Liam's reaction.

"Liam, how are you? Good to see you."

"I'm well, thank you."

"I'm planning to come to your concert when it arrives in Rome soon," Marco said.

"Do you live in Rome?" Vesta asked.

"No. We have a flat there that I use. I am usually at our villa about an hour outside of the city. I oversee our vineyards there. It's beautiful but sometimes lonely."

Vesta's eyes widened on his final word. She wished they hadn't. Marco smiled again.

"I live here in New York," Vesta said trying to distract from her schoolgirl behavior.

"Yes, I'm aware of that. Congratulations on succeeding so magnificently this time as CEO of Sybarite. Your home goods are first class. I have purchased a number of them for my residences."

"Thank you. I haven't officially been reinstated as CEO and chairman of the board but it's almost certain I will be soon."

Vesta felt a nervous twitch flash through her head to toe. She looked away from Marco so as not to seem too foolish and noticed the other members of the Parrino family watching the conversation from their perch on the balcony.

"I heard how badly Rasputin went off the tracks with his allegations. I'm glad that's all behind you now," Marco said.

"Yes, everything will be fine except for the fact that my uncle is dead."

"Your uncle was a fine man. I was very sorry to hear the terrible news."

"We've gotten Raz thrown off the Sybarite board. Now we just need to get him back in jail and then prison."

"It may be difficult with the Russian extradition laws."

"Extradition? What are you referring to?" Vesta cocked her head.

"He's returned to Russia."

"Liam! Why didn't you tell me?"

"I didn't know," Liam said shaking his head. "It must have just happened because otherwise Jared would have told me when we spoke by phone this morning."

"Jared doesn't know everything despite what he and others may believe," Marco said coldly.

Vesta shot a surprised glance at Marco. Silence fell between the three of them for a moment.

"I apologize," Marco said. "It was rude of me to be so blunt. It's a sticky little trait we Parrinos seem to have."

"So how did you know he returned to Russia?" Vesta asked.

A rapid beeping began inside Marco's jacket. He pulled a mobile phone from his pocket.

"Excuse me," he said and answered the phone.

Vesta looked up to the balcony again. The three Parrinos who remained watched her every move. The one Liam called Giovanni had his mobile phone up to his ear.

"I'm sorry, but I must go now." Marco said still holding the phone. "It was my complete pleasure to meet you Vesta, again and for the first time." Marco said and kissed her hand once more.

"And I look forward to your performance in Rome, Liam." Marco gave a slight bow.

"Thank you," Liam said with a salute of his hand.

"Nice meeting you Marco," Vesta said. "Have a safe flight back to Italy."

"Actually from here I go to our vineyard estate in Napa for a few days. So I'll be around."

"Oh. That's nice." Vesta grimaced to herself knowing how lame that sounded.

Marco smiled again, teeth gleaming and deep brown eyes shining.

"Ciao," he said.

He turned from Vesta and walked with such grace but confidence that she watched him all the way to the stairs.

"Ground control to Vesta Beauvais." Liam leaned in a few inches toward her.

"I'm here. Shut up."

"I can only imagine the hot roll the two of you are going to have one day soon."

"You think?" Vesta asked.

"My pet, I'm afraid there's no avoiding it."

CHAPTER 3

The remainder of Sunday afternoon Vesta drank martinis with Liam as they mingled with guests at Raymond's memorial gathering. He managed to get her to eat some of the food while slowing her down on imbibing Russian vodka. As a result she maintained a stable conclusion to her day and an early arrival to her bed for a decent night's sleep.

The next morning the email from Jenny was a complete shock when Vesta logged onto her laptop. She hadn't heard from her former assistant since Raymond died. Sandor hired Jenny after she was fired from Sybarite saying it was to keep her from going to work someplace else. While that may have been the truth, it was also a fact that Sandor never liked to let a great person out of his hands, especially when they were smart and attractive. He did respect boundaries but being the Magician he had ways of seduction that were beyond what any measly mortal could contend with. Vesta figured that would be the last she would hear from her sterling employee.

Jenny's email alerted Vesta that Jared had contacted her by phone. She had accepted his generous offer to return to Sybarite as Vesta's assistant and would be in their old office Monday morning. That meant today, Vesta realized as her pulse quickened. She checked her mobile phone. It was nine-thirty. Did that mean Jenny was there now? Why did she wait until last night to send the message?

An alert popped up on her mobile phone indicating she had a voice message. It was Jared asking if they could meet at her office as soon as possible that morning. The message had been left last night. She returned his call but got his voice mail. The message she left was short, she would meet him there in an hour. It didn't matter that it was a last minute request or that obvious planning had gone on without her knowledge. What mattered was that she was headed back into her office. A shot of adrenaline raced through her body. No High Priestess of the tarot or any supernatural crap would stop her, she was headed back into the world she knew and loved.

With an attitude that bounced between giddy prom queen and Spartan general, Vesta strutted into her closet to pull out the perfect outfit. Something that screamed, I'm in charge, was called for. Of course, nothing does that better than one of her Sybarite light wool suits, perfect for late September. Her hands landed on a dark gray skirt and jacket that had been expertly tailored to her body. Next she chose a white silk Donna Karan blouse that always looked spectacular with a suit. Simple but chic black Manolo Blanik's were the only other things she needed to grab. Fifteen minutes later she walked out the door of her Lower Manhattan apartment, down the elevator and into the lobby. The doorman greeted her.

"Good morning Ms. Beauvais." He tipped his hat to her. "Have a lovely day."

"Thank you. Could you hail a cab for me?"

"My pleasure."

A minute later Vesta slid into the backseat letting a sigh escape her lips.

"Fifty-third and Third please," she said. They pulled from the curb and the adrenaline flowed through her again like a facet turned on full blast.

Traffic was brutal. One last barrier, she thought, one final hurdle to jump before Sybarite was hers again. After what seemed like hours but was only forty minutes, they turned onto 53rd Street heading to Third Avenue. Vesta grabbed her Louis Vuitton handbag, laptop case and overcoat. She stroked each item in the crook of her arm unconsciously as they inched closer to her destination. At last the driver came to a stop.

Vesta stared for a moment at the towering edifice with its graceful curved corners. She loved that the building resembled a gigantic sexy red granite, glass and steel tube of lipstick opened up to the world. A lot of other people who looked at it felt the same way because it had been nicknamed the Lipstick Building since its opening ten years earlier.

She paid the driver and got out. More than three months had passed since she stood on that sidewalk. It was the spot where she had screamed at Jared. Never could she remember being so angry or feeling so betrayed. Minutes earlier she had been voted off the Sybarite board and relieved of her position as CEO. Her office door had been locked with her personal effects delivered to her home. Raz had in a matter of half an hour destroyed with a rash of lies everything she had worked all her life to accomplish. And why had he done that? To keep her from finding out the truth about who she was.

He was almost successful in his mission to keep her identity hidden. Raz knew that once she was again in full possession of her abilities she would, through her InSight, see the sex slave ring he had created. She had already caught glimpses of it when his accomplice shook her hand. That's why he trumped up the false accusations about illegal financial activities by her within the company. He knew it would distract her from doing anything but trying to get her job back.

After she had described her vision to Amara, all of the trionfi who were close to her, Uncle Raymond, Jared, Sandor and even Cyrus set the trap for him at Liam's concert. Their plan almost worked until one of Raz's hired killers grabbed a gun and shot Raymond. Vesta shuddered. Now her uncle was dead. And the whole situation seemed completely impossible and ridiculous. These characters depicted on tarot cards, reincarnating life after life, running around trying to save the world from villains. And now she was supposed to be an integral part of the group. She had a much different plan at the moment.

Vesta looked around her at the street scene. People in business attire walked past, many on their mobile phones, some toting cups filled with coffee. Taxis pulled up to the curb then dashed away, voices and car engines, the sound of a siren in the distance. This was her reality. Where she stood right now. It was time to get back to the business that she worked so hard for and that needed her.

The enormous steel-banded pillars in the lobby lead her to the bank of elevators. With an exhale that signaled complete confidence in herself she pressed the button to go up. Emerging on the thirty-fourth floor she stepped into the wide hallway. Bright morning light filtered through the wall of windows as she walked past them toward her office. She could feel eyes upon her as she passed. The designers and office assistants, the marketing and public relations employees, they all silently watched her from their desks and tables. At the end of the long walkway Jenny stepped from behind her desk.

"Oh my God, I'm happy to see you!" Jenny's fingers fluttered like little birds.

"Let me hang up your coat. I will bring you an espresso right away. And Mr. Schultz is waiting in your office."

Vesta smiled and handed her coat to Jenny. "Thanks. It's good to see you too."

A sense of being home spread over her as she turned the knob and pushed open the door to her office. There was her desk at one end of the room so she could see the both the door and the wall of windows looking out onto Manhattan. A familiar pulse in her body began echoing the pulse of the city outside as she walked toward her desk. Jared was gazing out of a window and turned as she entered.

"Good morning," he said.

"Good morning."

"Welcome back."

"Why didn't you tell me yesterday that you hired Jenny again and wanted to see me in my office this morning?"

"You didn't give me the chance."

"And you didn't really try." Vesta said as she stepped behind her desk and sat down. "I looked for you at the party later. It seems there's quite a lot that you know but I don't."

He exhaled audibly and stared at her for a moment before he spoke.

"Yes, we have to talk. And I took the liberty of inviting someone else to join us."

After two solid knocks on her door, Cyrus walked into Vesta's office.

"Good morning," Cyrus said as he walked over and shook Jared's hand.

"What are you doing here?" Vesta asked.

"Bringing you a heavy dose of clarity my daughter."

His ever-present swagger brought him close to the desk. Both men sat down across from her.

"Why do I get the feeling I'm being ambushed?" Vesta said.

"You're not being ambushed. Cyrus has first-hand knowledge of things that I thought he could better explain."

"And you couldn't tell me this yesterday?"

"Yesterday was a day to pay our respects to Raymond. This business could wait," Cyrus said.

"Really?" Vesta said focusing her gaze steadily on Cyrus. "I don't recall seeing you there. Oh, that's right, you don't attend funerals of family members. You weren't there for my mother's funeral so why would I think you would have been there for her brother's."

"Vesta, enough of that," Jared snapped. "There's no time for your petty grievances today."

"You in your arrogance call them petty? You grew up with a loving father who took care of you and your mother. Try growing up without knowing your father except for an occasional visit when it fits into his precious schedule. You never knew what it was like to be poor and feel abandoned, alone except for a fragile mother that you felt responsible for."

Vesta heard a slight groan from Cyrus as he shifted in his chair.

"Your self-imposed ignorance has damaged all of us Vesta. If you were aware of any of our history you would know that hasn't always been the case in my life, or yours," Jared said.

"Oh, that's right. I'm the insufferable member of this elite little group who cast a spell on herself so she wouldn't remember in this life who she really was. Some pretty shitty lives must have led up to that, I'm thinking. And you're the almighty Emperor of the pack who never makes any mistakes. Did I get that right?"

Vesta stared at Jared who returned the look without words or emotion.

"And you," she said turning to Cyrus. "You're represented on the cards as The Chariot from what I'm told. Oh yes, and half of the Lovers according to Uncle Raymond. That's a great joke, isn't it?"

There was another knock on the door. Jenny peeked into the office.

"Pardon me. I have your espresso," she said.

"Sure." Vesta replied. "Please bring it in."

Jenny set it on the desk. "Gentlemen, can I get you anything?"

Both men shook their heads. Jenny smiled and exited the room closing the door behind her. Cyrus stood up.

"Vesta, I can recommend some well-trained therapists if you need one, or several, to help you work through your childhood angst." Cyrus leaned forward on her desk. "In the meantime, we need to discuss a couple of matters with you."

He walked to the row of windows and looked out. Vesta felt a flush of anger race through her body that rendered her speechless for a moment. Jared took advantage of the opportunity.

"Raz was released on bail two days ago and immediately took off in one of his private jets for Moscow. The FBI with the help of the CIA, no doubt, is now getting involved to extradite him."

"I heard this news yesterday," Vesta said.

"From who?" Jared asked.

"It doesn't matter," she said. "I thought Scotland Yard arrested him and that he was in custody in London or something."

Cyrus turned to face Vesta.

"He was but his attorneys got him transferred to U.S. jurisdiction and the court here set bail at their request. We're going to have to pry him out of Russia now to face this murder charge. This is going to take some time because he's a Russian citizen."

"I don't care if he's from Mars. He murdered my uncle and he needs to be sitting in a jail right now."

"We're working on it," Jared said.

"I'll call my attorney." Vesta grabbed her mobile phone from her handbag.

"They can't do anything more than what is being done right now," Jared said.

"We'll see."

"Vesta, stop!" Cyrus bellowed from across the room. "Didn't you hear what the man just said? What makes you think he and I haven't covered this ground already? We have. It's time for you to listen rather than talk."

Vesta stood up and began walking toward Cyrus.

"Do you think you can just waltz back into my life after all this time and start telling me what to do? You can't. I don't know you from any other obnoxious man who wants to throw his weight around."

"Hear this daughter, I am your father. And just because I wasn't sitting around that log cabin of your mother's changing your stinking diapers doesn't mean I haven't been looking out for you and the others. You have no idea what I'm responsible for and I'm in no mood to tell you. Stop your pathetic whining and pay attention, there's something you need to know."

"And we need your help." Jared added as he turned in his chair to look at them both.

Vesta stared at one then the other for a long moment. There was so much she wanted to say but she also wanted to know what information they had.

"Make it quick," she said walking back to her desk.

"Raz is involved in more than sex slavery," Jared began. "We know that he's bringing drugs, opiates, into this country and others. He has help though and we need to know who it is."

"It's probably that little toad who shot Uncle Raymond," Vesta said.

"No, it's not him. He's just Rasputin's lacky. He's still sitting in

Scotland Yard. He doesn't know anything except to jump when he's told to." Cyrus moved closer to the desk.

"If you try, you can see who it is," Jared said putting his hand on Vesta's desk.

"What do you mean see? How?" Vesta asked.

"Your gift is your sight beyond the veil. Raymond had it too but now that he's gone for a while, it's all up to you," Jared said.

"I must have wiped my mind clean," Vesta said. "Because I don't have this sight you're talking about."

"You do," Cyrus interrupted. "You just need to remember it."

"Amara can help you," Jared said. "She was trying to spur your gift when you were in Tofino through the kundalini sessions and walking the labyrinth."

"I don't need Amara's help," Vesta said.

"Yes, you do," Jared said. "And we need yours. We have to stop what Raz is doing. He's using all of his powers to network these drugs throughout the world."

"And what are his powers? I know he's represented as the Devil on the tarot cards, which I can totally understand, but what does that mean?"

"It means," Cyrus began. "Rasputin was given the gift of making the human race aware of the pitfalls and dead end of being obsessed with material things. Of being consumed with aspects of life that distracted them from their true callings. His power rests in his superior ability to attract people to that which doesn't serve them. The result was supposed to be that he takes those who need to be shown to the point where they realize their poor judgment and change direction toward service. Unfortunately, Rasputin's train came off the tracks several lifetimes ago and has since been hell on wheels raining chaos down on us for his putrid pleasure."

"Why haven't you stopped him before now?" Vesta asked.

"We have. Many times," Jared said. "But sometimes he

causes monumental destruction before we catch on to what he's doing and stop him."

"History books are filled with his fine handiwork," Cyrus said.

Vesta looked at both men trying to grasp all they were telling her.

"So you want me to find out what he's up to now by tapping into my gift?"

"Exactly," Jared said. "We found out from your vision at Amara's fundraiser that he was forcing young women into sexual slavery. When some were rescued they told of being drugged on a daily basis by an IV concoction that sounds like an opiate mixed with something else. This is something new that he's beginning to sell. We need to know who's helping him transport this drug around the world so we can shut it down."

"My sources have taken me as far as they can," Cyrus said. "That's why Raymond sacrificed himself so you would agree to allow him to break his promise to you."

"Sacrificed himself?" Vesta repeated.

"Yes, he knew that was the only way you would listen to him."

"What do you mean, the only way I would listen to him was if he was dying? Are you saying that his death was my fault?" Vesta almost screeched the words.

"Don't lose your wits again. Stay with us," Cyrus said.

It was too late. Vesta's eyes flashed and Jared leaned back in his chair.

"Vesta, wait," he said.

"My uncle did not sacrifice himself for me. That stooge shot him from point blank range at the command of Rasputin Dragomirov who parades around as some powerful demon. To hell with him! And to hell with the both of you. You don't know my uncle. I'll find out what Raz is up to but I don't need your help or Amara's. Jared, am I reinstated as CEO and chairman of the board at Sybarite?"

"There are documents that some of the board members still have to sign, but yes, you provisionally are."

"Great. Well, I've been gone for a while and I have a lot of catching up to do. You gentlemen need to excuse me now."

"Yes, but what about getting back up to speed on your gift and seeing what's going on with Rasputin?" Jared asked.

"I will be in touch when I'm ready. Now leave my office."

"She has to make a big show," Cyrus said turning toward the door.

"Cyrus, why don't you disappear for another twenty years?" Vesta said as she picked up the phone on her desk and punched a button. "Jenny, can you come in please?"

"Don't let your emotions get in the way of what you're here to do," Jared said. "Rasputin has to be stopped but we have to find him and his network first. This is where your InSight comes in. We're counting on you."

Vesta turned her back to Jared as he followed Cyrus out of the door. Jenny passed them as she pranced into the office holding a huge bouquet of peonies in a Tiffany Atlas crystal vase.

"Check these out," Jenny said.

Vesta whirled around. The pissed expression on her face softened.

"Peonies. My favorites. They're gorgeous."

"They just arrived with this card."

Jenny set them on Vesta's desk and handed her the card. She gazed at the white and pink petal bombs for a moment. These were the only flowers that could make her swoon. Quickly she opened the card. It said simply, *Welcome back. Marco.*

CHAPTER 4

Vesta's mobile phone was ringing as she slid into the back seat of the cab just after sunset.

"Yes?"

"Did you get the flowers?"

She recognized Marco's deep soft voice.

"I did. How did you know so quickly that I was back in my office? And, how did you get this number?"

"So many questions. But the important one is, will you be my guest in Napa this weekend? Your reinstatement requires a worthy celebration."

"Marco, I'm just settling back into the rhythm of my job. I can't leave so soon."

"There's no work that should be done after Friday until Monday. Everyone deserves some rest. Especially you. I will have my jet waiting Friday afternoon. You can shower and change on the flight and be here in the evening. We will have a late supper and time to get to know one another. I will have all the details sent to your assistant."

"I, well, alright, I guess," Vesta stumbled for words.

"I look forward to seeing you then. Ciao bella."

"Ciao," Vesta echoed as she pressed the end button on her phone.

The cab plodded through traffic as Vesta tapped out her thoughts with a finger on the Day-Timer open in her lap. She had written the date on her calendar, but what was up with her agreeing to fly across the country to stay with a man she didn't know? And only a week after returning to Sybarite? She wasn't usually so dumbstruck by men. Of course this was no ordinary man. Marco Parrino was devastatingly handsome, wealthy and suave. European mothers taught their sons how to treat women, Vesta believed that. And she had always thought American mothers should take note and do the same.

Marco's mother, Valentina, however came from the African continent. What did they teach their sons? A chill passed through Vesta as she pulled her overcoat tighter. That was why she also wanted to go to see Marco. Something about his mother and father tugged at her thoughts. There was something she needed to know but she wasn't sure what.

Vesta stared out the cab window without seeing anything. The spot between her eyes whirred creating a tingling under her skin. She wished she hadn't drunk so many martinis before she saw them standing on the balcony of the Plaza's ballroom the day before. Alcohol messed with her InSight; she knew that. There was something, a message or vision maybe, trying to come through but she couldn't grasp it. She looked at her Day-Timer.

Taking the weekend off was no problem. She had already planned to be at her office for long hours Monday through Thursday then work at home during the evenings. The damage done by Raz's CEO designate, Alyona, during her absence hadn't been as bad as she feared. Everything would be back in order by Friday.

A sense of caution spread through her. Marco's invitation

was all too easy and wonderful. In her experience life wasn't like that. Not for her. But she wanted to feel like her old life was back again, not the new foreign High Priestess gig filled with expectations she had no idea how to fulfill. She yearned for the life she had carved so carefully for herself free of this second self.

She knew she wasn't just going to Napa Valley for sex with Marco, although she hadn't had great sex for months, not since she and Jared spent that afternoon in his Silicon Valley office. Maybe if she relaxed a bit this weekend, she would figure out what to do next.

An image of Raz popped into her mind. The life-size Porky Pig dressed in an expensive suit. Her fingers trembled and the spot between her eyebrows spun faster. There was a sense of him somewhere on her periphery as if she was observing him in real time. He was walking somewhere but darkness surrounded him making any location impossible to detect. Yet she could hear the lapping of water as it splashed against what sounded like metal.

She wanted to hone her InSight to find Raz but she wasn't going to ask Amara for help. And she had no intention of helping Jared and Cyrus. Taking on the responsibility of being this High Priestess person was more than she was willing to do at the moment but if she could use this newfound gift to put her uncle's killer away for the rest of his life, then she was up for the task.

THE REMAINDER of the week flew by. Vesta worked twelve-hour days to make up lost ground at Sybarite. The spring collection had been shown during her absence. Alyona made a complete mess of the collection overriding everything that had been finalized. Vesta made amends with Neiman Marcus, Macy's and

Bergdorf's to send them photos of the collection they should have seen. She knew that everything would work out but only because she had forged great relationships with each of the buyers over the years.

They had all heard the gossip that was put out for public consumption, that board member Rasputin Dragomirov had marshaled a hostile take-over based on false accusations. They knew Vesta had been cleared of all charges but had unfortunately suffered the loss her beloved uncle to a random killing during that time. All the buyers were glad to have Vesta back at the helm and order was restored.

It was on that satisfied note Vesta boarded Marco's jet waiting for her at La Guardia airport at four o'clock on Friday afternoon. She was the only passenger and Marco had taken the liberty of having a masseuse and manicurist on board to pamper her on the transcontinental flight. She heard a champagne cork pop as they taxied out to the runway. The flight attendant handed her a bubbly glass just before it was their turn in line to take off. Sipping Dom Perignon Vesta watched out a window as the jet took off in a mad dash to catch the setting sun.

Objects below began shrinking in size finally becoming boardgame pieces. Maybe that was what life was all about. Perhaps all of it was simply a cosmic game dreamed up by the creator. Every decision made was destined by a controlling entity. Each event was pre-ordained. Free will was non-existent. If that were true, she mused as she sipped more champagne, then why did she work so hard? Why not just sit back like she was at that moment and relax about her life? Drop the agony of trying to figure out how to incorporate her new life, actually her old life that just seemed new to her, with the life she's living right now. The two were complete opposites of each other.

She adored her life full of high fashion and finance, sex and sparkling wine. That's why she went in search of a portal or something that would show her how to come back in the next life as the same person in this one, not some dreary life as the High Priestess of some archaic tarot cards. That thought lead her to the ominous question that had been lurking in her mind for days. What had been so terrible about her previous life that she was compelled to take the drastic step of casting a spell on herself to forget who she was when she was born again into this life?

Vesta stared out the window into the distant cloudscapes. Her thoughts were deep inside and drew all elements of her awareness to that place. She had to know. What happened that made her wipe out all her memories? Uncle Raymond told her it was because she had burned out from such heavy obligation. Cyrus made her feel like she let the trionfi down in some horrible way. Liam said he understood why she did it, but no one had really told her more than that. She needed to find out.

More champagne was poured. She watched the bubbles soar to the top of the fluted glass with the pale wheat color of the wine below. In a flash the image of the champagne glass morphed, in its place a different scene emerged. The pale wheat color smeared out to flood the entire lower half of her vision. Bright blue, like the sky, covered the top half. An odor of damp earth clung to her; a thunderous noise filled the air. Vesta flinched. The image disappeared and the champagne flute returned to her sight, sitting on the tray table as before.

She noticed her breathing had become shallow with her pulse racing. A spark of something akin to a tiny electrical charge coursed up and down her spine setting the spot between her eyebrows spinning. As she regained control of her breathing the charge faded away and her third eye quieted down.

Vesta stared at the glass. Had she recalled a memory? It felt so familiar to her, but it wasn't from this life. She searched her mind trying to make the memory or vision return but it was gone. She leaned back in her seat.

Maybe she should ask Amara to help her retrieve her memories. She said she could do that, but asking her would register as defeat. Reclaiming her gift of InSight should be something she could do on her own. And she wasn't even sure she was ready to take on all the obligations of that job yet. Taking care of Sybarite and finding Raz were her priorities at the moment.

Vesta winced as she recalled the image of her uncle lying lifeless on the cold stone rampart of the castle in Spain. Did she cause that to happen like the crazy Egyptian tarot card reader Madame Kali said? That whacky old woman in Cairo certainly made her feel like it was her fault with that prediction. Was Madame Kali also one of the trionfi? Or was she just a good card reader who picked up on something?

A sigh slid from her toward the glass of champagne. She picked it up and drained it. Alcohol wouldn't help her regain her InSight, or remember her past lives, but it would dull the pain she felt at that moment.

The jet had been at cruising altitude for a while. They were probably sailing somewhere over Illinois. Vesta stood up and announced that she was ready for her massage. The flight attendant directed her to a changing area adjacent to the bedroom suite near the rear of the plane. There she found a silk robe and slippers laid out. A massage table stood ready behind a screen nearby. She heard a knock on the door the attendant had slid shut.

"Come in," Vesta said.

A gorgeous man in his mid-twenties stepped into the area. His black skin on muscled forearms shimmered like ebony. He gave her a dazzling smile.

"Hello, I'm Laurent. I'm your massage therapist."

"Wonderful." Vesta's eyes twinkled.

Sleep overtook her not long after Laurent began his intense but delicious back rub. Dreams of ships drifted through her mind as they pulled into deserted ports. Palm trees surrounded one, flat wilderness another, a mountain range behind a third. All docking under the cover of night. She could hear waves lapping against metal as she stood close to one. A voice spoke and she wondered if it came from the ship with the heart pierced by three swords painted on its bow.

"Ms. Beauvais," the voice said. "Would you like to roll over on your back now?"

Vesta felt herself being sucked off the dock and through a dark doorway back onto the jet.

"What?" She opened her eyes. "Oh, sure."

Laurent discreetly lifted the linen sheet so Vesta could flip over. She closed her eyes again wanting to go back to the dock. There was something important there. What was it? But like a breaking dawn its steadily increasing light wiping away the shadows of the night, her dream faded fast into memory not to be recaptured. She tried harder to again see the image of the heart with the three swords thrust into it. But it was no use, she had lost her grasp of the scene. She exhaled.

"Where are we?"

"We're about an hour and a half from landing."

CHAPTER 5

Darkness permeated the Napa County Airport. Even though it wasn't quite eight o'clock, the sun was beneath the hills in the distance when the jet landed. Vesta felt relaxed and refreshed after her massage and shower during the flight. The pilots stood on the tarmac at the foot of the jet's steps along with the rest of the crew when she disembarked.

"Ms. Beauvais, I hope you had a good flight." The pilot tipped his hat to Vesta. "There is a car here to take you to Signor Parrino's estate."

"It was great. Thank you," she replied.

A woman with long shiny black hair dressed in a well-fitting black Chanel suit studded with pearl buttons emerged from a black Mercedes sedan. Her caramel skin punctuated her large dark eyes and luscious red lips. She looked like an Indian goddess of the modern age as she marched in her Jimmy Choo stilettos toward the group.

"Ms. Beauvais, I'm Saffron. I will be driving you to meet Signor Parrino. Are you ready?"

"Yes, I am," Vesta said.

Moving with short, quick steps the flight attendant carried Vesta's luggage down the narrow stairs of the jet placing it in the trunk of the car. Saffron opened the back door of the Mercedes for Vesta then got into the driver's seat. They sped away from the tiny airport and began an odyssey through twisting dark roads. The thought crossed Vesta's mind that they must be passing fields of grapevines because no manmade structures popped up on the horizon, just contrasts of lighter black in the sky against darker black below. After twenty minutes of no conversation, no music, no clue of where they were, the car began a steep climb up a narrow mountain road pulling to a stop at the summit.

Soft golden spots of light waved back and forth in slow motion revealing glimpses of an open-air pavilion. Underneath it, Vesta spotted couches and a table set with the only source of light, hurricane lamps sheltering long glowing white candles. Vesta's car door opened. She stepped out.

"Thank you," Vesta said to the goddess in the Jimmy Choo's. Saffron bowed her head slightly, and without a word got in the car and left.

Vesta turned back to the pavilion. Only as her eyes adjusted to the scene did she see Marco standing off to the side in the thin slice of penumbra between the darkness and the light.

"I wanted to observe you like this before you moved any further," Marco said as he approached. Stretching out his hand he took hers and pressed his soft lips against her palm. "How good of you to come."

"Thank you for sending your plane, and your car for me."

"You must be exhausted from your long flight. Please join me for some champagne and a special supper I asked my chef to prepare just for you."

Marco placed his hand on the small of Vesta's back guiding her inside the pavilion. Wide slabs of limestone lay underneath a large Persian rug. On top of it sat a small sofa and two club chairs dressed in kid leather. In the other half of the space a small round table held dinner settings of crystal and china, peonies burst from a vase in the center.

"This is beautiful," she said.

"I'm afraid you haven't seen anything yet," Marco replied as he grasped a champagne bottle and popped its cork. He filled two glasses with the palest golden bubbles handing one to Vesta.

"Please come," he said motioning for her to join him on the far side of the pavilion. She followed and caught her breath at the view from their vantage point, the summit slipping away into a rolling slope down into a valley below. A waning moon peeked above the mountain range far in the distance. Even though only two-thirds full, the brilliant silver light illuminated the landscape in spectacular fashion displaying vast rows of grapevines stretching up the mountain and across the valley. Above she could see the inky black sky to the west dotted with diamond-bright stars thick as cream in the Milky Way. And there standing beside her she got her first good look at Marco who seemed absorbed by the scene. His black hair wasn't slicked back like it was in the Plaza ballroom. Tonight, there were large close-cropped ringlets covering his head, his thick black eyebrows framed his clean-shaven face. Whether he felt her gaze or not, he turned his attention to her in that moment and she fell into the large dark eyes that glittered with moonlight. His mouth spread into a smile so inviting.

"It's beautiful, no?" He asked.

"Yes. Just beautiful."

"To you, Vesta," Marco said raising his glass to hers. "Welcome back."

"Thank you." She touched her glass to his and sipped the wine. "Are you saying that because I'm back at Sybarite or because I'm back to knowing who I am in the trionfi?"

"Both perhaps. It is up to you to decide. It must be a very

difficult thing to be in the position you are right now. So much happening in your life that seems confusing."

"You can say that again," Vesta said as she took another sip of her wine.

"What am I thinking? You must be famished. Let's not talk of these matters. Let's enjoy the food."

Marco escorted Vesta to the table a few feet away seating her with a view of the moon now fully above the mountain. A moment later a van pulled up from the road with only its parking lights on. Two men got out and swung open the rear doors. They carried large trays to a buffet table hidden behind the sofa. The man in the white chef's coat began quickly assembling things from the trays as the other watched. Then he approached the table.

"Good evening signora. I am chef Rinaldo. I have been serving signor Parrino for several years now. It is a pleasure to serve you tonight. With your permission I would like to begin with the first course, lobster bisque."

Vesta looked at Marco who smiled at her.

"Well, yes certainly. It sounds delicious," she said.

Chef Rinaldo moved back to the buffet table and the other man came forward.

"Signora, good evening. I'm Giorgio and I will be your sommelier tonight. May I pour some rose for you to enjoy with the bisque?"

"That would lovely." Vesta said realizing that she was in for a treat of gourmet proportions.

Giorgio picked up a bottle from an ice bucket nearby. He presented it to Marco who nodded his head. He popped the cork, sniffed it for a moment then poured some of the wine into his sommelier's silver cup that hung from a silver chain around his neck. After tasting it, he gave a pleased nod toward them and poured a taste for Marco. Signor Parrino swirled his glass vigorously for a moment then put it to his nose and inhaled deeply.

"Ah, yes. This was a promising year."

Giorgio poured the wine for Vesta then more for Marco. He placed the bottle back into the bucket and joined Rinaldo. Together the two men brought small bowls of bisque to the table setting them down in front of Vesta and Marco at the same time. Heat from the bisque released the gentle aroma of garlic and paprika. Hunger aroused itself within her as she realized she hadn't eaten since lunch in New York City, ten hours earlier. Looking at Marco sitting across the table so handsome in his crisp white button-down shirt with the sleeves rolled up to his elbows, his dark eyes and hair in gorgeous contrast with his shirt and smile, Vesta knew she was starving for everything this evening had to offer.

Following the primo was the secondo of papperdelle with langoustine accompanied by a contorno of grilled baby eggplant. The food was extraordinary. Chef Rinaldo concluded the meal with his version of melon basil sorbet served with the vineyard's sparkling wine and a demitasse of espresso. Vesta drank both and at last leaned back in her chair, a smile spread across her face.

"We can turn out the lanterns when you smile like that," Marco said.

"Well, you've given me a lot to smile about. Dinner was superb."

"It is just a small thing. I wanted the opportunity to get to know you and for you to feel relaxed and welcome."

"I think you've accomplished all of those things."

"We have a nice start."

Marco raised his hand. Vesta heard shuffling behind her. He stood up and pulled Vesta's chair out just as the Mercedes sedan made a stealth approach.

"Shall we retire to the main house for an after dinner drink and a swim perhaps?"

"Sounds fabulous."

Saffron had been replaced by a handsome gray-haired male driver. He didn't speak but nodded graciously to both Vesta and Marco. As they pulled away from the pavilion, she made sure to catch a last glimpse of the soft golden spot on the mountaintop surrounded by the sea of darkness, the contrast vivid, mesmerizing. She felt drawn to the light yet also to the dark and for the same reason, each held potential. Revelation cannot be experienced second hand. And what is life if it isn't filled with revelation, she smiled to herself.

CHAPTER 6

Sitting in the backseat of the black Mercedes the cool ink of the night blotted out all objects except for the hobbled moon, Vesta studied it with fascination as she gazed out the window.

"It's amazing how bright it is even though it's only two-thirds full. You never see a moon this bright in the city."

Marco leaned toward her so he could see through her window. His right hand gently touched her left thigh before resting on the center console. Vesta sighed with a sound so slight that it was only a whisper. Marco's mouth spread open a fraction, his own exhale coming soft and warm.

"She is a goddess, no? Even in her waning times she exudes beauty, casting her light on lovers so they may know the pleasures she enjoys."

Vesta felt a flame spiral up her spine from her navel to her cheeks and spread throughout her body. She sensed Marco's face close to hers. He smelled like musk and sandalwood with the slightest hint of citrus. It was more intoxicating to her than the wine. She turned her head to face him. His dark eyes shimmered with the lunar glow. He had recognized the goddess and now it was her turn. She stroked his lean, tan cheek then reached her hand behind his head and drew it closer to her. He brought his lips to hers in a soft embrace that deepened into alchemical territory in a flash. Vesta drew his hand back onto her thigh guiding it underneath her skirt. She moaned as he touched the moist center he found. The car slowed and made a hard left turn. Marco withdrew gently from the kiss, and took her hand.

"We've arrived at my home, Villa Spada di Napa," he said as the sparkle in his eyes danced. "It would be my honor if you would come inside to be my guest."

Vesta smiled at Marco. "I would love to."

In a swift, elegant motion Marco hopped out, walked to her side of the car and opened the door. He bowed, extending his hand to her. Taking it and sliding out of the backseat Vesta got her first look at Villa Spada. Bathed in shades of silver and the palest blue from the adoring moonlight the front façade looked like a palace where a goddess from Rome would have lived. Three wide arches supported by columns sheltered the front door. Smooth stucco walls with ivy clinging in several places still allowed massive, bare wall space above and beside the columns making it look like a well-kept ancient ruin. And the moonlight teased it with her kisses.

Marco led Vesta to the massive front door that swung open to reveal a tiny elderly woman dressed from head to toe in black with her hair pulled back into a tight bun.

"Ah, Donna Maria, what are you doing up at this late hour?" Marco asked as he and Vesta walked inside.

The old woman grunted before she spoke. "I wanted to greet your guest." She stared up at Vesta eyeing her from head to toe. She grunted again.

"Yes, well," Marco began. "May I introduce you to Vesta

Beauvais. Vesta, this is our house manager Donna Maria Savonarola."

Vesta took a step closer to shake the woman's hand.

"No. No need for that." Donna Maria waved her away. "I just wanted to see for myself. I saw." She made a snorting sound followed by her now final grunt as she walked away.

Both of Vesta's eyebrows peaked as she turned to Marco. "What was that?"

Marco glanced at the floor for a moment shaking his head then returned her gaze.

"That was Donna Maria."

"I got that part. Who is she?"

"As I mentioned, she's the house manager of the estate."

Now it was Vesta's turn to shake her head. "She's so old. I'm surprised she had the strength to open the front door, let alone run a house like this."

Marco smiled which made the sparkle in his eyes dance again. "I understand what you mean, but you would be amazed at what she can do."

"Well, she certainly is charming." Her tone as flat as two-day-old champagne. "Is she one of us? A tri-phony, I mean."

Marco cocked his head to one side. "A what?"

"Sorry. That's my little name for us. Does she come back every life as Donna Maria, your servant?"

"Ah, no. She is not a member of the trionfi. She doesn't reincarnate as this person each time. But we do have close ties with her family and they have been loyal to us for many generations."

Vesta nodded as she scanned the huge room where they stood. "Nice place."

"Oh, yes. Please. Welcome to my home." Marco bowed slightly again, his arm making a sweeping arc as he escorted Vesta into a two-story room. Swallowing a sizable portion of one wall was a towering fireplace. Above it an enormous mounted shield was painted with a coat of arms. Three white crosses dominated the middle section with a black knight's helmet on top. Underneath the crosses was a castle that reminded Vesta of the one in Spain, the one where Uncle Raymond had been murdered.

"Is that your family crest?" She asked.

"It is. And it's even older than Donna Maria." Marco said with a little laugh.

Vesta nodded a couple of times without expression.

"You could park an SUV in that fireplace."

"My father has always preferred a large fire in the winter."

"Yes, it does get really cold out here in California." Vesta said as she walked toward the wall of windows looking out on a patio area.

Marco laughed again except this time with a bit of hesitation.

"Your home is so beautiful that Architectural Digest could just walk in and begin shooting right now."

"They did enjoy being here." Marco paused, studying Vesta. "I have something special for you. A very old cognac from my grandfather's vineyards in France."

"Older than Donna Maria?"

Marco smiled and his head bobbed a few times. "Maybe the same age."

He walked to a bar area in the corner of the room as Vesta wandered around looking at the unique assortment of antiques while he prepared the crystal snifters and warmed the cognac. She had no doubt that everything in the space was a treasure of some sort costing a fortune.

On a thick base of dark wood stood a hand carved out of marble with a fragment of wrist attached. Vesta reached out her own hand to touch it. The stone felt cool, the jagged edges along the wrist worn down to a polished nubby state.

"I am told that came from Pompeii," Marco said from the bar. "It was uncovered when they excavated the remains after Vesuvius."

Vesta nodded as she continued her journey through the private art collection. On a table heaped with oversized books she recognized a Tiffany bowl. Even though she knew it was available at any of their stores, she also knew it cost twenty thousand dollars. As her eyes traveled over the tasteful table arrangement they widened when they landed on something she had never seen in person before. Moving in for a closer look, she asked, "Is this what I think it is?"

There, next to the Tiffany crystal bowl and giant art books, sat an extravagantly decorated large egg. And it wasn't just any overly decorated egg, it looked like an authentic Fabergé.

"It was made by the famous Russian jeweler," were the last words Vesta heard from Marco as she reached out and touched it.

A flash of white light engulfed her vision and her hand felt like she had stuck a metal knife into an electrical outlet. The current zipped through her body. She froze. Everything froze. Voices from far away, muffled, spoke in her left ear.

"Priceless," one voice said.

"Worth the price," another said. "Collateral damage to be expected."

"Handled it myself. Must continue."

"Hidden well on the ship. Vesta."

She strained to see beyond the sheet of white before her eyes. No images came into view, but one of the men spoke again. Vesta. Vesta. He was saying her name. How did he know her name?

"Vesta!" Marco's voice sounded panicked as it ripped through the fabric of the other voices.

She shook her head then blinked her eyes several times.

Marco stood in front of her in the living room, his hands on her arms.

"What? I'm here." Vesta shook her head some more. "At least, I think I'm here."

"Are you alright?" Marco's eyes scanned her face. "Come. Let me take you to a chair."

Marco led her to an elegant fauteuil. Its arms and legs covered in a gold-looking foil and dotted with what looked like pearls where the upholstery studs usually were. Vesta sank into the chair. Her head pounded as if Thor himself were wielding his hammer on it, her third eye blazed like it was on fire. She knew it was telling her about something hidden on a ship but she didn't know what. It had everything to do with that egg and two men. And she knew it related to the dream she had on the plane about ships docking at night. Someone in his family, maybe even Marco himself, was involved in something bad enough that her InSight kicked in without her even trying to initiate it. A shiver ran through her. Whatever it meant, one thing was for sure, it felt like pure evil.

Vesta looked down at her hand that touched the egg. An odd sensation throbbed from it like her hand was swollen. She rubbed her fingers to make the twitching stop. What happened must remain a secret from Marco, but she had to discover what was going on. Honing her InSight might also help her locate Raz. Finding him was her priority. First though she had to distract Marco from this episode.

"Is this original Louis the fifteenth?" She tried her best to create a casual tone in her voice.

"Vesta, you had a most strange look on your face over there." Marco said as he knelt beside her. "You began breathing with heavy breaths. Your eyes were far away."

"I really must compliment your decorator." Her trembling hand fingering the fine carving on the arm of the chair.

"Shall I call a doctor?"

Vesta pushed herself upright in the chair commanding the chill in her body to leave.

"A doctor? Absolutely not. I'm fine."

"Please let me contact someone who can help you."

Vesta steadied her gaze on Marco. With unblinking, focused eyes but with a headache raging inside she replied, "I told you, I'm fine. No doctor is necessary because there's nothing wrong."

She saw Marco eyeing her with the caution of a man dismantling a time bomb.

"This is such good news. I was so worried about you. Please tell me what happened."

Vesta flinched. The slightest recollection made her hand twitch harder.

"A headache slammed into me. It did a hit and run. It's gone now." Vesta said maintaining a steady gaze. "I could use that cognac now though."

Marco looked over to the table where the snifters stood.

"It must be cold by now. I will heat it again," he said standing up.

"Not necessary. Warm, cold or with a straw, I know it's going to be just what the doctor would have ordered."

Marco retrieved the cognac and handed a glass to her.

"Sante," he said as he touched his snifter to hers. "It means to your health."

"Yes. Sante." Vesta replied as she put the snifter to her lips and drained the glass.

The caramel-colored liquor flowed through every cell sending instant relaxation to her afflicted hand and the rest of her body. Its anesthetizing quality numbed her finer tuned awareness bringing back her focus to the moment at hand dulling her headache somewhat. She let out a sigh as she set the glass down. Back to business. "So, you were saying that is a real Fabergé egg?"

She could feel Marco's awareness heighten.

"Well, yes. It is. But we should speak of other things since the source of your pain emerged from there."

"Oh no. I don't think that was the case at all." Vesta said realizing that a game of trying to outwit the other had begun. "It was a fluke. The egg had nothing to do with my headache."

Marco sat on a sofa next to her chair. He leaned back sipping his cognac. Vesta couldn't decide if he was looking at her with contempt or lust. It quite possibly could have been both.

"And the egg, have you had it for a long time?" Vesta pressed on.

Marco's face was calm, not a muscle out of place. He smiled but there was no sparkle dancing in his eyes.

"Not that long. Not like other things."

"Did you purchase it in Russia?"

Marco crossed his legs and leaned forward a bit. "It was a gift to my father actually. From a friend of his."

"I wish I had friends who gave me gifts like that," Vesta said as she picked up her empty snifter.

"Ah, you need another drink." Marco said.

"No. What I need is a nice quiet bedroom, hopefully with black-out shades." She stood up, corrected a tiny wobble in her head and tucked her short blond hair behind her ears.

Marco stood up and as he came toward her with a move she had witnessed countless times before from sophisticated men, with one easy motion he removed the glass from her hand wrapping his arm gently around her waist. He brought his cleanly shaven, perfectly tanned face with the chocolate kiss eyes close to hers.

"Now that I know you are feeling better, I would very much like to rejoin where we left off earlier."

Vesta smiled at Marco, the High Priestess at the Page of Swords, a careful dance taking place. She needed answers about what she heard when she touched the egg. They wouldn't come from him. And she was certain he knew she received a message from beyond the veil, something secret. He was trying to seduce her into talking. Vesta's eyes remained calm and determined as she gazed at Marco. While it was true that handsome men could distract her for an hour or two, they were certainly not to be trusted nor were they any match against her own manipulation skills.

Leaning in close so her mouth grazed the tiny soft hairs of his ear, she whispered, "Marco, my handsome host, that ship has sailed."

CHAPTER 7

Sunlight made its way to Vesta's bed in paw prints that crept across the carpet. When it leapt silently onto her pillow she awoke. The drapes had been drawn closed before she went to sleep, but the adamant morning found a crack in between allowing light to spill around the leafy bushes outside and into her room.

Vesta sat up and swung her legs over the side of the bed. The headache from the previous night had disappeared, but the new day brought a new headache. A throb began at her temples. As she stood up it took center stage. With a hand pressed on her right temple, she walked around the room opening doors until she found a bathroom. The shower looked like it was larger than her first apartment in New York. She stepped inside it and pulled levers for the steam option to begin. Billowy clouds puffed from all directions inside the glass walls. Peeling the spaghetti straps from her silk Vera Wang nightgown from her shoulders and letting it fall to the floor, she sat down on a tile bench and leaned her head back. Slowly she inspected the fog that had accumulated outside and inside her.

The vision from the night before was clear in her mind. As

she sorted through the details of what she heard, she realized that more information had been added to the mix. Did she download the additional details while she slept? Maybe that was part of how her InSight worked. She rubbed her temples as she mentally filed everything in order.

Two men were talking but the sound quality wasn't good. It was like they were speaking with blankets over their heads. The challenge in understanding them was exacerbated by the fact they both spoke with accents of some sort. One mentioned something priceless. Maybe he was referring to the egg. The other said it was worth the price. There were a few garbled words before one spoke of collateral damage to be expected. Did that mean there was injury or death from obtaining the egg? The other said he would handle it personally. Were they stealing priceless antiques? Then the other replied that it was hidden well on the ship. That could mean they were using their ships to smuggle stolen goods.

Rocking her head from side to side against the warm tile wall, Vesta knew her special tri-phony powers had kicked in for a reason. The Parrinos could be smugglers. They were obnoxiously rich and displayed rare ancient Roman statue fragments and Fabergé eggs like they were knick-knacks on a drug store shelf. They owned a fleet of ships that moved goods around the world. Maybe they were stealing cultural treasures, smuggling them out of their countries of origin and selling them on the black market.

But if that was true, that the Parrinos were smugglers of antiquities, was that such a horrible crime that her InSight would kick into gear? The act of stealing then smuggling was bad certainly, but the last time she had such a catastrophic reaction to one of her visions was when she saw the young girls being drugged and used as sex slaves. That was when she shook the hand of Raz's stooge at Amara's party and the vision hit her mind like a lightning bolt. Smuggling antiques wasn't on the same level as trafficking humans and drugs. Something didn't add up. Why did a piece of decorative art from Czarist Russia cause such a reaction when she touched it? Vesta shook her head.

Two things she knew for sure. One, touching the egg caused the voices to start. And two, the Parrinos were involved somehow. Whether Marco was mixed up in it directly or not she hadn't decided.

Marco, she had been rather impolite to him when they said goodnight. He had plied her for information and she had denied him. He had probably counted on her being unaccustomed to her InSight kicking into gear as a neophyte High Priestess and just blurting out what she heard.

Vesta looked down at the sweat beading up on her body. She may not like this new gig that was thrust upon her but she wouldn't let anyone play her for a fool. It was no different than having dinner with a competitor where each wiggled around to avoid giving out any information but tried to find out vital bits from the other. Vesta was a master at that game and knew exactly what to do.

It was a chilly trip to the bedroom to retrieve her mobile phone and two Advil but worth the effort. Within minutes Marco rapped on the door of the bathroom.

"Come in," Vesta said from her steamy perch.

She heard the door open followed by a cough.

"Good lord. Am I inside a cloud?" Marco asked.

"Please come in." Vesta emerged from a bank of mist glistening from head to toe. Marco stared at her naked body. She closed the bathroom door and took him by the hand.

"Thanks for getting here so quickly. Let's unbuckle your seat belt because you're about to be at cruising altitude."

As Vesta lay on the huge soft towel Marco spread out for her, she was sure she'd had sex in a steam shower before, she just couldn't remember when or with whom. It didn't matter at the moment because she was more than satisfied with how this time went. Marco's hairless chest and six-pack abdomen had sweat streams crisscrossing each other. It was new territory she had gotten to know well over the past hour. As he lay back on his own towel, propped up on his arms with one leg bent and the other outstretched, Vesta could see him being immortalized as a statue in that white marble the ancient Romans were so fond of. Who knows, maybe he was. But that wasn't what she was interested in now.

Marco reached his hand to her breast and stroked it. "I was worried about you last night."

"I think the wine after the long plane ride from New York got the best of me. I feel great now."

"I'm very glad to hear that but you were staring as if you were lost in a trance. As if you weren't here but somewhere else. What happened? Were you someplace else?"

Marco moved his hand down to her navel and began splashing a finger in the tiny water puddle. Vesta gave him a crescent smile, closed her eyes and moved his hand down a bit further.

"You know, my headache is finally gone. I'm giving you full credit for that." She guided his hand to a spot that was wetter than all the steam the shower could ever muster.

"I don't want to stress my brain by thinking about that moment any longer." She pushed his finger into the depths of her pleasure.

"I just want you to talk to me in that sexy accent of yours. Tell me about your family. Did you say you were in the shipping business? Wine, I suppose. Maybe some olive oil too?"

Vesta leaned up, propped by one arm, using her other arm and hand to grasp Marco by his tall, straight soldier who was ready for action again. It was his turn to close his eyes and utter a low moan. She knew how to dominate the battle and was on her way to winning the war.

The sun was high in the sky and lunch was being served when Vesta appeared in the outdoor dining area. She was steam cleaned as never before, her vintage Yves St. Laurent halter dress exposed as much skin as it covered. And Marco looked spotless in his white button-down shirt with the sleeves rolled up to the elbows. His dark eyes were dancing again. He greeted her with a quick kiss on the cheek before pulling out a chair for her.

"Do you like salmon? The chef has prepared some which just arrived from Oregon."

"I love salmon."

Vesta sat down and allowed the sunshine to be her second lover of the day as it caressed her shoulders and arms. Marco sat down beside her and reached for a bottle of white wine sitting on the table in front of them.

"May I? It's a trebbiano. Light so it won't interfere with the fish."

She nodded her head. "Yes, please."

Vesta reclined in her chair letting the warm sun run its fingers up her legs. The temperature was perfect and so was the company, and for that matter, the setting couldn't have been more idyllic. Knobby rolling hills studded with grapes ready for picking sprawled beneath a royal blue sky. She wondered how long it had been since she felt this relaxed, and dare she think the word, happy. Vesta exhaled slowly as a smile slid across her face.

"How long since you did analysis on the western slope?" Vesta's body tensed and her head turned as a growling voice that sounded faintly familiar with a thick Italian accent approached. She sat straight up in her chair and watched a part man, part bear lumber to the table. She recognized him from the balcony of the Plaza Hotel but he was much bigger up close.

"Ah, Papa. You are joining us for lunch?"

"Unless you have objections that I should not."

"No. No, of course not. You are most welcomed." Marco stood up and motioned to a woman standing near the house doorway who was wearing a white apron.

"Please bring another setting for lunch," he said to her.

"Make that two. Senora Parrino will be joining us," the old man said. The woman nodded and hurried indoors.

Vesta watched the sun totally eclipse as the round bald head of Marco's father loomed over her. Marco stepped in close to Vesta.

"Papa, may I introduce you to Vesta Beauvais. She is our guest for the weekend. Vesta this is my father Senor Francesco Parrino."

Senor Parrino leaned down, took Vesta's hand and delivered a heavy kiss that felt like a hot dog cut in half being squashed on top of her hand.

"It is a great pleasure to meet you." He snorted as he rose up again to his full height. Vesta did her best to temper the recoil instinct of her hand. She slipped it out of his and reached for her wine glass.

"Senor Parrino, it is good to meet you as well."

"Please call me Francesco. We must not waste time with such formalities." The old man moved heavily toward the chair at the end of the rectangular table. He sat down with a grunt.

"Now, tell me about yourself so that I may know you better." Francesco leaned back in his chair allowing a tuft of mangled black hair to protrude above the top button of his white shirt looking like a baby bear trying to claw its way out. Vesta observed more black hair on his arms exposed by his rolled-up sleeves along with hairy little patches sprouting in clumps around his neck. His bushy black eyebrows were the crowning touch as they protected the tiny pin-points he had for eyes. It was quite a contrast to his large hairless head. Vesta wondered how someone as handsome as Marco could come from this Neanderthal.

"You must have an interesting story to tell," Francesco said stirring Vesta from her thoughts.

She shrugged. "I grew up in Colorado with nothing. I had a scholarship to go to college and worked into the position of CEO and chairman of the board of Sybarite, a luxury fashion and goods line based out of New York City. Independent, determined woman makes good. Really kind of a boring story I guess."

"Yes, I had heard that you were doing these things. I meant recently though."

Vesta blinked with the flash of a smile. "I would say my life has definitely gotten more interesting recently." She took a sip of wine. "Did you know me before?"

"Before?" Francesco asked.

"Before this life we're all running around in now," Vesta said.

"Ah, yes. I did."

"You will have to excuse me then since I'm just coming online with this new, yet old, role of being the High Priestess."

"We all have our reasons for doing things," he said.

The woman in the white apron reappeared. She poured a glass of water for Francesco and set the place in front of him with a napkin and silverware as well as a place to the left of him.

"You're not drinking wine," Vesta asked.

"My father doesn't drink wine. It is ironic, we know, but it isn't good for his diabetes," Marco said.

"A wine exporter who doesn't drink wine," Francesco snorted and laughed at the same time.

Vesta raised her eyebrows. "Well, I'm a High Priestess who

doesn't do anything priestly." She cut her glance over to Marco who gave her a quick smile in return.

Francesco leaned forward heavily resting his arms next to the silverware. Vesta heard a groan. She wasn't sure if it was from him or the table.

"You know, we can help you. We are here to serve you. There are many questions we can answer. And many ways we can help." Francesco stared at Vesta unblinking.

"Lots of people like you have offered to help me already."

"What people like me? You mean Marco?"

"Marco has been entertaining me. Showing me a great time. I'm referring to the others of the trionfi like Jared, Cyrus, Sandor and Amara. They're all wanting to help me, show me, enlighten me."

Francesco made the loudest snorting sound Vesta had heard so far and acted like he was spitting on the ground.

"They know nothing. They act like ancient gods who are now extinct. And for good reason. They don't know how to deal with the modern RanChans."

"RanChans?" Vesta furrowed her eyebrows. "What's that?"

Francesco cocked his head. "You don't know that American word?"

"Papa, that's a word made from two American words." Marco looked toward Vesta. "It means random chance. The trionfi call all those who are not born life after life with the same purpose to fill and the same gifts RanChans. Some American member of the trionfi came up with that name a few lives ago and it stuck."

"Jared Schultz has no idea how to deal effectively with RanChans. He is the great Emperor yet he rules like a stable boy. I can show you how to use your formidable power to create vast riches for yourself and your family." Francesco leaned back in his chair again his eyes not leaving Vesta.

"My family is dead. And I haven't decided how or when I want to learn about my power."

"Your uncle was a man who did not listen to good advice in this life. He could have lived much longer if he had listened to me."

"My uncle was murdered by Rasputin's assassin. There was nothing he could have done to avoid it. He was gunned down at a party."

"It could have been avoided. And that is what I am saying to you. I can show you how to live a good life, enjoy the good things."

"I'm doing well on my own."

"Be a smart woman in this life Vesta. There was a reason you put that spell upon yourself last time."

"Maybe she chooses to have the rest of this life be a challenge too."

The hair on the back of Vesta's neck sprung up. A prickling sensation sent chills cascading through her body. On her left she saw a woman approach whose skin was the color of caramel candies handed out at Halloween. She was petite in size but walked with the gait of someone over six feet tall. She glanced at Vesta, her bright green eyes piercing into private depths. Vesta gasped; her eyes widened. She regretted both gut reactions and, in an instant, tried to mask them which made her expression even more contorted. The emerald eyes narrowed and a viper's grin creased the caramel.

"Mother," Marco stood up and moved quickly around the table to pull out a chair for her. "I would like to introduce you to," Marco began.

"No introduction is necessary my son. Vesta and I just met."

"Of course. Very good." Marco positioned his mother in her chair at the table. "May I pour some of our trebbiano for you. It's quite exceptional."

"Yes, I will have some."

Marco poured the wine while Vesta felt herself being scanned by the woman. Pulling herself up to her full height in her own chair, straightening her back and lowering her chin, Vesta returned the steady gaze. The hair was still standing stiff on her neck as she reached for her wine glass. This was the woman who could read minds. And chances were more than good that she was reading hers at that moment. Time to think of boring subjects.

"Senora Parrino, did you and your husband just arrive?" Vesta asked.

"We flew in from New York a few hours later than you last night."

"You flew commercial then?"

"A common assumption. But no, we have several jets in the attivita commerciale."

Francesco nodded and picked up his wife's glass of wine and brought it to his nose.

"No Franci, no." She said giving him her full attention and taking the glass from his hands.

"Valentina, I want only to smell the terroir."

"It is the same as the vintage before this. No different." Valentina said as she placed her glass in front of her.

"Papa, I will take you into the cellar where these barrels sit. You will be embraced by the smell of the earth the moment you walk in," Marco said. "I will take you after lunch."

The old man nodded without eye contact as he fingered the silverware by his plate. Vesta studied every movement he made.

"And so, now you are back with us," Valentina said returning her spotlight on Vesta.

"Actually this is my first visit to your estate."

"I refer to your rediscovered awareness of your identity."

Vesta felt her third eye begin to spin. There was another

sensation too, one that seemed to course through the veins of her body. Almost electrical in nature she tried to identify it but it was lost in the recesses of her mind. Other thoughts, vital ones, seemed to be lurking on the perimeter too but she couldn't draw them close enough. The tension made her feel off balance in a physical way. Vesta reached for her glass of wine and drank more than a sip before setting the glass down.

She looked at Valentina as steadily as she could. The age of this woman perplexed her. She could have been fifty or seventy-five. Her hair was piled into a turban of blood orange silk. Heavy gold earrings that looked like shields or emblems dangled close to her multi-colored silk caftan. She was tiny, thin and had wrinkles, but not many. Usually a woman's hands scream her age but Valentina's were smooth yet bony. The gargantuan ruby ring on one finger almost appeared to drip blood when the sun hit it. Vesta shivered. She could feel Valentina's eyes scratching every inch of her body.

"I must be the talk of the trionfi these days," Vesta said.

"The question of your ability to assume your duties has been raised."

"As I was saying to your husband when you arrived, I've done very well for myself so far."

Valentina picked up her wine swirling the golden liquid so that the sun glinted in the glass yet her eyes remained on Vesta.

"No comparison can be made between selling dresses and being the High Priestess of the trionfi."

Vesta's body stiffened. She was formulating a stinging reply that was never launched because a plate of grilled salmon and fresh salad greens was set in front of her and Valentina. Two more followed for the men. Water from a crystal pitcher was poured into tall glasses. Marco nodded at one of the women of the waitstaff when she finished at the table, then he picked up his wine glass.

"I would like to propose a toast to our honored guest today," he said. "May your memories of our family be fond ones."

Vesta almost laughed out loud but held it in. If there were any good memories of her day so far it would be the magnificent sex she had with Marco that morning. A smile grazed her face as she looked at him across the table.

"Thank you." Vesta sipped her wine then began to enjoy the freshest salmon she had ever tasted now that the grilling was complete. Light conversation about food and wine was conducted by Marco for the remainder of the meal.

Lunch concluded as clouds shoved the sunshine away from the table. A chill, this time from the weather, set in. Vesta checked her watch and looked at each of her hosts.

"This meal was exceptional. Please tell your chef how much I enjoyed it. Now I must grab my bag and get to the airport. Marco, I believe you said my plane left at 3 o'clock."

"It is at your disposal for any time today, but yes, we had agreed upon three."

Marco stood up, walked around the table and pulled out Vesta's chair. Francesco motioned for Marco to come help him stand. After an awkward series of movements and grunts the mission was accomplished. Valentina rose from her chair, waving her son away when he tried to assist.

Vesta walked toward the family who were standing at the end of the table.

"Thank you for opening your home to me today Senor Parrino."

She shook his hand.

"Francesco." The old man said as he nodded.

Vesta turned toward Valentina extending a hand. Her fingers began to tingle like she had dunked them in icy water.

"Senora Parrino," Vesta said. Valentina raised her hand to block the motion.

"It is an ancient custom of my people that you do not touch royalty unless they initiate it. One of many things you must learn in this life."

Vesta's eyes opened wide. She dropped her hand to the side and the tingling stopped.

"Royalty?" Vesta took half a step back and smiled. "So who's royal? You or me?" Vesta grabbed the most sarcastic tone she could muster. "I'm confused."

Valentina's green eyes flashed bright. Vesta felt a wall of invisible sand blast her face then her entire body. It was a psychic shredding on a molecular level lasting only an instant but left Vesta stunned. She blinked to recover visualizing a wall of energy springing up between her and Valentina to protect herself. An urge to grab the bony brown hand of the old woman breaking it in two surged through her but evolved into a promise. "I will do whatever it takes to bring you down as hard as I can. I know that you and your family are smuggling something and I will find out what it is," she silently pledged.

A grunting sound distracted her thought as Francesco cleared his throat.

"Valentina comes from the Kongo culture. We call them First Blood because they are the oldest of our kind. She is the only one left so we treat her with the deepest respect."

Francesco moved between Valentina and Vesta taking her hand again. Once more it felt like two halves of a hot dog were pressing on her when he kissed it.

"We hope you come to understand our ways in this part of the trionfi family. We can help you Vesta. Tell me what you want. We can provide it. That's the way it works."

Francesco turned loose of Vesta's hand.

"You hold hope where there is likely none," Valentina said. "Just because the High Priestess obliterated her memories this time to forget her past mistakes does not mean she will demonstrate any wisdom now."

Vesta locked a gaze on Valentina that spoke of hatred on a level she had never conjured before. The ancient First Blood soaked in the dark energy with pleasure almost like she fed off it. Francesco waved his hand at Vesta.

"You help us and the world is yours. We make sure of that. You will see. If you don't join us, then you will see the other side. But I think you are a smart woman in this life. You have already shown it by not obeying your old ways. This is better, no?" The old man nodded. "Just tell us what you want." He grunted once more before leaving the table.

Vesta watched as he struggled to shift his weight from one foot to the other walking into the house.

"The only thing I want," she thought to herself. "Is to have another hot round of sex with your son, this time wearing my favorite Laboutins." Vesta smiled to herself but made it look like she was smiling at Francesco.

Marco ran his fingers through his curly black hair as he walked up beside her.

"I will call the flight attendant now to make sure everything is ready. Excuse me please."

Vesta watched Marco with his smooth tanned skin moving easily beneath his white button-down shirt. He pulled out his mobile phone from his pants pocket as he walked to the pool area. She noticed Valentina standing at the edge of her view, a stick figure wearing flowing silk and priceless gems. Valentina lowered her chin diving beyond psychic barriers with her words.

"Yes, he is a very handsome young man," she said. A viper's smile slid across her face. "Intelligent too. Beautiful, youthful women line up and are his at any moment he chooses. He works, but he takes time for his pleasures too. Many here at this house even. How inferior you must feel having sex with such a young, virile man being close to ten years older than he. Even when wearing your Christian Laboutin."

CHAPTER 8

Mindreading existed in Vesta's world up to that point as a lame sideshow trick. What Valentina pulled wasn't a trick. Liam warned her. Now there was no doubt the old witch read her mind. Learning to block her entry meant tapping into her tri-phony powers and asking the others for help. She hated the thought, but the bit of conversation Vesta heard when she touched the Fabergé egg needed unraveling. It would illuminate the path to wrecking Valentina's smuggling venture. Whether it manifested in the end as something petty or grand, Vesta didn't care. She wanted to make the enterprise come crashing down around that turbaned head. Focusing on this didn't mean her search for Raz would falter. Refining her High Priestess skills would help find him. In the meantime, she had hired investigators, the best in the business according to her research who were on his trail in Russia. As soon as they found him, she would enlist, bribe, whatever was necessary and whomever she needed to pull his scum-drenched carcass out of Russia and back into a jail. That was her primary goal but since there was nothing else she could physically do at that moment about him, she would turn her attention to what flared up her

InSight. Handling more than one major project at a time had never been a problem.

The idea that Sunday was a day of rest was absurd to Vesta. Only the lazy or those lacking ambition regarded it as such. She abhorred lying in bed past seven o'clock, whether it was hers or someone else's. Even though she slept only four hours after returning from Napa Valley, a day full of possibility beckoned. Cold clouds clotted the sky as she walked to Battery Park from her apartment. There was no better way to get rid of jet lag and a mild hangover.

Vesta drank too much on the flight home. Valentina reading her thoughts sent a panic through her. Waves of anger followed by fear ebbed and flowed in her brain. Being on board one of the Parrino's private jets meant there were cameras, no doubt. If she drank enough wine, according to her reasoning, maybe Valentina would only get a jumble of images or words out of her. That was her strategy anyway, plus it deadened her pain of feeling so inferior to such a raging bitch.

An icy wind pierced her sweatshirt and pants as it snapped from the river. She put her head down and walked faster. Cracks in the sidewalk reflected the cracks she felt in her life. She didn't want to be the High Priestess in some elite group of cosmic snobs. It interfered in her well-crafted career plan. She needed to be thinking about the summer collection and accessories for Sybarite's new luggage line, yet despite that she stayed focused on how to topple everything in Valentina's life. She knew it smacked of a childish vendetta, but she didn't care. Even if she didn't want to be the High Priestess of the tarot cards, she rejected the notion on all levels that this woman would get the best of her. She would take care of the Valentina problem in record time.

As she walked, she made a mental list. Several things were learned from her InSight when she touched the egg. She heard something real, it wasn't a dream or fantasy, it was a conversation, as if she had listened at a keyhole at a door. Furthermore, not only could she hear what was going on but she got a sense of the place too even though she couldn't see anything. A certain essence existed when she received InSight. Something like a mild electrical current ran through her and permeated the vision. Now she could recognize it, distinguish it from daydreaming.

The final realization dictated that she must take action. Even though she didn't know for sure the job specifics for the High Priestess, she knew having visions was part of it. And once a vision like this came to her, action had to be taken to deal with it. But she had no idea what to do next.

Vesta's fast walk turned into a slow run around the tip of Manhattan. She ran to get rid of her jet lag, her hangover and the frustration over this new responsibility. How much time would this new project require? She knew she had to start getting some answers, but she hated the idea of asking for help.

All the remarks from the trionfi, the tri-phonies, about her being fun in this life began to echo in her ears. She must have been such an insufferable bore before. The image of her as a homely earth mother wandering around in Birkenstocks worn with socks and shin-length skirts popped into her mind. A shudder ran through her followed by a wave of nausea. That could never be who she was in this life or any other. Yet she knew making nice with the other major arcana members was necessary to find out some practical application steps in her quest to defeat Valentina and locate Raz. But that meant being cordial to the traitor Jared, Miss Perfect Amara, Sandor the magnificent jerk and worst of all Cyrus, the miserable excuse for a father.

It also meant they would want her help in finding Raz. She was determined to find him, but she didn't necessarily want to help them. He was lying low somewhere in Siberia probably. After he was apprehended again, she would make sure the authorities knew about the sex slave ring and the drugs. She could handle Raz on her own, the trionfi didn't need to be involved.

Vesta put her head down and ran harder. The memory of Uncle Raymond asking if he could reveal the secret to her seeped into her awareness. He knew he was dying and she would be the only one left to see the visions averting disaster for the regular humans, or RanChans as Francesco called them. The weight of that responsibility felt overwhelming but he was counting on her.

Vesta stopped running and looked out into the harbor. She had to do the High Priestess gig for Uncle Raymond if no one else, it was that simple. Vesta exhaled.

"Well, shit," she said out loud.

"It's your double-edged sword."

"What?" Vesta spun around to look behind her. Sandor waved from a nearby bench where he was seated. "Are you following me?"

"I've been sitting here for ten minutes. You ran right past me."

"I don't believe you. And what did you mean by double-edged sword?"

"Being the High Priestess has some definite rewards and some huge responsibility," Sandor replied.

"How did you know I was thinking about that?"

Sandor stood up and walked toward her.

"Darling, you're new at this job. Or at least new in this life at it."

Vesta put her hands on her hips and leveled her gaze at him. "I'm glad I can amuse you. So you can read minds. No one mentioned that you could do it too."

"Only a little. But you're so easy to figure out."

Vesta squinted her eyes at Sandor. She wanted to say something insulting but couldn't think of anything fast enough.

"Sounds like our ancient African queen got under your skin a little bit in California, huh?"

"You don't have a clue what you're talking about."

"Valentina didn't read your mind?" Sandor said as he walked closer to her. "She didn't diddle around in there." He pointed to her head and made a swirling motion with his finger.

"What do you want Sandor? Get it over with and tell me why you followed me."

"Vesta, all kidding aside," Sandor stared straight into her eyes without blinking. "We need to know what's going on with Rasputin. He's gone off the radar since he was released into Russian jurisdiction. You are the only one who has InSight."

"I can't just make it pop out of me at will."

"Sure you can if you learn. And baby, we really need for you to learn, or remember, how to do that."

"I'm not your baby." Vesta turned away from Sandor but was excited at the notion of being able to call it into action at any time she wanted.

"How do I learn?"

"Well, Raymond would teach you since he was usually older than you each lifetime. But that's not going to happen now. I'm sure Amara can help you. Maybe some of her meditation techniques and yoga, and walking around that circle thing."

"It's called a labyrinth. Yeah, I've done all of that and I don't want Amara's help right now." She was lying but hoped Sandor hadn't caught it. Learning how to use her gift was essential but she didn't want to appear too eager. The thought of being needy to anyone in that group was revolting to her.

"You need somebody's help cause you're no help to any of us like this."

"I'm no help to you? Like you've been help to me?" Vesta whirled around to face Sandor again. "Why didn't you tell me who I was before Uncle Raymond was shot? You could have saved his life. You knew what was going on."

"Honey, you cast one hell of a spell on yourself to forget who you were in this life. You made Raymond promise not to tell you. Then you made him get an oath from the rest of us not to tell you. You tied it up real nice with a bow there. So what were we supposed to do? We did everything we could to stop Rasputin but he's one wily asshole. He sure got you off track of finding your portal. Isn't that what you were calling it?"

The truth of his words and the smirk on his face cut deep.

"Shut up Sandor. What I want to know is why did I put a spell on myself in the first place? What was so damned bad about my last life?"

Sandor's expression softened his stretched grin disappeared.

"No one was finer than you last time." Sandor looked down at the ground. "I'm really not the guy you should talk to about what went down last time. Not to dodge the heat but," he said as he shifted his gaze to the harbor.

"But you are," Vesta finished his sentence. "And I'm not surprised. Then who will tell me? Cause I need to know right now."

"I can tell you."

Vesta swung her head around toward the park to see Cyrus walking up.

"Okay, this is beyond creepy. You're both following me. Do you have cameras in my apartment too? Do you watch me pee in the morning?"

"Sandor and I came together. There's no big mystery. Or cameras."

"I seriously doubt that. I know you're really anxious to get information out of me because I've seen you more in the last three months than I have all my life." Vesta pushed her hair behind her ears. "But first you're going to answer some questions for me. What happened Daddy Dearest? Why did I put a spell on myself to forget who I was in this life? Nothing makes sense right now. Everything I thought I knew about myself has been scattered like a deck of cards in the wind so I don't know which end is up."

Sandor walked closer to Cyrus.

"She always had a way with words," he said to Cyrus, then looked at Vesta. "Great analogy there." He finished by giving her a thumbs up.

"Shut up." Vesta's blue eyes flashed at Sandor with an energy she could feel shooting from her toes through the top of her head.

"Darling, if looks could kill," Sandor said, "this minor god would be laying on the sidewalk right now."

"Now Sandor, give Vesta a break. You're enjoying this advantage way too much. Vesta needs our help and we need hers."

Sandor raised his hands in surrender. "Okay, fine. Just joking with our esteemed High Priestess. Just trying to lighten the mood a little."

Cyrus lowered his eyes to Vesta almost as if he was bowing to her.

"Let's continue your walk, if you don't mind."

Vesta relaxed her gaze and nodded her head. The trio walked in silence for several moments before Cyrus began speaking.

"I know Raymond was able to explain a little bit before he died this time. The origins of the trionfi stretch back long before we were depicted on the Italian cards in the early Renaissance. That's when we went underground, to use a tired phrase. The Catholic Church became aware of our existence and was afraid we would usurp their power. While not being able to catch and kill all of us during that time, they did create some major obstacles for us."

"Yeah, and you were a huge bad ass during part of that era. Even I was amazed at what you came up with," Sandor said as he leaned his head close to Vesta's.

Cyrus gently pushed Sandor away from her.

"Now let's not get off track. That's another story for another day," he said. "Vesta, we were anointed with these unique gifts by benevolent beings who don't normally call our planet home."

"Extraterrestrials you mean? Yeah, Uncle Raymond sort of mentioned this but I have to say that's hard for me to swallow."

"I could insert a crude joke here, but I won't." Sandor said as he raised up his hands. "I won't." Cyrus glared at him.

"Love how those killer looks run in the family. All right. All right. I'll stop." From his sports jacket pocket Sandor pulled out a stick, a ridiculously long stick. Vesta's eyebrows furrowed as she watched a three-foot long polished piece of wood emerge from his breast pocket. Sandor waved his free hand at Cyrus. "Go on. I'm listening."

"Any way, yes, we were each chosen by these beings that wanted to ensure our planet not only survived but thrived. They wanted us to develop without outside interference from other non-local beings so they gave each of us certain gifts. While we each obtained stunning abilities, the Enlightened Ones, also called the Elders, structured it so that no one person could protect the planet and its inhabitants without the help of the others. No one had supreme power over the others."

"Checks and balances, see?" Sandor said as he walked using his stick as a cane.

"Right," Cyrus said. "In some lives one of us might have more to do than the others. It depends on the state of human evolution, societal situations and environmental conditions."

"I was very busy during the Great Depression," Sandor said.

"Yes. And Amara was vital to many of the human rights laws that were initiated a thousand years ago in England, in France during their revolution and here in the US in the mid-eighteen hundreds."

"Okay," Vesta said. "I get what you're saying about that but I want you to back up a minute. Francesco called Valentina First Blood and said she was the oldest of our kind. Liam told me that too. How can that be if we were all given our gifts at the same time?"

Cyrus stopped walking. He looked at Sandor who shrugged his shoulders and pointed his walking stick toward Cyrus.

"Valentina comes from the first line created by non-local beings. Before humankind spread across the globe they were centralized mainly on the African and Australian continents. The beings that gave Valentina and her line their gifts were not as careful in the way they structured them. The First Blood each received the same powerful abilities. Their gifts weren't divided up as they were when we were created. As human history progressed, the First Blood expanded around the earth and settled their own civilizations. Eventually however they began warring, killing each other and found the way to stop their line from reincarnating. Valentina destroyed the last of her kind many lives ago."

"Her powers aren't as sharp as they used to be because her line is so old. But she can still royally fuck you up if she wants to." Sandor pointed his stick at Vesta.

"Yeah, that whole royal thing sounded like bullshit," Vesta said.

"It's not. Trust me," Cyrus said.

"So does Marco have the same powers as his mother?"

Cyrus shook his head. "No. In fact no other members of the royal families have the gifts Valentina does."

"Royal families?"

"When you do finally look through a tarot deck, you'll see that there are four royal families in it," Sandor said.

"Our main protector and benefactor in the fifteenth century, Filippo Visconti, the Duke of Milan, came up with the idea of not only of having us and our gifts painted on cards," Cyrus said. "But granting large estates to four minor trionfi families who swore allegiance to us."

"Yeah, they're gifts weren't strong enough to last through the centuries so their extra human stuff basically dwindled to nothing. But the old duke was sympathetic to their situation and set them up with money and land."

"Are you saying Marco doesn't have any super powers like us?"

"You tell me," Sandor said with a wink.

Vesta rolled her eyes at him and turned to Cyrus. "That means neither Francesco nor Giovanni have any special powers either."

"Only in so far as a heightened awareness, a super sensitivity, in certain areas," Cyrus said. "That's all that remains of their gifts."

"The Parrinos are the house of Swords, so they're the bad assess who like to pick fights," Sandor said.

"It's their mental acuity that sets them apart," Cyrus said.

"There's some blood lust in there too," Sandor said. "You have to admit that."

"Valentina brought that with her when she killed the Queen of Swords with one of her potions, stopped her reincarnation and took her place a long time ago."

"How did she do that?"

Cyrus shrugged. "Some sort of special concoction she came up with. It's how she stopped the other First Blood from reincarnating too."

"Francesco wasn't about to argue with her because he knew the same would happen to him," Sandor said.

"Do they reincarnate like us with the memories?"

"Only vaguely," Cyrus said. "They're schooled, more or less, in what's expected of them. They learn their family history, the trionfi history, and from personal diaries they pass down. If they pursue interests that spark their innate talents, they succeed in stunning ways."

"And they're supposed to shelter and protect us in times of need. That's why they were given the estates and cash to begin with," Sandor said. "Only two of the four families would actually do that now."

"What do you mean?"

"Well, you now know you can forget about any protection from the Parrinos unless you play by their rules. And the same goes for the Garcia family. Javier will steal the shirt off your back if you're not paying attention."

A black Cadillac SUV pulled up on the street beside them. The passenger window slid down and Amara leaned her head out.

"Good morning! How is everyone? Would you like to come have brunch with us? We know a great place in Chelsea."

Vesta walked over to the car in looked inside. Jared was in the driver's seat.

"I really loathe the entire notion of brunch," she said.

"Vesta, can we please go somewhere to eat and talk?" Jared asked.

"You guys really have this all timed out, don't you?" Vesta shook her head but opened the back door and got in the car followed by Cyrus and Sandor. They maneuvered through the Sunday streets arriving at a restaurant a few minutes later.

Walking inside felt like entering a secret garden. The front door was the same as every other old warehouse-looking door on the block but once on the other side you were transported to an English terrace of some lord's manor house. The hostess smiled bouncing up and down a few times when she saw Amara. Sandor made sure to cast an award-winning smile at her.

"Hi! It's so great to see you again so soon. I have the table on the balcony for you. I think it's the best one in the place," she said.

"Thank you, Heather," Amara said returning the beaming smile.

"I thought we were going someplace like a diner. I'm wearing a sweat suit," Vesta said looking down. "They're going to kick me out."

"Not when you're dining with the owner," Amara replied over her shoulder as they headed for their table. Vesta rolled her eyes.

"Since when did you go into the restaurant business?"

"My foundation decided to invest with this group of women who wanted to raise money for saving the Amazon rain forest. We're going on a research trip there next month. Want to join us?"

"No," Vesta said picking up her menu then shutting it seconds later.

"That was quick. You know what you want already?" Sandor asked.

"Yep. They can't screw up a cheeseburger."

"Oh," Amara said. "This is a pescaterrean restaurant. The only meat served is fish. But we do make an outstanding burger with portabellas that tastes just like beef."

Vesta shook her head. "Fine. Whatever."

Cyrus set his menu down and addressed the table.

"Sandor and I have been reacquainting Vesta with our roots. She had some questions that we wanted to answer."

"Before we get back to that, I want to know, since Jared is now in our presence, where is Raz? And what have you done about getting him back in jail?" Vesta asked knowing that the best defense is offense.

Jared cleared his throat and looked directly at her.

"Rasputin is in Russia again, and without going into too much detail being that we're in a public place, I can tell you that he has disappeared for the time being. We don't know what he's doing or exactly where he is. That is where we need your help."

"Why me? Don't all of you have your super powers ready to jump into action?"

"Gentlemen," Amara said. "It might be helpful if we describe in simple terms what each of us can contribute so Vesta will better understand how this works."

"I'll go first to bring the old girl up to speed," Sandor said. Vesta glared at him. "There goes the arrow again," he said as grabbed his chest.

"Just get on with it," Cyrus said.

"Okay, so as you know, I'm called the Magician in the original deck of cards. Why? Because I make magic things happen with all my trusty tools." He held up his walking stick then set it back on the floor.

"Whether it's business or money matters, negotiating a conflict, or sometimes creating it," Sandor smiled. "I'm the go to guy who can manipulate beneficial results with a full toolbox of resources."

"Isn't that what most hedge fund managers do?" Vesta stretched a fake smile across her face.

"Precisely," he said. "I can also disappear for a minute or two but it's exhausting."

"Sandor's abilities stretch wide but not too deep," Cyrus said.

"Are you calling me shallow?" Sandor asked.

"I knew that before I even knew about you being a tri-phony," Vesta said.

Amara raised her hand.

"Vesta, I'm known by the cards as the Empress, you know that. I realize it's a lofty title but my gifts translate into nurturing all life. My main focus since the Industrial Revolution has been protecting our environment. Humans have wreaked horrible damage on our beautiful Gaia."

"The damage would have been far worse without all you've done over the past few centuries," Jared said placing his hand on top of hers.

Vesta rolled her eyes again for all to see.

"Jealous much?" Sandor asked poking her gently with his walking stick.

"Touch me just once more with that stick and I'll break it in half."

"It's a wand," he said. "Don't you know what my tools are according to the tarot? They are a wand, a pentacle, or coin as I prefer to call it, a cup and a sword. Be glad I didn't prod you with the sword. Oh, that's right, you've already had some sword action this weekend."

Cyrus exhaled deeply drumming his fingers on the table. "Maybe we should explain why we all have specific gifts. Sandor and I told her about the First Blood."

"Everything?" Amara asked.

Cyrus gave Amara a quick glance of warning and shook his head. Amara blinked acknowledgment and changed the subject.

"Vesta, would you like a deck of tarot cards," she asked sounding slightly flustered. "So you can become more familiar with the major and minor arcana?"

"No. What did that exchange of looks between the two of you mean?"

"Darling, you can run but you can't hide. And you need some heavy on the job training right now," Sandor said.

"I'm not running or hiding from anything."

A young man walked to the table and asked if they would like to order their meal. Vesta sat back and eyed the group as they decided what they wanted to eat. The crazy reality dawned on her that the Emperor, Empress, Magician, High Priestess and the Chariot were pausing in their conversation about how to protect life on the planet to order food and drink from an unsuspecting waiter. The whole concept was still almost too much to grasp but she had to admit the energy was palpable swirling around the table. It invigorated her and made her feel strong. The waiter looked at her.

"Ma'am, what would you like?"

"Whatever is the closest thing to a cheeseburger here and a spicy bloody Mary."

"Thank you," the waiter said then took orders from the rest before leaving the table.

"Another hangover?" Sandor asked. "That's a sure-fire cure."

"Do you have any clue about how to mind your own business?" Vesta asked before turning to the others. "So Cyrus, I'm told you're the Chariot. Isn't that a thing rather than a person?"

Cyrus gave a quick half smile in response. "Technically, yes. Images and names were painted on the original cards for story-telling purposes so that trusted humans wouldn't forget us. The names they gave us referenced what our gifts are. They couldn't come up with one name to express "the guardian who has the ability to hold things together when they're completely falling apart" so they symbolized me as the charioteer and called the card the Chariot."

"According to Uncle Raymond you're also on the Lovers card with my mother."

"I am."

Vesta shook her head as she stared at Cyrus unwilling to let him off easy. "That's ironic, isn't it?"

"Vesta," Jared began.

"It's okay, Jared. Vesta only knows what she's seen in this life from an outsider's perspective."

"What I saw was my mother struggling to make ends meet while we lived in a cabin without heat or running water on the side of a mountain in Crested Butte, Colorado."

"That is how Enid has chosen to live for many lifetimes. Even after those conveniences were invented she eschewed them in favor of living close to the land, as she liked to say." Cyrus leaned forward across the table from Vesta. "Has anyone told you yet what Enid's individual card is?"

"Not yet. Please enlighten me." Vesta replied in a dull monotone.

"It's Strength. And if you were familiar with the tarot deck and what each card symbolizes, you would know that Strength represents relentless fortitude, courage and the ability to withstand all of life's challenges whether they be physical, emotional or spiritual."

"I guess that came in handy this time since you abandoned her, and me."

"Don't you get it?" Jared interrupted. "She chose that life. That's what she wanted. That's what she always wants."

"Vesta, Enid and I are very similar in needing to be close to the Earth." Amara paused as if she cut her sentence short. She looked at Cyrus who returned her gaze and nodded after a few moments.

"What?" Vesta asked. "Again, what's with the secret eye communication?"

Jared leaned back in his chair and ran his hand through his hair.

"What?" Vesta demanded.

The waiter arrived with their drinks. Their conversation paused. He placed a bottle of imported beer in front of Jared who picked it up and drank it dry without hesitation. He put the empty bottle on the table.

"I'll have another please," he said.

"Yes, sir." The waiter headed toward the bar.

"Okay, he's gone. Now tell me what's going on," Vesta said.

"Well, you see Vesta," Amara began. "In the major arcana our relationships to each other pretty much stay the same life after life. We remain related by blood to who we were in the beginning. Situations always vary though. Sometimes we know each other from childhood and sometimes we don't. Sometimes our parents tell us who we are in terms of the trionfi, and sometimes they don't until we're older."

"So, who else is blood related here? The only one I know about is Cyrus being my father."

"That's right. He has always been your father. And Enid has been your mother since the beginning and Raymond has always been her brother. You see the Enlightened Ones chose an entire family to receive their special gifts because they already exhibited extraordinary natural abilities. The gifts they gave each one added to the significant ability each one already possessed. So, it was like super-charging the uncle, the father, the mother, and the two daughters."

Amara paused. Vesta could feel the eyes of everyone at the table watching her as she stared at Amara. She was replaying in her head what Amara just said. Something needed reviewing because it didn't add up on the surface. Then it clicked together in her mind like discovering a missing puzzle piece. She froze in her chair, then lowered her head still staring at Amara.

"Wait. Are you telling me," Vesta paused. "We're sisters?"

Amara nodded her head. "I am."

Jared drew his breath in and looked down at the table. Vesta scanned the assembled group one by one. No one seemed to be breathing.

"But how can that be?" Vesta began. "You have different parents. You were raised in Connecticut and I didn't even meet you until I was in college."

"That was the situation this time. But I was born to Cyrus and Enid. They put me up for adoption when I was two months old. You were only a year old, so I'm sure you don't remember."

"What?" Vesta heard the words Amara was saying but they weren't making any sense. She picked up her bloody Mary and drank it dry in seconds. She waved her empty glass at Cyrus.

"You were even worse than I thought. At least you let Enid keep me." Vesta stared at Cyrus shaking her head. He returned the stare with eyes that would freeze an Eskimo.

"No. No, it wasn't like that at all Vesta," Amara said. "He and Enid discussed it with Raymond who drew upon his InSight and they decided the best way for me to have the most impact in this life, given the current socio-economic situation was to have a wealthy couple adopt me so that I would grow up with the resources to help places like the rain forest and groups of young women who were going to be in great need. It was a brilliant idea, really."

Vesta studied the wet ring on the table left by her glass. She began nodding her head. The waiter arrived with Jared's beer.

"Will you bring me another right away please?" Vesta asked pointing at her glass. The waiter nodded and left.

"Okay, let me get this straight. You and I are blood sisters?"

"Yes."

"And Cyrus and Enid put you up for adoption by an extremely wealthy east coast couple, who as I recall were old for first-time parents, right?"

"That's right," Amara said. "They had given up after years of trying, so I was a real blessing to them."

"I'm sure you were," Vesta said. "And they both died when we were in college, right?"

"Unfortunately, yes, but they had nice long lives."

"Yes, and you inherited hundreds of millions of dollars when you turned twenty-one."

"That's right. And that's when I began Conscious Evolution Partners with them named as co-founders."

"Of course your private school education from kindergarten on up prepared you for doing something like that."

Amara nodded. "And I had made a lot of contacts with people who helped me enormously in creating those."

"Right. Bono, Bill Gates and Oprah, to name just a few." Vesta looked at Cyrus. "And I was left with Enid to grow up without a store-bought dress until I earned enough money working at the Loose Moose coffee shop after school to buy one."

The waiter set Vesta's bloody Mary in front of her. She picked it up and drank it dry in less than ten seconds and set the glass on the table.

"You people are something else." Vesta stood up. "You all just wrote me off and left me there to fend for myself. After all, I was no good to you. Casting a spell so I wouldn't remember who I was. It was a toss-up if I would make anything of myself, right?"

"It wasn't like that. We were trying to protect you because of the spell," Amara said.

"Vesta, sit down and let Amara explain," Jared said.

"Nope," Cyrus said picking up his vodka martini. "She's about to make one of her grand exits."

Vesta smirked. "You are so astute Daddy-o."

She walked out of the door of the enchanted garden and onto the dirty New York sidewalk. She could have hailed a cab but she wanted to let the cold air freeze the thoughts running through her head, freeze the hatred and sorrow, freeze the ridiculous life this hand had dealt her.

CHAPTER 9

A sound coming from her jacket pocket signaled a phone call coming in jolting her out of her rage-stupor. She recognized it as Marco's number and hit the accept button despite not really wanting to talk to anyone.

"Hello Marco, what's up?"

"Good morning. Did you receive the flowers and small gift I had delivered to your home?"

"No, but I've been gone since eight o'clock."

"In my mind I was treasuring the time we spent together and I wanted to thank you for coming all the way to Napa Valley."

"It was easy with your private jet. And thank you for the weekend. Parts of it were fabulous and other parts were interesting, to say the least."

"Yes, I wanted to apologize for something my senses told me was happening at lunch. My mother can be a bit demonstrative at times. She only seeks the welfare of our family. If she appeared less than cordial to you, I sincerely apologize."

"Marco, you're a nice man, but your mother made it quite clear to me that she thinks I'm too old to be carrying on an intimate relationship with you."

"Age makes no difference to me."

"I understand that you feel that way. I do too. But how old are you?"

"I'm thirty."

"Well, I'm thirty-nine. Some, like your mother, would call that age gap too big."

"I don't."

Vesta stopped walking and stood in a shop doorway to block the wind.

"Look Marco. I'm going to be really straight with you here. I enjoyed our time together but I know that you and your family want me to cooperate with your business somehow. Even though I don't know what that means exactly. And I think you're just using sex as a way to get to me. I won't let you play me like a fool."

"Vesta, while it's true that my father has asked for your coop- eration and my mother has been rather curt with you because of your hesitation, I assure you that my intentions are only to enjoy more time with you. You enliven me in a special way that I would like to explore further."

Vesta resented the responsibility imposed on her as the High Priestess but she could certainly use the InSight that came with it to find out what the Parrinos were smuggling and ruin Valenti- na's high and mighty life. And if she had another sizzling night with Marco again, that would be okay too. A plan began to form in her mind.

"Well, you have to come see me then."

"I'm telling you, do not fuck with her." Liam's raised eyebrows and wagging finger meant he was more than serious.

"Valentina has you spooked. She's some moldy leftover from

an ancient age who can barely keep that turban balanced on her wrinkled old head." Vesta reclined in her chair.

"I told you she could read your mind, and she did. Don't you think she's going to find out about this plan of yours?"

Vesta leaned across the two-top table at Le Bernardin and spoke in a low voice.

"You also told me she isn't able to read my mind unless I'm in close proximity to her. That means as long as I stay at a good distance, she won't have a clue what I'm doing."

Liam waved his Gilpin's and tonic at her. "You're playing with real fire, Love," he said.

"Besides, you're going to teach me how to block her from reading my mind." Vesta leaned an inch closer to Liam.

"You just block her."

"Well, that tells me absolutely nothing." Vesta picked up her martini glass.

"Look, you blocked that Madame Kali from roaming around in your head when you were in Cairo, right? It's the same thing."

Vesta remembered how the tarot card reader popped inside her psychic space that day in her shop. It was the strangest thing she'd ever felt, someone occupying the realm of her awareness with her, dwelling in her most private sanctum. She recalled the shock of realizing what happened and psychically slammed the door shoving Madame Kali out. Whatever that meant, she still wasn't sure.

"I don't know what I did to kick her out." Vesta shook her head.

"Doesn't matter. Just do it again."

"You're a lot of help."

"I am," Liam drained the last of his cocktail and waved to a waiter for another. His wave caught the attention of two women following the maître d' to their table. "Oh my god, it's Liam Spencer," one said to the other. Both women paused as they approached him but one caught Vesta's evil eye piercing their scrawny frames and nudged her friend forward.

"It's the price you pay for being out in public with me." Liam smiled like a cat that had eaten more than one canary.

"That's why you're perfect for my plan. And Marco told me when he was at my place last night that he was really looking forward to your show." Vesta leaned back in her chair eying the room. "Nobody would pass up backstage access and front row seats to your sold-out show at the coliseum. Not even our prune Queen Valentina."

"What makes you so certain she will invite me to one of her villas while I'm in town?"

"That's what Italian etiquette demands." Vesta polished a spoon with her napkin. "And she will want to show you off to her friends and cohorts."

"And my rowdy bandmates?"

"Especially them." Vesta lowered her voice. "They will be just the distraction I need to check out a few things in Villa Parrino."

Liam shook his head cautiously, his eyes never losing contact with Vesta's. "My pet, you are asking for some serious shit to hit the fan by doing this."

"I know what I'm doing."

Liam's drink arrived along with their lunch.

"Another Wild Thing for me, please," Vesta said to the waiter.

"You are a wild thing," Liam held his cocktail up to salute Vesta who bowed her head with a smile.

"And I'm just getting started."

DOING the bidding of the trionfi wasn't on her agenda. Vesta had no intention of helping them find Raz. Her detectives were on the case but even better, she would learn how to use her InSight to find him. Vesta held her breath for a long moment, her body rigid as she stared out the window. They had watched her muddle through a childhood of poverty, ignorant of who she really was, while her secret sister Amara had the best of everything growing up.

Vesta paced in her penthouse apartment downtown, rage growing inside her as she turned away from the skyline view and East River in the distance. They knew about her plight, freezing through winters with Enid. The thought froze her step. Enid. She didn't blame her mother who never understood the value of money, who didn't understand why people clamored for it. Her whole world was centered on that mountain and all the plants and animals. And even though Vesta couldn't have cared less about those things, she respected her mother's feelings. She saw how much relief Enid brought to the town of Crested Butte with her herbal remedies. The children in town called her Enid, the ghost, because of her marshmallow white skin and thin, wispy white hair that floated like a halo around her head. The fact that she wore only white clothing accentuated the effect to an extreme. If it weren't for her aquamarine-colored eyes, celestial sapphires, she would be invisible on the hillside on a snowy day.

A special pain was created for thoughts about Enid. Heaviness in Vesta's heart accompanied by a mild nausea in her belly was the sensation reserved for Enid alone. There was also a tear that always made itself present at the corner of her eye, a reminder of the guilt that would never go away. Why didn't she return to visit her mother that winter? Maybe she could have prevented her cold, lonely death in that dreary cabin.

Vesta shook her head like a viper's tail to rattle the thought loose enough to slip out of her mind. No time for regret. She must execute her plan, but for her plan to work, she had to learn how to block Valentina from reading her mind while she was at the Parrino villa. Liam told her to do what she had done when Madame Kali invaded her mind. But what was that? She just psychically slammed the door shut to her mind. She had no sense of how to recreate that move. Vesta exhaled hard and fast as she closed her eyes.

Her eyes flew open a second later because an idea was born to her, as all genius ideas are, out of nowhere. If she couldn't prevent Valentina from reading her thoughts, then let her thoughts be about something so confusing and distracting to the evil old witch that she couldn't make sense out of them.

The mobile phone rang. Her eyes sparkled as she looked down at it on her desk and she began nodding her head. She picked up the phone and answered the call.

"What is it you fool?"

"Be careful what you ask for. They're all coming. All my rowdy mates."

"I've been waiting a week to hear from you. Did she invite you already?"

"Indeed my darling. Just like you said."

"Told you."

"Senora Parrino is hosting a cocktail party in our honor the night before our show in Rome. Wait till she sees I've included you on my guest list."

"She will be thrilled, I'm sure." Vesta began pacing again.

"You sure you've got it all sorted?"

"I'm sure."

"How are you going to handle that, um, little problem we discussed last week?"

"Don't worry, I've come up with something that will work

perfectly. Let's meet for dinner the night before to go over some details."

"Well, that's going to be in Paris then. And two nights before the party we'll be playing before we leave for Rome. You'll come to the Paris show too?"

"No problem. There are a couple of restaurants I've been wanting to go to in Paris anyway."

"Take care of yourself. You are my favorite misfit mogul after all."

"Don't worry about me. Break a leg in the U.K. and I'll see you a couple of weeks."

Vesta hung up the phone and laid it down. She picked up her Walkman and popped a cassette tape of Liam's top-selling album Fool's Paradise into it as she chuckled under her breath. "You just wait you wrinkly old bird. I've got something special for you."

CHAPTER 10

One of the assets of climbing to the top of the corporate heap is to know how to do a little bit of everything. Vesta learned early in her life not to count on anyone following through on anything. Understanding each facet of her job, and the jobs of her employees, was essential. With her focus now set on the discovery and destruction of Valentina's smuggling operation, Vesta turned to her dusty skills of computer hacking. A programmer she hired earlier in the year to check for system vulnerabilities in Sybarite had taught her the basics. She wasn't a certified nerd like he was, but she understood enough to accomplish the task.

As she packed her bags for France and Italy, she recalled how the hacker introduced her to the dark web. It was fascinating to watch him prod the digital monster. His fingers flew over the keys as though he were a piano virtuoso. One screen of jumbled letters and numbers flashed for a second before he jumped to another. He rattled bits of nonsensical info to her as he went. An algorithm he called BackRub was used to search for keywords associated with Sybarite. He kept lamenting that something called Google wasn't out of beta yet but that he could really use it to speed up his research.

Vesta didn't pretend to understand what he was saying, but she did sit beside him for hours watching the screen and listening to him babble. In the process of protecting her company's confidential information online, she learned the basics of hacking simple systems. It was illegal, but in her mind, not unethical. This family was smuggling something and she was going to find out what.

Sybarite was not only stable but thriving. Within a month of returning to her job as CEO, Vesta ironed out the fashion line's wrinkles for the design of next year's summer collection. She boosted production of the luggage line finding a quality leatherette material for those wealthy clients who didn't want to tote around animal skins.

Vesta recalled staring at Amara with her mouth open when she first mentioned leatherette luggage for Sybarite.

"Leatherette? Doesn't that really mean plastic?"

Amara assured her it wasn't plastic but fabric coated in a special polyurethane that could be molded into any shape desired. It took a while but Vesta embraced the suggestion when she found out how many models and celebrities were eschewing leather goods. And how eager those people were to carry in public, around photographers, Sybarite bags, a beautifully crafted luxury brand that was ethically conscious.

"We're setting the trend, once again," she had announced at the board meeting the previous week. To top off her list of rapid-fire accomplishments, Sybarite was leading the pack in being animal friendly.

A smile spread across her face. Her company, her baby, was healthy again. Raz hadn't had time to do much damage. He didn't want to run Sybarite anyway, except into the ground. He only wanted to get her fired so she would stop looking for the portal which he feared would lead her to discover her true identity.

A dark cloud drifted over Vesta's smile. Her true identity. Confronted with that thought again, she tried to shove it to the back of her mind.

"I may have been the High Priestess for countless lifetimes, but I'm the CEO and chairman of the board of Sybarite in this one. And that suits me just fine."

She would use the information she gained from the trionfi, same as she would use her minor hacking skills, but that didn't mean she had to embrace either profession. Vesta nodded to herself and continued packing her luggage. The intercom from the lobby rang.

"Yes," Vesta answered.

"Ms. Beauvais, we have a delivery of flowers for you. Shall I send them up?"

"Certainly."

Vesta smiled. Marco knew she was leaving for Paris that evening. Sending more peonies for just a few hours enjoyment was a crazy Italian indulgence.

She opened her front door, then walked into her bedroom to grab some cash for a tip. The door buzzer rang.

"You can just put them on the kitchen counter. I'll be right there." She walked out of the bedroom to see Sandor standing there with two-dozen red roses cradled in his arm.

"How did you get in here?"

"The front door was open. You told me to come in."

"I know, I opened it for the delivery guy bringing me my peonies from Marco."

"No, you were opening it for me to bring you these long-stemmed beauties." Sandor pulled one of the roses from the bouquet and handed it to Vesta.

"Those have giant thorns." Vesta waved the flower away from her. "Put them in that vase over there by the refrigerator."

She closed her front door. "I'm going to have to talk to my doorman about who he sends up here. You don't look like a delivery boy."

"I'll always be your special delivery boy."

"You may think you're God's gift to women," Vesta said moving a step back from him. "But I'm here in this life to throw cold water all over that idea."

"That only makes me harder when you talk like that." Sandor winked at her then walked into the kitchen. "Got anything to drink?"

"Seriously," her eyebrows raised. "How did I ever think you were attractive in those previous lives of mine?"

Sandor smiled, his Brad Pitt good looks on full display. "You were so hot for me all the time that I could barely get any of my work done."

"Right," Vesta looked at him with a side-ways glance not giving an inch to his ego. "I'm sure you're telling the truth."

"That's one of the advantages of you blotting out your memories. You'll never know."

"Is that why I wanted to scrub my mind?" Vesta walked into the kitchen and pulled a bottle of Russian vodka from a cabinet. "Here you go." She plunked a high-ball glass next to the bottle.

"Aren't you joining me?"

"No. And you still haven't told me why you're here."

Sandor poured a generous shot of the clear liquid into the glass and culled some ice cubes from the otherwise empty freezer.

"I brought you this peace offering." Sandor said pointing to the roses. He picked up his drink swallowed it in one gulp and set the glass down, ran his hands through his well-coifed brown hair then leaned both hands on the kitchen counter. "Look," he said finally dropping the act. "I didn't know about the scheme Cyrus came up with to send Amara away to be adopted as a baby this time until after I met you as an adult."

Vesta turned away from Sandor toward her row of windows overlooking lower Manhattan. "Don't make excuses. You were all in that together."

Sandor walked over to face her. "Hey, you obliterated your mind for this go-round. I didn't think you would have any business with the trionfi in this life. What was I supposed to do? We all took an oath not to tell you the truth because that was what you wanted."

Vesta's blue eyes opened wide to gaze at him. "What happened that made me do something like that?"

"That's not why I'm here today." Sandor glanced down at the floor and shook his head. "And I told you, I'm not the one to say."

"Then who is?"

"I'm here to offer my help in bringing you up to speed on your gifts," Sandor ran his finger along the edge of the window frame. "And to, uh, discuss your responsibilities."

"My what? My responsibilities?" She took a step closer to him. "Did any of you ever consider what your responsibilities were to me? Or the fact that maybe I wanted just one life where I wasn't this High Priestess with a load of responsibilities?"

"We tried to play it your way. You made it almost to forty without having to honor any of your duties. I would say that's pretty damned good."

The usual playfulness in Sandor's eyes had dulled into two dark brown holes staring at her, his easy, enticing smile gone. His presence in the room now caused an uneasiness to creep inside her making her arms and legs stiffen, her head hurt. She wondered if this was one of his Magician's gifts in action, the one he mentioned of being able to negotiate beneficial results. It wasn't negotiation, it was coercion. Resistance by a RanChan would be futile against it, she could tell. Recognizing the mental manipulation he was trying to force on her mind she psychically shoved it out. She wasn't sure if he had picked up on how she was combatting his action, or not.

"Sometimes this world is easier to deal with than at other times." He continued to talk. "But there's always some shit going on somewhere. And it's often stirred up by Rasputin. And sometimes, like now, it's bad enough that all of the trionfi can feel that world-changing events are on the line. We're geared to pick up on these things. It's our job."

His gaze redirected from her toward the skyline.

"We learned about the sex slave ring he had going through you and your unwitting comments about your visions. We wouldn't have known otherwise. But we were already tracking this drug cartel he created. Now that he's hiding somewhere, probably Siberia, a place we've heard about in the Urals, we've lost his trail. He has to be working with someone else though because we hear about more drug deliveries being made from our sources."

He turned to face her again. "We need your help. You must learn how to control your InSight to find him."

Vesta smoothed her short blonde hair back from her face, then smoothed her skirt commanding no nervousness to be apparent in her movements or voice. "I'm very busy on another project right now." She walked into the kitchen and poured herself a shot of vodka. "I have my own mystery to solve at the moment."

"I see you're packing for a trip. Sybarite business?" Sandor walked into her bedroom and thumped her suitcase with his forefinger.

"I'm not at liberty to discuss it." Vesta drained her drink. "But I do need to return to my packing."

Sandor walked into the kitchen nodding his head. "Okay. Still not going to cooperate, huh? Okay. Raymond trusted you would do the right thing. He believed in you. Are you really going to let his last dying wish go unheeded?" Sandor reached out for Vesta's hand. She pulled it away and took two steps back.

"Don't lecture me about my loyalty. I'm going to learn to control my gift. I want to find Raz even more than you do. He will pay for murdering my uncle."

"Raymond was counting on you. This is bigger than your vendetta."

Vesta strode to the front door and opened it.

"I told you that I'm working on finding Raz and I'm sure that will help you stop his drug running but that in no way means that I'm going embrace you all like one big happy family."

Vesta looked out into the hallway. "My family is dead."

CHAPTER 11

A long plane ride was always a respite from the constant tugging Vesta felt for her attention, whether from someone at Sybarite or now the tri-phonies. Somebody constantly needed something from her. A slow, heavy breath seeped out of her parted lips as she leaned back against the airline-provided pillow. When cruising at thirty-eight thousand feet she could ignore all forms of communication, close her eyes and rest.

Being unplugged physically from the world below allowed her a deep sense of relaxation. Her most vivid dreams occurred then, and this flight adhered to that standard. In the dream, she saw herself walking barefoot on smooth, cold stones at night. The location was obscured because of the thick black air pressing against her. It wasn't uncomfortable but it was persistent. There was a nagging quality about it that provoked her temper because it wouldn't leave her alone.

"No," she said aloud and shifted positions in her jet bed. The blackness made it impossible for her to see where she was walking but she kept following the black line on the floor beside her feet, which was even blacker than the black surrounding her. The anger within her eased as she sensed a growing vibration beneath each step she took. Solace overtook the irritation. The stones flattened out merging into one surface of tiny undulating peaks and valleys, a slow rhythmic beat began matching her pace. Was she hearing it, or just feeling it underfoot? She wasn't sure. It was a comforting sensation, whatever it was.

Vesta drifted further into her dream. Her logical mind no longer worried or cared that she couldn't see where she was going. The pressing blackness had become her silent companion. She walked on the cool, smooth surface grateful for each nuanced pock until the black line at her feet vanished. Searching to pick up its trail again, Vesta's gaze landed on a pair of bare feet standing next to hers. She gasped. A hand reached from the impenetrable blackness for hers. It was warm and gentle as it pulled her forward. With a first instinct reaction she resisted the tug. The grip became firmer insisting she follow. Her feet obeyed even though her mind challenged the action at every moment. One more inch forward she stepped and the blanket of night lifted into a golden glow of light.

The face of Peter flickered into focus. He was holding her hand. Vesta smiled as her heart felt like it opened with a thousand flower petals blooming at once, a sigh echoing from inside her but also outside of her.

"Where have you been?" She asked. "I looked for you."

Peter drew a smile so gentle across his face that Vesta began to cry. "I know," he said. "I'm here now, with you."

She gasped for air in the darkened first-class cabin and bolted upright from her bed grabbing at nothing. Staring at the floor of the airliner for several long moments, Vesta's thoughts were in as much disarray as the man's littered seat across the aisle from her. As her eyes wandered over the napkins and wine glasses strewn about the floor space of his area, with the plastic bags from his airline-provided socks and headphones spilling into the aisle, Vesta demanded that her mind sort dream from reality. It wasn't such an easy task at that moment. She could feel the warmth of Peter's hand, and see the kindness in his eyes.

How did she know Peter was kind? She had met him only once, and for a brief moment at that, when he was standing in the center of the labyrinth in Chartres Cathedral. He told her about the beau vis, the cosmic energy that was supposed to inhabit the labyrinth. She thought at the time it was strange that the French words for it were so close to the spelling of her last name. Madame Kali told her to go there to avoid a disaster, which happened after all with the death of Uncle Raymond. Vesta hadn't thought about Peter for a long time, but she had felt so protective of him even though they had just met. He had this beautiful innocence about him yet he reminded her of a tragic character from some Shakespearean play.

Vesta shook her head and reached for a bottle of water. Her dream life was retreating fast into the ether eclipsed by her waking reality. She was feeling normal again. Rattling sounds in the galley area behind her signaled that the crew was preparing coffee and breakfast. Vesta stood up, stretched, and strolled in that direction to clear her brain.

"Good morning," she said to a flight attendant. "Coffee ready yet?"

"Yes, ma'am." The young man in the navy-colored suit of the airline handed her a cup with steam billowing from the top.

"Thank you." Vesta scanned the counter beside them for sugar and cream. Her eyes landed on a post card lying next to both. It was a photo of the exterior of the north side of Chartres Cathedral. Vesta blinked, and wondered if she was still halfway between her dream and being awake.

"Have you been there?" She asked pointing at the card. The flight attendant looked up from his clipboard and then at the card.

"No. What is it?"

"It's Chartres Cathedral. I thought that was your postcard."

The man looked back down at his clipboard. "No, it just appeared there a few minutes ago. Maybe someone left it when they came by for a drink."

Vesta looked back at the card. "Yeah, maybe."

LANDING IN PARIS was always a thrill, no matter how many times Vesta had done it. She adored being immersed in the French culture, steeping herself in the language, food and wine to the best of her ability. She had stayed at many places over the years. When meeting clients she opted for the Cesar Ritz or George V, necessary indulgences to send the correct message in business matters. Yet despite her pleasure of being catered to beyond reason at those hotels, she preferred the more low key ambience of the Hotel Du Jeu De Paume on the Ile Saint-Louis. Royal tennis courts from the seventeenth century had been converted into a small boutique hotel and her idea of the perfect place to stay. Within five minutes she could walk to the rive gauche, two different metros or stand in front of the glorious Notre Dame de Paris.

Vesta closed her eyes as she stood waiting at the carousel for her luggage in Charles de Gaulle airport. She recalled the Easter service she attended at the cathedral years earlier. Not being Catholic, or even religious, she was surprised at how transfixed she was by the spectacle. When the priests, decked out in their finest robes and birettas, walked into the transept for mass waving their thuribles billowing clouds of incense Vesta was hypnotized. It took a while but after some serious searching she found the Cire Trudon candle Spiritus Sancte that smelled very close to that moment. Still she could hear the choir harmonizing the medieval chants that lilted through the thousand-year-old space. Vesta smiled. She didn't know why that memory was so special to her, but it was.

Luggage flopped down the chute toward her. Spotting her Sybarite Amazon green crocodile bags was effortless in the sea of black rectangles sliding down. Vesta grabbed each bag and walked out to the taxi stand in the pale Paris morning. Tolerating fall's icy embrace in this city was a honed skill. Even though it was only October, the bone penetrating cold had already arrived. That was what Hermes wool scarves were made for. Vesta wrapped her Jaguar Quetzal cashmere shawl close to her neck and handed the luggage to her driver.

Settled into the hotel room, Vesta set about planning her day to wander, eat and drink before meeting Liam that evening. In preparation for her trip, Jenny had purchased a ticket for her to see the exhibit of The Havemeyer Collection: When America Discovered Impressionism at the Musée d'Orsay. The entry time was two o'clock, meaning an early lunch somewhere near the Quai was called for.

Dressed from head to toe in vetements francaise, even down to her panties and bra, Vesta stepped out onto rue Saint Louis en l'ile. A taxi was waiting for her but she chose to walk. The wind was calm with a temperature chilly but manageable. She wanted to steep every sense in Paris. Making her way across Pont de la Tournelle connecting the Ile Saint-Louis to the rive gauche, the Seine river looked like corrugated metal as it dipped and rose against its embankments steady and unyielding over the millennia to kings, revolutionaries and artists. It flowed past them all with typical unsympathetic French dismissal of their corporeal value. Vesta smiled to herself thinking about all the famous people who for more than a thousand years had crossed the river in that exact spot.

A few blocks away was Shakespeare and Company, the venerable bookseller who also weathered countless political storms to remain open and welcoming to all. Vesta considered going in but decided her appetite for food and drink outweighed her thirst for books at that moment. Around the corner from the museum was a family-owned café with a salad niçoise worthy of a four-star restaurant. Vesta hungered for it, and their traditional braised leeks. Superb French food existed in New York City but simple dishes prepared to an old French mother's standards were harder to come by. Those and a glass, maybe two, of a local white burgundy would set the pace for the exhibit.

Two o'clock arrived faster than Vesta calculated. An extended conversation with a couple at the next table about Paris versus New York live theatre performances, and three glasses of white burgundy, sent Vesta at a brisk pace down the Quai Voltaire and up to the museum doors. Crowds were the rule at Musée d'Orsay. Vesta waited in line, then bolted across the main gallery to arrive at another line to enter the exhibit. At last she entered the small rooms housing the exhibit.

The Havemeyers were some of the first Americans to collect Impressionism paintings by the masters Cézanne, Manet and Courbet. They were normally on display at the Metropolitan Museum of Art in New York and Vesta had seen them there. What was special about this exhibit was that it was presented from a French point of view.

She walked up to her favorite painting in the collection, Claude Monet's Four Trees. Gazing at the four slender poplar trunks stretching beyond the top of the canvas with the reflection of them below in the water, she mused at how daring he was to not include the tree tops in the painting. And she was mesmerized by the ethereal pink and yellow mist filtering through the sunlight as it rose from the ground that Monet captured with his genius brush strokes.

As she stood transfixed by the work of art, something out of the corner of her eye snagged her attention. A brief glance at first extended into her full attention. At her far left, along the wall stood a tall, thin man wearing black pants that were too short, black loafers and a black turtleneck sweater. His large brown eyes were staring at her. Vesta froze. She knew that face; the ill-cropped brown hair, the soft gaze and lips that looked like they should be either laughing or crying. Vesta blinked to reboot her brain. It was Peter.

The moment the recognition registered in her brain, a group of people speaking German walked in her line of sight and she lost eye contact with him. Vesta scrambled around two, three, four people only to look into the faces of more people she didn't recognize and didn't care to know.

"Where did he go?" She muttered to herself.

Moving rapidly through the crowded room, she sorted through faces one by one. No Peter. She glanced at every person in the other rooms of the exhibit. None of them were him. Twenty minutes passed. Vesta stood in the gift shop at the end of the exhibit wondering if she had imagined him. She hadn't expected to see him, so why would she imagine that she saw him? He was staring at her when she looked his way. They made eye contact. Vesta gazed at a cheap print of the Four Trees hanging on the wall next to the register without even seeing it.

"Why did he run away?" Vesta shook her head. None of it made any sense.

Vesta walked out of the exhibit into the main gallery. She looked toward the giant clock that told time to passengers when the museum served as a rail station at the beginning of the twentieth century. No one in the crowd below was Peter. She swiveled her head looking in the direction of the muses holding the world on their shoulders. Her eyes searched between the snow-white marble statues and into the petite dark galleries. Upstairs she checked the restaurant moving across the room through its exterior doors to the rooftop terrace overlooking the Seine. People posed for their prized vacation shots, but not Peter. He had vanished.

Vesta's head drooped as she walked over to lean on the balustrade. The twenty-minute search, the jet lag, the wine at lunch, the thrill of seeing Peter and losing him had sapped her energy. All she wanted to do was lie down and sleep. She didn't want to see the rest of the exhibit, shop along Saint Germain Boulevard or do anything that could possibly give her any plea-sure. Vesta pulled her scarf out of her coat pocket and wrapped it around her head as she watched a tourist bateau bump along the gray river.

The wind picked up blowing Vesta's Celine wool coat open. She turned from the river making her way back through the restaurant, through the main gallery and out the front door. The walk to the hotel held no magic. The sidewalk vendors with their eclectic selection of books and prints held no allure. She didn't even glance at Shakespeare and Company when she passed. If she had, she would have seen Peter standing inside by the window perusing a copy of Gravity and Grace by Simone Weil. He watched her pass by offering a slight smile when she reached her closest approach to him then returned to his reading.

Vesta threw herself onto the bed in her hotel room. She left instructions with the concierge to call her at six o'clock. There would be time for a bath and a cocktail before she met Liam. Until then, she wanted to shut out the world.

The mystery of Peter continued. The irritation she felt

mounted. Why she was drawn to him on an emotional level? And why did he come to her in her dreams but then run away from her in real life? She didn't have the patience for the melodrama to drag on but at the same time she felt deeply compelled to follow it.

Two short rings from the phone woke Vesta from a deep dreamless sleep. She stretched her arm from the bed to answer it.

"Oui," she said. "D'accord. Merci." Vesta dropped the receiver on the pillow. She glanced around the room from her sideways view. It was dark except for a narrow column of light from the interior courtyard squeezing its way through the drapes. Pushing herself up from the bed she noticed she was still wearing her Chanel blouse, skirt and tights. Dismantling all of that, taking a bath and reassembling a chic outfit for dinner plus hair and make-up would take some time, and a cocktail. Vesta called room service for a trés frois Russian vodka and asked them to deliver it to her bath. In France they did things like that without batting an eye. Vesta could think of nothing finer at the moment than a hot bath and a very cold martini.

The steaming water eased Vesta's back muscles but not her thoughts. With an elbow propped up on the bathtub's edge and her head nestled in her palm, Vesta examined her pedicure at the other end of the tub. She felt numb.

The door buzzer sounded twice.

"Entre," she shouted. The door to the room opened and she heard someone walk through the bedroom and toward her in the bath. A young man dressed in black pants and jacket with a crisp white shirt entered.

"Bonsoir, madam." He pulled a small table from the dressing area beside the bathtub and placed a silver tray with a small ice bucket, cocktail shaker, cocktail glass and a bottle of fine

Russian vodka down on it. The he proceeded to mix a perfect, and very cold, martini for her.

"Merci beaucoup, monsieur," Vesta said as he handed her the glass. The young man bowed.

"A votre service, madam." He closed the bathroom door as he left.

Vesta let the crystal liquid slide in its entirety down her throat. She set the glass on the table, leaned her head back against the tub and closed her eyes. A long deep sigh slipped from her parted lips. She needed to think about her plan when she got to the Parrinos villa and she wanted to think more about Peter, but she just couldn't do either at the moment.

The art of dressing to kill for a night out when you don't feel like even moving a finger takes a lot of practice, but Vesta had mastered it many years earlier. Full days at Columbia University sent many students home to study and sleep. Vesta knew she needed to study and sleep, but she needed to drink in the night life of New York City, literally and figuratively even more. Growing up in Crested Butte, Colorado, meant she experienced no fun past dark, ever. Her high school classmates who hung out on the creek bridge in town slamming cheap beer didn't interest her. Urinating and puking over the railing into the icy water below classified as the main entertainment for them. Vesta bet that thirty years later, they were still doing the same thing.

When she received her scholarship to Columbia, Vesta moved to New York one week after her high school graduation. She found a job at a coffee shop near the campus. Lots of students hung out there and soon she knew all the coolest places to hear live music in the city. The days of the Mudd Club and CBGB's were in full swing. Knowing someone on the inside was essential. Vesta bonded with several of the bartenders and guys at the front doors. They liked her street smarts and no bull-shit way of doing things. She dressed like a minor slut but talked like their best friend from childhood. It was on one of those nights she met Liam for the first time.

Vesta smiled as she stood up from her now tepid bathwater. Yes, she knew just what to do. Dinner at a fancy Paris restaurant held pleasures beyond explanation or expectation. French women excelled at dressing in a simple yet elegant style with a bit of slut thrown in for good measure. For years, Vesta studied how the Parisian women robed themselves for 3-Michelin-star dinners. Without bragging, she could now teach them a thing or two.

The valet unpacked her bags when she arrived, steaming her dresses to unlock any wrinkles. Vesta scanned her choices in the closet for the evening selecting a black Yves Saint Laurent smoking jacket, matching cigarette pants and a white Chloe crepe de chine blouse. The requisite Christian Louboutin black pumps she pulled from the closet floor.

She dressed with care admiring each garment she put on. Looking in the full-length mirror she unbuttoned her blouse to just below the fold of her breasts. There she dabbed with devoted attention Chanel No. 5. If she could meet anyone from history it would be Coco Chanel. Vesta admired her rags to riches story, she worshipped her fashion sense. There was no woman more stylish, independent or brilliant in her mind.

Walking over to the room safe she extracted her custom jewelry case. Never a fan of yellow gold, she drew out a pair of white gold drop earrings, slender strands of the precious metal with hunks of blue sapphire on the end of each. She took out the ring Liam gave her long ago when his first album went platinum. He took her to Tiffany's in New York. Together they chose a platinum band studded with emerald-cut diamonds. She remembered him saying, "This isn't an engagement ring, and certainly not a wedding band, but if I were ever to marry, you would be my only choice." Vesta admired the light refracting in a thousand different directions on the stones, and her heart embraced all former lovers who became life-long best friends.

A final check in the mirror confirmed that she bowed down to no one. The French cab driver waiting curbside seemed to agree as she slid into the backseat. Restaurant Guy Savoy was close by her hotel but the driver sensing her attitude of romance and holding the world at the end of a string drove a bit out of the way so that they passed by the Louvre en route. Vesta gazed at the ancient buildings sheltering the modern giant glass triangle constructed by Mr. Pei. The greatest collection of art work on the planet slumbered peacefully inside. Crossing the Pont Neuf, the lights along the Seine sparkled in the water. Paris at night dazzled all the senses and set hearts on fire. Vesta invited it all in.

When they arrived at the restaurant a dashing older man with flowing milk white hair opened the cab door.

"Bonsoir, madam. Bienvenue," he said with a bow.

"Bonsoir, monsieur. Merci bien." Vesta slid out of the back-seat like a snake from its skin.

She entered the former Paris Mint on the Quai de Conti marveling at the transformation. While it still held the original beauty of its sky-scraping windows and massive moldings, the space, no doubt, housed an elegant restaurant now. Following the maître d', Vesta moved through a dining room overlooking the river and the Ile de la Cité. There by the window, framed by gentle pops of pale streetlight, sat Liam. From the next table a woman wearing a long black leather Versace gown with an enormous sparkling blue cross on it stopped talking to him when he stood up.

"Lovely to see you my pet." He took Vesta in his arms and kissed her on both cheeks. She greeted him in the same French manner and let him pull out her chair. The entire room watched every movement they made without looking directly at them, a trick the French perfected long ago. Looking at them would break about a hundred French rules on dealing with celebrities within this crowd of wealth and taste. Instead it was as if they absorbed each minute action through their pores as though they came genetically modified with this ability. Vesta had seen it before and found it to be quite an extraordinary talent.

A sommelier appeared at her right side. "Madam, voulez vous du champagne?" Vesta nodded.

"Certainment, merci." Vesta noticed the 1985 vintage Dom Perignon bottle as the wine was poured. She looked at Liam with raised eyebrows.

"1985 was a very good year." Liam raised his own glass. "I think that's when my third album went platinum."

"That's the year I became project manager at Sybarite. Yeah, it was a good one." Vesta picked up her glass and touched it to Liam's. "But it wasn't 79."

Liam smiled reaching for her ring, rubbing it between his fingers for a moment and staring at it.

"No, it wasn't 1979." He drank his glass dry. The sommelier who stood close by refilled it immediately. "Oh my god, how much fun we had back then."

"I was twenty-one that year. I felt like I had seen and done everything possible." Vesta laughed out loud. An easy smile spread across Liam's face as he looked at her.

"You are still as fabulous now as you were then." He tipped his glass toward her. Vesta's cheeks burnished a slight rose but recovered in record time. The woman in the Versace gown strained to hear their conversation from the next table. Her husband did not look amused.

"And your attitude is as infectious as always." Vesta tipped her glass toward Liam.

"Infectious? Lovey, I took medicines and got rid of all that years ago." They both burst out laughing. The eavesdropper straightened in her chair and cleared her throat.

The headwaiter arrived at the table. He bowed to Vesta and then to Liam. "Monsieur Spencer, Monsieur Guy Savoy would like to present you and madam with a chef's menu tonight. He asked if that would be fine with you."

Liam looked at Vesta who nodded with excitement.

"Please tell Monsieur Savoy that we would be honored." The waiter bowed at Liam again and left.

What began next was an odyssey of food and wine unparalleled in the personal histories of either Vesta or Liam. From the freshest oysters and smoked salmon, to the lightest leek and gruyere soufflé, to the most tender filet mignon and delicate cheeses all washed down with French Montrachet and Bordeaux wines. Both were moments away from food comas when chef Savoy arrived at the table. Liam stood up applauding. Vesta stayed seated but applauded with gusto. Guy Savoy smiled with a simple bow. The entire restaurant joined the pair in applause. Liam requested a bottle of Dom Perignon for each table in the room and for the waitstaff then offered a toast when all had been delivered and opened. The festive mood expanded into something that would rival the liberation of Paris. Normally smug Parisians wandered to other tables to say hello to friends and acquaintances, and everyone stopped by Liam's table to thank him.

The woman in the Versace dress seized on the opportunity to approach their table as she and her husband were departing. As she gushed to Liam about how wonderful she thought he was, a sad smile crept across Vesta's face. She admired Gianni Versace as a designer and his tragic loss was still fresh. His clothing was rule-breaking, visionary and instantly classic. As she eyed the soft black leather and gigantic glittering cross, she thought about another loss that happened in Paris barely a month earlier when Princess Diana died in a car crash inside the Pont de l'Alma tunnel. Vesta looked down at her lap. She wasn't the only one who had suffered a heartbreaking loss that year.

After more thank-yous from other diners, at long last the room began to settle as Vesta and Liam drew their chairs closer together so they could talk without anyone overhearing them.

"You know you spent a fortune tonight not only on our meal but champagne for everybody in the place." Vesta leaned in whispering a bit too loudly due to her high consumption of wine.

"No worries. The tour will pay for it. Worth every penny for the press I'll get out of this in the morning."

"Ah, so it wasn't just generosity. You had an ulterior motive."

"I wouldn't say that at all." Liam waved his arms around. "I loved doing this. How often can we get stuffy French aristocrats to loosen up like they did tonight?" Liam sipped the last of his wine. "It was a vibe like the old days."

A waiter arrived with a cart and prepared warm snifters of cognac for them. Liam handed one to Vesta and took the other.

"Did you ever think we would end up like this back then?" Vesta asked.

"Definitely not." Liam swirled the amber colored liquor around his glass. "This has been one of the most fun lives I've had. Some of them were bores and some rather nasty, but this ranks as one of my favorites. Not the least of which is because you are who you are in this one."

Vesta stared at Liam. "Was I really that much of a shrew before?" Her eyes pled for an answer but feared one at the same time. Liam stared back at her for a long moment then burst into laughter. Vesta looked surprised but soon dissolved into laughter too.

"Horrible," Liam said. "Sometimes you were just horrible."

"What do you mean? Give me an example."

"Well, I wouldn't say horrible necessarily. Just boring." Liam stopped talking and cocked his head. "Yeah, boring. That's a good way to describe you."

"God, no wonder I cursed myself."

"Everyone was terrified you did it except me and Ray. We understood."

"Uncle Raymond wasn't angry with me?"

"Your uncle adored you. You could do no wrong in his eyes. He knew you had a good reason for everything you did." Liam took a deep sip of cognac. "Speaking of which, are you sure you have a solid plan in mind for this upcoming caper?"

"Well, I know I need to find out what that family is up to." Vesta leaned in close to Liam.

"And this is because the grand dame pissed you off with her comments about your age?" Liam lowered his head and locked eyes with Vesta.

"Not at all." Vesta looked down at her glass. "It's because I'm supposed to be doing things like this. Right? I mean that's my job in this tri-phony world."

"I think the rest of the group would say the greater need is finding you know who."

"I have people searching for him. They're the best at what they do. They'll spot him."

Liam cocked his head. "Not the same as you putting your talent to work on it."

Vesta raised her hands palms up. "I don't know how to just turn this on and off like a faucet. What do they expect? And now that I know how they screwed me over in childhood I don't feel like I owe them anything."

"They thought you were out of the group for this life. And they were also trying to protect you from the others."

"So, they just left me penniless on the side of a mountain to fend for myself." Vesta sipped her cognac.

"You've done very well this time Love."

"No thanks to anyone else. That's why I don't care if I ever help them. They never did anything for me. Besides I'm working on finding Raz right now. My team is on it. And if they don't come up with something soon, then I'll figure out this InSight stuff and do it myself. He won't get away. But this is first. I'll have it handled within the week. And I don't want Amara, Jared, Sandor or most of all Cyrus involved. They need to stay out of this."

"You know you risk not only getting caught but you will incur the devastating wrath of the head bitch when she finds out you've been diddling in her affairs."

"When she finds out," Vesta put her hand on Liam's arm. "It will be too late." She gave her drink a quick swirl and drank the glass dry. "She will know that I can stop her little smuggling ring. And I don't need to be wearing my priestly robes to do it."

"You're talking about bringing the whole house down. Don't you think you're going to need some back up?" Liam's voice was just above a whisper.

"Sure. I have you and your band."

Liam shook his head. "I don't want to foul things up for you on this because they probably are up to no good that needs to be stopped. But," Liam shook his head. "I'm not a very strong player here. My gift in this group is for opening the door to new things. I keep everyone in touch with the time we're in."

Vesta's eyebrows furrowed as she squinted her eyes at him.

"Right. I know that's vague, but it's a really important role." Liam shrugged his shoulders. "And I'm the most fun of the group. But I'm not good in a fight."

"Who said anything about fighting?"

"When you go sneaking into their business you could very

well be discovered. If that happens," Liam nodded with vigor. "Trust me, there will be a fight." He poked Vesta in the ribs with his finger. "They represent the royal family of Swords on the tarot. What do you think they do with those long pointy things?"

"They're not going to know what hit them until it's too late."

"I wish I had as much confidence as you." Liam waved his arm at a waiter across the room. "D'autre, sil vous plait." He motioned to both his and Vesta's empty glasses. "I'm going to need a little more confidence before we do this."

CHAPTER 12

Dawn in Paris spreads infinite potential from her celestial robe at the beginning of each day. The magnificent city filled with century upon century of glorious architecture, art and people thrilled Vesta every time she woke up there. Liam's concert would begin around eight o'clock that evening, plenty of time to shop, say hello to a couple of clients on the rive gauche as well as along the Champs de l'Elysee. But first she needed coffee, lots of coffee, to reboot herself from the indulgent night before.

The weather maintained its crisp chill but the skies sparkled vibrant blue. Vesta pulled a Comme des Garcons coat out of the closet. While Rei Kawakubo's label was technically Japanese, one of her two main bases resided at the Place Vendome. Vesta determined that she still adhered to her French couture vow even with this choice. Besides, she chose a Chanel sweater, skirt and boots to wear underneath.

If Paris were a cocktail, she would have been drunk by noon. Immersed in the language, attitude and culture for hours, Vesta wondered why she didn't live there. One day she would, she promised herself. After a working, yet sublime lunch at L'Orangerie inside the courtyard of the George V with two clients from Printemps who carried Sybarite's couture and luggage line, Vesta returned to her hotel to regroup for the show.

Pairing her 1988 vintage Christian Lacroix t-shirt with the huge bejeweled cross in the center with some skinny jeans and black Laboutin boots sent Vesta's mind tripping back to the moment she first saw it. Anna Wintour took a huge risk putting a thousand dollar t-shirt on the cover of Vogue magazine, but it resonated with readers and represented a turning point for Vesta. It clarified who she wanted to be and what she wanted to do. Fashion coursed through her veins, style meant everything to her. And risk she gobbled up with a spoon. Vesta couldn't afford the t-shirt when she first saw it, but she vowed that she would buy it for herself one day. Two years later she purchased the shirt from a Sybarite client who had worn it just once. Tonight, she admired it in the hotel mirror with the same love as the first time she saw it. That defined her drive to accomplish her goals and reflected the era of work, party, repeat she mastered so well. A dab, or two, of Madame Coco's iconic perfume behind her ears completed the package.

Returning work phone calls dominated the cab ride to the Palais des Sports. In New York it was lunchtime, and the fact it was Saturday made no difference to Vesta. If something needed communicating, she didn't care if it was Christmas. Three conversations, one with Jenny to check in for anything that needed attention since her absence on Friday, one with David who oversaw Sybarite's luggage line and wanted approval to add a new back-pack design in vegan leather, and a quick one with the CFO Charles to let him know that 1998 budget amendments would be to him in a week.

Blowing out a satisfied exhale knowing she was on top of everything job-related, she gazed at the gigantic crowd filing into the aluminum-domed arena as her cab passed by. She smiled.

Liam still possessed the magic. Older crowds adored him and the younger ones felt like they had discovered an iconic heartbeat of rock.

Vesta hopped out of the cab and walked through a back entry designated for employees and sports teams. Earlier in the day, Liam's press agent sent all access credentials over to Vesta at the hotel. She waved them at the security guards as she headed for the throng of young women gathered around a door at the end of a long fluorescent-lit hallway. Giggles and sighs echoed off the cinderblock walls as boobs and butts wiggled stretching to get a peek inside.

Vesta saluted a grizzled scarecrow figure blocking the doorway as she approached.

"Hello Vestal," he shouted in his cockney accent.

"Hey Oz," she said. His real name was Jimmy and had been the manager of the roadies for Liam's tours for as long as Vesta could remember. He bestowed the nickname Vestal on her decades earlier when he noticed how picky she was about the men in her life. Even though she was about as far from a vestal virgin as one could get, the similarity of the names stuck. She returned the favor by calling him Oz since he reminded her of the movie character made of straw from the Wizard of Oz.

"Move aside ladies." Oz had a gentle but firm way, culled from years of practice, to relocate eager groupies. "The queen of everything has arrived and you have to let her through."

Vesta threaded her way past the girls listening to them comment in French, asking each other if that was Liam's wife. A young woman wearing a tattered New York Dolls t-shirt said, "Who cares? I want her shirt."

Vesta stopped and looked at the young woman with a steady gaze replying in French, "You can have it one day but first you must do what you love and work hard at it." The girl's eyes opened wide in surprise, her face acknowledging her understanding of Vesta's words. "Merci," she said nodding.

Vesta hugged Oz when she reached him at last. He picked her up with a tight squeeze as he always did. "You never age lass."

"You're looking good too." Vesta regarded the girls who clustered back together like a gaggle of geese at the door. "And you're still in charge of the door I see. Not a bad gig."

"Especially at my age." Oz winked and scratched at his gray stubby beard.

Vesta opened the door to the dressing room and walked in but called out over her shoulder, "Don't do anything I wouldn't Oz."

"Well that leaves it wide open then, don't it?" Oz cackled.

Vesta surveyed the space. Bowls of the requisite jelly beans and popcorn sat on a table beside liter bottles of Evian. Liam hadn't changed his rider in twenty years. Sweet and salty bites, a perfect metaphor for him. Somewhere behind a folding screen a champagne cork popped. Liam emerged with the bottle in hand. Vesta stared at him. The deep lines on his face gave the Grand Canyon a run for the win. Dark circles under his eyes spoke of the previous night's revelry.

"I heard the virgin queen arrive." Liam put his hand up to his ear. "And hark, she wants more champagne."

Vesta laughed and nodded. "Indeed I do because God knows I didn't get quite enough last night. But it looks like you did."

"Nonsense." Liam waved his hand in the air then filled two glasses and handed one to her. He picked up the other and paused like he was lost in thought for a moment. He raised his glass high in the air.

"Here's to the best of friends through the ages. Through thick and thin, always and forever."

"Such a somber sounding toast." Vesta raised her glass.

"Sure, best friends through thick and thin." She touched her glass to his and they drank their flutes dry. Liam refilled their glasses.

"I think we should do the toast you used to do before you went on stage at CBGB's or the Mudd Club." Vesta looked up at the ceiling. "How did it go exactly?"

Liam raised his glass. "Here's to a show to end all others, if not then fuck the mothers."

"That's it!" Vesta laughed and raised her glass. They each took a sip and set their glasses down on the counter. Liam looked at Vesta.

"You know we used to finish a whole bottle before I took the stage." Liam sat down on a stool in front of a mirror.

"Do you think I would ever forget those nights?" Vesta leaned on the counter beside him. "All I had to do was dance. You're the one who had to perform."

Liam opened a small black case pulling out a cosmetic brush, powder and a stick of black eyeliner. "Some nights I would just make up words to my songs because I couldn't remember them, I would be so drunk. Other nights I would stick the mic in some fan's face and let him sing a couple of bars for me because I was so high."

He began spreading a thick black line across his eyelid. "I'm more responsible now. Although, last night was one for the books and my bedraggled face is paying for it tonight." Vesta leaned over taking the pencil from him.

"Let me do that. It's going to take some expert work." She applied a perfect line along the lash above the eye then one below it. She repeated the process for the other eye. "Why don't you hire someone for this?"

"I don't like the way others do it."

Vesta dusted powder on Liam's face then dug around in his case to find a sponge. She applied a heavy coat of powder.

"Maybe one of those pretty babies outside is a make-up artist." Vesta said as she checked her work.

"Please, I don't want any entanglements with those nymphs. Only trouble there. Trust me." Liam stared at Vesta. "Speaking of which, are you ready for tomorrow night?"

Vesta nodded.

"Because I don't really know what you're planning to do, and I don't think you know either. We could end up in some serious merde going off half-cocked like this."

"I know exactly what I'm going to do. And I'm going to watch Valentina's face melt into a puddle of merde." Vesta stared back at Liam. "Why are you so concerned? I've never seen you act like this. Usually you just roll with the punches and couldn't care less what happens."

Liam's eyes widened as he wagged his finger at Vesta. "You don't know these people. They will fuck you up if they have a mind to."

"So I'm stepping into a scene from the Godfather with their Italian accents and everything? Is that what you're saying?" Vesta flicked her hand back like she swatted at a fly. "Don't you think I've come across their type before?"

"I don't know how much help I can offer you my pet."

"All I need is for you to act like a fool. You can manage that, right?" Vesta picked up her champagne and handed Liam his. She touched her glass to his then drank the contents in one swallow. "The only question I have is, are you ready for tonight?"

Liam drank his champagne and stood up. He stretched his arms out twirling around for Vesta. Dressed in a skin-tight red and black jumpsuit with a large harlequin pattern splashed on every inch, Liam looked like a rock and roll fool. His shaggy locks framed his black lined eyes, his dazzling smile made him irresistible even with the Grand Canyon crevasses beside his mouth.

"It's my homage to Freddy tonight. What do you think?"

"You know I love it."

There was a knock on the door. Oz leaned his head in. "Ten minutes okay with you, mate?"

Liam gave Oz a thumb's up.

"Do you want to go around to the front row or stay back here?" Liam asked Vesta as he gave a final check to his makeup.

"It's been a while since I sat backstage here in Paris."

"Well, that means you escort this tired old fool out there then."

Liam grabbed a black top hat from behind the dressing screen and tapped the brim against his knee. He gave a deep bow to Vesta then extended his arm to her then opened the door to screams of joy from the waiting throng. Oz ran the girls off telling them they could stand next to the stage on the floor if they hurried.

Down another hideously-lit fluorescent hallway, Liam walked with a jaunt nodding with a smile to the road crew and arena staff as they passed. Vesta strode with confidence beside him, the energy of inescapable excitement bubbling up. They heard the swelling cheers of the crowd as the band took the stage, stamping feet echoed off the walls, the rhythm matching their pace as they approached the stage. The entire scene electrified. Vesta felt all the power of the crowd merge into one ball of energy surging from her feet, racing through her body and out the top of her head. She released herself to all the moment offered. Liam turned to smile at her as they reached the stairs ascending to the stage. Vesta hugged him then kissed him on the cheek.

"Break a leg you awesome man," she said with a final squeeze.

The audience exploded into a cacophony of cheers as Liam walked into the spotlight and the first guitar notes of one of his biggest hits, Thought I was Dead, blasted through the speakers. Vesta climbed the stairs peeking beyond the heavy black curtain dividing her from the vast auditorium. Liam was waving his top hat around and bowing. Thousands of fans with their hands in the air were pulsing to the beat, even the seats at the top and on the far edges of the auditorium were pounding to the rhythm. Vesta found a spot on the back corner of the stage where she could stand but still see the show and the audience's reaction. A few minutes later Oz dragged a plastic chair over so she could sit.

No hint existed that Liam was forty years old as he strutted, bobbed and twirled on the stage like someone in their twenties. The freedom he loved so dearly to express himself without hesitation, without fear or risk of disapproval was on full display at that moment. His voice was clear and strong belting out his timeless songs.

Vesta gazed out on the audience to watch their adoring faces and to try to spot the French groupie girls who Oz had told to hang out by the side of the stage. She saw clusters of young guys and older couples sprinkled in with dozens of cute girls. They were all in sync with the music except one person she noticed who was off by at least half a beat to the rhythm. As her eyes rested on the challenged rhythm figure Vesta realized it was Peter. She held her breath as she leaned forward squinting her eyes. Swaying in an awkward way, dressed in a cheap white turtleneck sweater and too-short black pants with black loafers, Peter sensed her gaze. He looked directly at her extending a timid wave. A lightning bolt of adrenaline flew through her head and out her feet. Jumping up, Vesta knocked the chair over and ran off the stage down the stairs. Oz ran after her.

"What's wrong lass?"

"Oz, how do I get out to the front row?"

"You go out to the hallway and take the third door to the left. Is something the matter? Do I need to call security?"

"No. No." Vesta yelled over her shoulder. "I see someone out there I must talk to."

She ran down the hall and plunged through the third door on the left. The instant wall of people reminded her of rush hour on the FDR back home. Working her way through the crowd was going to take a minute, maybe more. She employed her method of gentle but firm progress through the old people, young people, people who smelled great and those who did not. At last she made her way to the spot where she saw Peter. The girls from Liam's door stood there wiggling their butts and waving to the rock star, but Peter had vanished, again. Vesta looked around. A sea of unfamiliar faces, all looking up to the bright stage at Liam swaggering around with his microphone. It was no use to look any further. She knew it would be more futile than when she saw him the day before at the Musée d'Orsay. There were a thousand times more people and he clearly was trying to avoid her.

Walking to the hallway backstage, Vesta sat down in a chair by the security office to decide what to do next. She stood up a second later realizing they would have surveillance monitors of the crowd. After a short rap on the door, Vesta poked her head inside.

"Bonsoir." Vesta asked if she could view the crowd with them. The two security guards scoffed at her request. "Non, madame. C'est impossible." Going just a bit beyond the truth as she knew it, Vesta told them Liam's brother, who was a little slow in the thinking department, was lost in the crowd and didn't know how to join her backstage.

The guards discussed the matter between them for a minute then allowed her to look at the monitors. Fifteen cameras, at least, were pointed at the crowd. The monitors would shift between cameras every minute. Vesta scanned the screens for over an hour until her eyes grew hot and glazed over. No Peter. Not even a cheap white turtleneck in the crowd.

The show would wrap up soon and not wanting to be caught in the mass exodus, she grabbed her coat from the dressing room and walked out into the cold Paris night to a cabstand. She asked the driver to loop around the arena before heading to her hotel, her eyes searching and straining for any clue. But there was no sign of Peter.

The bar at the Hotel Du Jeu De Paume glowed with soft candlelight as she walked past it toward her room. Vesta slowed her pace then turned around. A club chair in a corner of the room looked more than inviting. She sunk into it. A waiter arrived and after ordering a large cognac, Vesta ran her fingers through her hair as she leaned back against the chair. Was Peter following her? Maybe it was just chance, or fate, that they were at the same place at the same time two days in a row. Things like that could possibly happen, it was a major exhibition at the Musée d'Orsay and Liam Spencer's show attracted thousands of people. But they had locked their gazes onto each other. He was staring at her at the exhibit before she even realized it. And he waved to her at the concert. Something didn't add up. Plus, the fact she had met him only once in the center of the labyrinth at Chartres cathedral but felt a deep connection and an urgency to find him after that day without any rational reason why, twisted Vesta's thoughts into a knot. She imagined them winding along the path of the labyrinth together, the image clear in her mind.

She sunk deeper into the thick padding of the chair and closed her eyes. A sigh pushed its way past her lips. The spot between her eyebrows began to spin.

"We must move faster. Our time is limited." A garbled male voice with an accent said.

"She is still ignorant and no threat to us." A female responded; her voice muffled.

Vesta's eyes flew open to see who was speaking. No one sat on either side of her, the other tables were empty. The bartender and waiter stood at the far end of the bar speaking French in low voices as they prepared her cognac.

She was certain she heard someone speaking English. Both a man and a woman and they had accents, his thicker than hers. Their conversation was muffled, like it was before when she touched the Russian Fabergé egg, sounding as if they were behind a wall. She pulled her phone from her evening bag and looked at it. It was turned off.

Vesta closed her eyes again listening intently for a minute hoping to catch more. Only the subdued conversation at the end of the bar grazed her ears. She opened her eyes and rubbed the spot between her brows. What she heard wasn't her imagination. Jet lag affected her a bit but not enough to hallucinate a conversation. It was her InSight kicking in. She sat up straight in the chair and tried to recall what lead up to it. Had she done something to cause the InSight to happen or was it some random occurrence? The waiter walked toward her with the cognac.

With her drink in hand, she swirled the glass thinking about what she heard. The man said they needed to hurry. But the woman said she was ignorant and no threat. Vesta swallowed some of the caramel-colored liquor. The voices weren't clear but they sounded familiar. Did she know the people who spoke? Each had an accent but they weren't the same accent. A prickling sensation began on her neck as it dawned on her that the woman's voice belonged to Valentina.

Her third eye began to whirr softly. Vesta took that as confirmation that she was correct. The Parrinos were involved in something illegal and the man was afraid Vesta was about to discover what it was. His voice didn't sound like Francesco who had a thick Italian accent. The one she heard was something else, it was familiar yet she couldn't place where she had heard it before.

Vesta sipped her cognac. Tomorrow she would fly to Rome. Her plan to sneak into an office area during the party at Villa Spada and hack into one of their computers needed more thought. Even though she told Liam not to worry, she knew that everything depended on getting in and out of the room undetected. What would they do to her anyway if they caught her? Kick her out of the house? No big deal there. The way she looked at it, she had everything to gain and nothing to lose by putting her plan into action.

CHAPTER 13

While Rome ranked a notch below Paris in Vesta's heart, it never failed to quicken her pulse the moment she caught sight of the ancient city from the air as it rambled over the millennia-worn hills. Landing at Leonardo da Vinci airport held special meaning for her. The great Renaissance painter had been one of her greatest inspirations since childhood. Born illegitimate to a prominent notary and a poor local girl in a town outside of Florence, da Vinci, without any formal education joined the studio of the renowned painter Andrea del Verrocchio at the age of fifteen. His talent impressed everyone from the start. Vesta thought many times about how such a genius at painting, drawing, inventing, writing backwards on a regular basis, progressed through life. Did he recognize himself as a genius early on? She knew he worked with constant diligence expanding the knowledge of human anatomy and giving the world its first concept of flying machines. His work ethic energized her own.

Vesta pulled her bags through the conundrum of disorderly order of the airport terminal. She smiled as she observed the airport's managed chaos, surely orchestrated by the Marx brothers. Somehow the airport staff got people where they needed to go, and for that she was grateful.

As she walked out of the terminal to find a cab, she wondered what da Vinci would have thought of a place that had hundreds of flying machines taking off and landing from it every day bearing his name? She was sure he would love it. Wasting time patting himself on the back would make no sense for someone like him though. Genius meant freedom from the constraints of trying to measure up to anyone or anything else. It resonated with the flow of an unregulated imagination, and the excitement and curiosity that came with it.

The J.K. Place Roma sat in the center of Rome's fashion district. Imbued with the luxury of a boutique hotel with impeccable attention by the staff and glorious rooms filled with tasteful touches of the old world and the new, it checked all the boxes of what she could want. Her favorite suite offered a spectacular view of the city from the sumptuous rosewood canopy bed anchored in the middle of the room.

Moments after she arrived into the suite, she stood at the window letting Rome work its magic on her. The secrets hidden behind so many of the walls, the history carved there by some of the greatest philosophers, leaders and mythological gods the world has ever known. The place deserved all the adoration it received. Looking down at her watch, Vesta calculated that two hours of free time remained available before getting ready for the Parrino's cocktail party. Their villa, located an hour's drive from Rome, near the town of Frascati required she wear something made in Italy. It was her requirement, in truth, and a perfect reason to run down the block in search of a suitable dress, one with an inside pocket to conceal her special treat for Valentina. Vesta nodded in approval as she turned from the window and headed for the door.

A temperate October breeze from the Mediterranean ruffled

her hair as she headed out on foot toward the Via Borgognona a few blocks away. There she found a stunning Brunello Cucinelli black jumpsuit that fit her like it had been custom made. Pairing it with a black Valentino jacket, in case the evening turned cool, and a fuchsia silk Elizabetta scarf for a pop of color she successfully completed the outfit. After returning to the hotel, from her jewelry case she pulled out a pair of Venetian drop earrings bought years earlier on the island of Murano. She followed it with a Sotheby's purchase made the year before of an antique cameo brooch said to be of Lucrezia Borgia writing a letter to a lover.

"Most appropriate," she murmured to herself as she headed to the shower.

Marco would certainly be at the party. Even after scrutinizing him, testing him and teasing him, she still hadn't decided if he was part of what she was sure was a smuggling operation.

"He has to be though, right?" She said out loud. He was deeply involved with the family wine business which included exportation on their ships. Logic made it evident that he would know about other family matters.

Regardless of how much she enjoyed sex with him or the way his eyes dazzled when he laughed, she would take him down with the rest of them if he was involved. And she would find out the answer to the question that very night.

The ride to Villa Spada took a long time. Once outside of the city the green-gold undulating hills reminded Vesta of some backdrop in a mythological play. In her mind she could see Venus and Apollo roaming merrily as they looked for their next adventure. It also created a fertile landscape for her to think carefully and do a final run through. Her plan to hack into one of the Parrino's computers wavered in her mind. She told Liam she knew down to the last detail what she would do, but that wasn't true. Playing it as she went sounded right. The layout of the villa needed assessing, Valentina's movements also. Did security monitor the offices? Answers forthcoming would determine what action to take.

Vesta fondled the palm-sized rectangle in her jumpsuit pocket. Without doubt Valentina would try tapping into her thoughts the minute she arrived. Vesta prepared herself by walking through all the doors in her mind and shutting them tight, just like Liam told her to. She even secured locks on them with keys she swallowed to keep safe in her belly.

"Name the things you see. See the words in your mind." Vesta drilled instructions deep into her subconscious while the car sped past hillside towns and fields of grapevines freshly picked.

At last they turned right onto a gravel road stopping in front of an enormous wrought iron gate. A man walked up to the car, conversed in Italian with the driver, Vesta picking out a few words in each sentence. The driver said he was dropping Vesta off for a party and gave the man her name. Access granted, the heavy gate swung open.

The driveway extended around a hillside dotted with stone pines, their flattened crowns stretching toward the valley below. A sharp turn to the left set them on a more narrow road lined with tall Italian cypress spaced in even rows which culminated at an ancient stone wall a few hundred meters beyond where the driver stopped. He got out of the car and opened her door as a large man approached from behind the wall.

"Keep the doors locked. Name what you see," she whispered to herself.

"Grazie," she said out loud as she paid the driver including a generous tip. He bowed and drove off.

"Senora Beauvais." The booming voice came from someone resembling a minotaur more than a man with his wide-set eyes and bulbous nose. Vesta stared at him for a moment.

Minotaur, she saw the word in her mind. "Yes, that's me," she said out loud.

"I'm Sergio. I'm here to escort you to the villa." He extended his burly arm. Vesta's mind recalled a glimpse of the Disney animated movie Beauty and the Beast, the part where the beast extends his arm to dance with Beauty. The scale was about the same.

Disney, the word formed clearly in her thoughts.

On the other side of the wall stood a crumbling staircase patched in places with modern stone and plaster.

"We have an elevator if you prefer, senora," Sergio said before they began the climb.

"No. This is fine."

Villa Spada came into view step by step. Faded white stucco walls soared three stories high with eyebrow-looking moldings framing almost every window. The entrance supported three huge arches leading into an alcove, much like the Napa Valley house. Above the arches on the roof sat a monstrous-looking god sculpted from marble who held a sword aloft in his hand. Vesta didn't recognize him from any books but noticed he kept watch over all who approached.

Monster.

Sergio led Vesta through the heavy wooden door into the villa. Niches holding marble busts of Roman men with beards lined a lunette entry. They walked further across the white marble floor coming to an enormous room filled with people smoking, laughing, and drinking. Sergio bowed and left the room. Vesta looked around.

Fellini.

A bar was tucked into a corner of the grand space. As she headed for it, Vesta realized the room had an identical layout to the house in Napa. Making her way toward the bar she saw

Marco's brother, Giovanni, talking to a group of men. He made eye contact with her but gave no recognition.

"Good evening, senora," said the bartender as she reached her destination. "May I pour you a glass of the house's wine?"

"No thank you. Do you have Russian vodka?"

"Yes."

"Could you mix a very cold martini for me?"

"Yes, of course."

James Bond, the Sean Connery version, faded into solid form in her mind. He would be perfect at a gathering like this dressed in his tuxedo, his eyebrow arched as he eyed the room. She scanned the scene for Marco but saw neither him nor Valentina.

"A Russian vodka martini senora." The bartender slid the drink to Vesta.

"Grazie."

"Prego."

Vesta picked up her martini just as an arm wrapped around her waist.

"There you are." Marco's smile and intoxicating scent moved close to her. "I didn't know you had arrived."

"I just got here." Vesta kissed Marco on both cheeks.

Sex in Napa Valley.

"How was your flight from Paris? You look incredible." Marco stepped back and admired every inch.

"Thank you. I'm fine."

"I was delighted when my mother told me you were one of the guests Liam invited tonight."

"Yeah, is he here yet?"

"No." Marco looked around the room. "Most of the people here are friends of my parents. Old acquaintances and business associates. Come, let me introduce you."

Vesta and Marco walked over to the group where Giovanni

stood. The older brother, tall and lumpy, a younger model of Francesco, greeted Vesta with kisses on each cheek and made introductions around circle. The three other men were in business with the Parrinos although none said what kind of business. All were vague when Vesta posed casual questions to them.

The three stooges.

One of the men, the shortest and widest with a mostly bald head, Curly, said, "We are looking forward to meeting Liam Spencer. I have listened to his music since my mother played his records when I was a child."

Vesta nodded. "Good."

"You have known him for a long time?" He asked.

"Oh yes, quite a long time."

A clatter across the room announced the arrival of Liam and his bandmates. Ian, the bass guitar player, had dropped his phone and some other metal sounding object on the marble floor creating a noise that drew everyone's attention.

This is Spinal Tap; Vesta saw the words type out. "Excuse me please," she said out loud and walked toward Liam who opened his arms wide for her. Dressed in a deep red silk shirt unbuttoned to mid-chest, requisite medallion hanging from a leather cord on bare skin, black leather pants and some kind of black snake skin wrapped on his boots, Liam had a broad smile plastered on his face.

"It's the goddess of the spindle!" He grabbed her up and planted a kiss on each cheek.

"That will do." Vesta said in a calm tone while taking inventory of each person in Liam's entourage. "Where's Oz? You invited him didn't you?"

Liam looked nervous. Vesta studied his face to be sure. Yes, he's nervous. About what? Vesta caught herself. Mick Jagger on stage, see him on stage prancing around, she commanded to herself.

"Of course I did." Liam looked around. "He's, um, he'll be along directly."

"Okay." Vesta eyed him closely. "Anything you want to tell me."

"I need a drink." Liam nudged Ian and the other band members. "Mates, you ready to kick this party off?" After rousing approval, Liam led them to the bar. Vesta watched him which confirmed her sense that something was amiss. He didn't have that careless gait she was so fond of. His body moved in an unnatural way for him, more like a banker or politician.

Mussolini. Ronald Reagan.

A cold chill grabbed her, running up her spine as if all the clouds on the planet converged over Villa Spada to block out the sun for the next millennium. She turned, already knowing what she would see behind her. Valentina entered the room.

Valdemort, the letters dripped blood in her mind.

Putting the martini glass to her lips, Vesta drained her glass then turned to head to the bar in the opposite direction. She began humming lyrics to Liam's hit Nobody's Fool. When she reached it, Liam was there and she sang the lyrics in his ear.

"You're being a tart this evening. Have another?" He pointed at her glass. She nodded but kept on singing as she turned to face the room.

She watched Valentina move through the crowd, her tiny, thin frame with impeccable posture balancing a turquoise turban with her caramel-colored head and flashing green eyes. Her floor-length silk caftan gave no clue to any specific body features as it floated from group to group.

Vesta hummed the words to Liam's song louder in her head and turned back to the bar.

"Here you go Love," Liam handed her a martini then picked up his Gilpin's neat. "I'm going to find Oz." An attempted smile straggled across his face then disappeared. "To make sure he didn't get lost."

Vesta frowned at him. "What is wrong with you?"

"Nothing!" He wiggled his head side-to-side in quick, abrupt motions. "I'll see you in a minute or two." Her eyes followed his tight, quick steps as he dodged saying hello to anyone making his way to the entry way of the villa.

Charlie Chaplin as the little tramp she pulled into her psychic view.

With another martini in hand and all of Liam's bandmates in tow, Vesta walked out on the terrace. No wind but a cooler temperature prevailed as the sun slid behind knobby sunbaked hills. A purple hue rose from the ground tinting the sky a shade Vesta had never seen before. Dusty, deep lavender permeated everything in her view creating an other-world scene.

The band began chatting about their gig in Paris, how great the crowd was, how hot the women were and how much champagne they drank. Vesta stared at the landscape. Something seemed odd. She couldn't say what, but a shift had happened without doubt since her arrival. It seemed impossible to say but it felt like gravity had intensified, as if two planets were about to collide, their enormous individual power pulling on the other and each resisting. Vesta steadied herself. No one else seemed to notice. She poured the martini down her throat.

The time had come to put her plan into action. After pulling the Walkman from her jumpsuit pocket, she took tiny headphones from her jacket, plugging them into the cassette player she popped the headphones on and turned up the music.

Fool's Paradise blasted between her ears. Turning to face the villa, Vesta saw the façade sway as if she observed it from underwater. She blinked and it regained its normal look. Something continued to poke at her reality. Something wanted through. Vesta shook her head. Time to focus.

The terrace stretched out to the end of the villa away from the party room. There were no exterior doors in that direction but she could see an outside staircase that led to the second floor. Vesta walked toward it with an easy gait as she sang the song lyrics under her breath.

"Don't think twice, you know you want to join me in a fool's paradise."

She scanned everything to her left then her right. No one in sight as she turned and climbed the wide stone steps landing in front of a heavy wooden door at the top. On it sat a large iron door knob, rusty and pitted from decades of assault by the elements. She grasped it with her hand and tried to turn it. It was locked. Looking up she noticed a camera aimed at the doorstep staring at her with its unblinking eye. Vesta tried to act surprised and mouthed the word "bathroom" at its steady gaze. She tilted her head in an exaggerated fashion to make it seem like she was on an innocent mission searching for the ladies' room. As she descended the stairs, she decided her next plan of attack would be to rejoin the party, find a bathroom and sneak through the house from there.

Groucho Marx dancing and singing Hello, I Must Be Going from Animal Crackers. The scene almost made her giggle as it played out in her interior film projector.

Dusk had settled rapidly, she noticed as she turned around to descend the stairs, casting everything around her from the deep lavender color a minute earlier into a surreal shade of blue. The hue reminded Vesta of cheap science fiction movies from her childhood. The kind they showed at the dollar cinema on Monday nights when humans landed on another planet and were observing the alien landscape for the first time. But she was seeing it in real life. The weird gravitational sensation continued pulsing through her but she realized she was growing accustomed to it as she walked down the stairs.

"There you are." Liam ran up to her out of breath when she reached the bottom. "I've been searching every nook and everyone's cranny for you." His eyes looked glazed with fear. Vesta pulled her headphones off and tucked them into her pocket along with the Walkman.

"What is wrong with you?"

"Nothing," he said but kept the wild-eyed stare.

"Then why are you looking like that?" Vesta began walking back toward the party.

"Like what?" Liam laughed in a high-pitched tone. Vesta stopped walking and turned to face Liam. He stared over her shoulder.

"You only laugh like that when something's wrong." Vesta took a step closer to him then recoiled. "And what the hell, you're full of static electricity." She pushed a finger toward him and heard a pop. "Ouch! You shocked me."

"Oh god, I've got to release this shit before it kills me." Liam began bouncing up and down shaking his hands. "Promise to forgive me. I did what I thought was best for you."

"What are you talking about?" Vesta swiveled her head to follow Liam's gaze. From the deep blue folds of shadow pressed between illuminated windows, four people walked toward them. One moment in darkness, the next in a pool of golden light they traveled across the terrace. Vesta squinted to see their faces.

"Who is that?"

"I didn't want you to get hurt."

The bodies moved in a familiar way but at first she couldn't place where she'd seen them before. One moved distinctly like a woman. Moonlight caught part of a rolled up white shirtsleeve on another. Vesta gasped and swung around toward Liam with a look that would mow down fifty men.

"Why did you call them?"

"You don't know that old desert hag. She'll turn your mind into a plum pudding if you aren't careful."

"I trusted you." Vesta's voice sounded like ice hitting metal. Liam looked down fumbling for a cigarette in his shirt pocket.

"Good evening Vesta," Amara called out when they arrived at a closer range.

"Why are you here?" The ice pellets striking with every syllable.

"Because you need some help," Jared said. "And we're here for you."

"I don't need any help."

Sandor held out one of two martini glasses that he held to Vesta. "Yes, you do. You just don't know it yet."

"I don't want that."

Cyrus cleared his throat. "Vesta, I realize that you still don't get the big picture here, but you're going to have to trust us on this one."

Liam moved closer to Vesta. He touched her with his finger and even though he didn't shock her, she pulled away from him. "Lovey, I didn't think you could manage this caper on your own. And the little help I could offer wouldn't get you far."

"Look at what you're all doing." Vesta raised her hands in surrender. "That crazy old bitch is in there right now reading my mind, knowing exactly what I was planning. All thanks to you geniuses."

"Not quite," Liam said. "I conjured that little electrical storm around you to prevent her from hearing a thing."

"She can't read the rest of us," Sandor said. "We learned how to block her lifetimes ago." He sipped his martini then pointed at her. "You taught me how."

"So, let me get this straight, you're here to help me bring down Valentina?"

"Actually," Amara said. "We're here to protect you."

"And talk you out of going through with your plan, if you really have one." Sandor nodded toward Liam. "According to little Sparky here, it sounds like you don't."

Vesta cut a laser gaze toward Liam. A zigzag smile smeared across his face. "I, uh, well you see, I was terrified that you were going off half-cocked."

"By that look she's giving you, I would say your cock is the one that could be in half if she gets her hands on you."

"Sandor," Amara said. "That's not helping."

"She's right." Jared said. "I'm sure the First Blood knows we're here. She knows something's up too. Vesta, you need to tell us every detail of the InSight you received."

"Who said I had an InSight?"

"You have to tell us, since you've dragged us into this," Cyrus said.

"I haven't dragged you into anything."

"You did the moment you decided to take her on. We need to know why. There has been a truce of sorts for years between the Parrinos and us. They've handled their successful import business where most of their dealings are legal, or at least tolerable." Cyrus put his hands into his pants pockets. "That's changed now."

"Chances are better than good that she knows you're up to something," Jared said. "We need to know what you saw so we can deal with it."

Vesta felt outnumbered. Liam betrayed her and if Jared was right, Valentina laid in wait for her.

A sharp pain like a pin poking into her forehead set her third eye on fire. She slammed her eyelids shut to stop the pain and saw a ship docked at a pier too tiny for the large vessel. Darkness cloaked all the action around it except for headlamps worn by men she saw unloading boxes of a uniform size from the ship. They carried the boxes to two vans. Three men with automatic weapons stood near the trucks. The vision faded away. Vesta opened her eyes.

"What did you see?" Amara asked.

Vesta shook her head and rubbed the spot between her eyebrows. The burning had stopped. She looked at Amara.

"How do you know I saw anything just then?"

Amara leaned in to Vesta placing her hand on her arm. "We are sisters. While I don't have the InSight gift, I can see it in your aura when you receive it."

"Stop fighting it Vesta," Jared said. "Tell us what you saw. We're wasting time."

Vesta looked down and studied her shoes for a moment. Manolo Blahniks really were comfortable despite the heels being so skinny and high. She sighed and looked up at the group knowing it was time to lay out her cards.

"It was a ship at a dock that didn't look like it was big enough to handle a boat of that size. It was very dark and guys wearing headlamps were unloading wooden boxes, all the same size into vans. Some other guys were standing by the vans holding assault rifles."

The trionfi exchanged glances between each other.

"I think they're smuggling antiques," Vesta said. "When I touched a Fabergé egg at the Parrino's house in Napa, I heard voices, both male, in my head talking about something priceless and there being collateral damage. One said they must continue. Then the other said he would handle it himself."

Cyrus nodded his head. "Thank you for sharing that."

"Look, I know you want me to help you find Raz, but this family is involved in something illegal. My InSight has focused on them for some reason. It keeps showing these smuggling scenes, these ships and their boxes of cargo. It's not like I'm asking for them to come to me or like I know how to control them."

"Vesta, listening to you describe that scene, it occurs to me that there might be a connection between," Jared began.

Liam interrupted by clearing his throat in a loud exaggerated manner and pointed behind them. The group turned around to see a thin stick figure in a billowing silk caftan walk toward them, a turban piled high on her head.

"To what do I owe the honor of your presence tonight in my home," Valentina said as she reached the group.

Jared gave a slight bow. "Senora Parrino, it is our honor to be invited into your beautiful home. I thought you knew we were coming."

"I knew," she said as her emerald gaze landed on Liam who replied with a flickering grin. "Our guest of honor invited many tonight," Valentina said.

"Well, it's been so long since I've seen this crew, I felt like it might be the right thing to do." He flashed another zigzag smile.

"And the High Priestess," Valentina continued. "Back so soon on our soil."

Vesta locked eyes with the First Blood not willing to pretend anything. "You gave me quite a welcome in Napa Valley. I wanted to get to know you better."

Cyrus stepped closer to Valentina. "Senora, we bear no ill will toward you or your family. We are here merely as guests at Villa Spada."

"So you say." Valentina walked toward the terrace railing then turned to face the group. "There is no place closer to me in my heart except for my beloved Nile. You shall respect our home or pay the price."

A breeze caught the long silk sheath she wore causing it to ripple like waves lapping on a shore. Clouds eclipsed the new crescent moon at that moment sending the terrace into darkness. Valentina walked away from the group back inside her villa.

"Well that was a cheery greeting." Liam pulled a cigarette from his pocket and lit it.

Sandor pointed at Vesta. "Don't fuck with her. She's playing nice right now. We have to let her think everything is cool while we decide what to do next."

"So this is a group project now?" Vesta said. "I can handle that one on my own."

"Love, you are truly no match for her." Liam reached his hand toward Vesta. She ignored his hand and his comment.

"Especially the state you're in right now," Sandor said.

"What's that supposed to mean?" Vesta cocked her head.

"What he means," Amara said. "Is that you haven't fully discovered your powers yet. You are an incredibly gifted and powerful woman."

"I know that."

"Don't let that ego bite you too hard on the ass," Cyrus said.

"Stop with the sniping everyone. Vesta you know yourself as the woman who worked hard to become a CEO and chairman of the board. But you really have no idea who you are as the High Priestess. You haven't begun to explore what you're capable of, what your duties are in that realm," Amara said.

"And what if I don't want to give up that life for all these duties? Am I supposed to just turn my back on my career, on my company and its employees?"

"We're not asking you to do that," Jared said. "We want your help locating Rasputin. To do that, you need to become more familiar with your abilities so you can tune into where he is and what he's doing. Although I might have an idea."

"I will find him. He killed my uncle. I won't stop until he's locked up for the rest of his life. His prostitution ring of teenaged sex slaves is out of business so he's not wreaking pain and destruction at the moment."

"Why this obsession with the Parrinos then?" Sandor said.

Vesta turned to face the rolling hills as the slender moonlight pierced the sky again.

"You just want to show Valentina that you're the Queen Bitch."

"Sandor," Amara said.

"It's true. She has never taken shit from anyone. You all know that. Hell, Valentina knows that. She's just playing the hand as it lays right now with Vesta at a distinct disadvantage."

Sandor walked close to Vesta.

"You're batting completely blind here. All those tricks you taught yourself to become a corporate head aren't going to help you with her." Sandor looked toward the villa. "No, it's like pissing on a grass fire until you remember what you wiped out of your mind."

Sandor patted her on the shoulder. Vesta recoiled from his touch. "Good luck with that. Oh, and we'll be around to help or clean up your mess. It's our job. We haven't forgotten."

Vesta squinted her eyes at him for a long moment. How she could have ever felt love for him in a previous life, not to mention marrying him, was beyond her wildest imagination.

"I'll be fine. You don't need to worry about me." She turned to look at Liam with an ice-cold stare. "And you certainly didn't need to travel this far to babysit me."

"Liam did what he thought was best for you," Amara said. "You must recognize that."

"I recognize that I need a drink." Vesta turned from the group toward the villa. Liam followed in step behind her. She stopped, turned and faced him. "Without an escort."

Liam stood frozen in place. The moonlight chiseled out deep lines beside his mouth and above his forehead. His gaunt frame looked bent at the shoulders, hunched over like a little old man. He stared at Vesta unblinking.

"I only wanted to help you," he said.

"You betrayed me." Vesta hissed the words.

"Never. I would never do that."

Vesta spun around and walked inside.

"You gave it your best shot. That's all you could do," Sandor said as he approached Liam and swung his arm around his shoulder.

"Oh do shut up." Liam flicked Sandor's arm away.

"She's unprotected in there," Amara said.

"We will just have to wait and see what happens next," Cyrus said.

"You know this isn't going to end well," Jared said. "Vesta thinks she's bulletproof and Valentina smells blood in the water."

"I'm more concerned about her unwillingness to assume her duties." Cyrus scratched the stubble on his chin. "We really need her InSight. And we don't know how long Raymond will be out of commission this time."

"Well, Enid's almost three, so we shouldn't have to wait too long," Amara said.

CHAPTER 14

The lights inside the villa cast a soft golden glow in the large room. The centuries' old tapestries that hung from the high plastered walls seemed to come alive in the light. The unicorns and troubadours, the maidens and warriors, all felt as though they had paused mid-step from their actions as Vesta walked in. Guests looking like they were borrowed from the cast of the classic Fellini film 8 1/2 filled the space with laughter and conversation. Knots of cigarette smoke tied halos around their heads as a man sang in Italian from a piano in the corner.

"At last, here you are," Marco said as he approached sliding his arm around Vesta's waist. "I have been looking everywhere for you."

"I was out on the terrace. You didn't look very far."

Marco smiled as he brought his mouth close to Vesta's ear. "I was hoping to show you some other parts of Villa Spada."

She paused for a moment letting the perfectness of how his suggestion fit into her plan wash over her. A smile spread across her face like the crescent moon outside. "I would love that." She couldn't have imagined a better scenario to get into the inner bowels of the Valentina's lair.

"Come with me." Marco offered his arm.

Hot sexy man. She filled her mind with images of naked Marco hoping Valentina was pillaging her thoughts.

He led her to a grand marble staircase on the far side of the entrance hall. As they ascended, she scanned the room for the First Blood but didn't spot her. Francesco sat on one of the sofas talking to other men. Even from a distance she could see that he was breathing with heavy puffs leaning all his weight on one side of the seat which seemed to groan in agony. Across the room stood Giovanni talking to a cluster of rough looking men and two well-endowed women whose plunging necklines were fighting a losing battle of containment. The group seemed to be hanging on every word Giovanni spoke.

When they reached the second-floor landing Vesta paused to survey the layout. It was without question a palace. Limestone walls displayed what had to be priceless antiques and artwork every few feet. Paintings hung next to more tapestries, marble busts and statues littered the wide hallway. She followed Marco as her gaze took in the splendor from each step. With the scrape of her heel she stopped next to a painting she recognized. The tiny hairs on the back of her neck sprung up. It was of a peasant girl touching the hand of a young nobleman, the brushstrokes careful and fine. She stared at the familiar scene.

"Hold on," she said. "Don't tell me you have a copy of a painting. I can't believe your family would stoop to such common standards."

"Oh, it's not a copy."

"Well, Caravaggio is one of my favorite painters and I know that only two versions of this painting, The Fortune Teller, was made. His first version hangs in the Musei Capitolini in Rome and the second in the Louvre."

"And his third here," Marco said with a slight wave of his hand toward the painting. Vesta turned her head to scan his face.

"You see," he said. "Michel was a friend of the family. He was inspired to paint this after he met my mother." Marco laughed. "He took some liberties with her appearance as well as his own, but nevertheless."

Vesta's jaw dropped as she tried to find the words to ask the questions racing through her mind. "Wait," she said. She looked at the painting again, her fingers stretching toward it. "You're saying this is an original Caravaggio, and that your mother knew him?"

"Yes. He painted this first, before the others. It was a gift to my mother as a way of saying thanks. She introduced him to his first patron, Marchese Giustiniani."

"And your family has kept this since the late fifteen-hundreds?"

Marco nodded. "Certainly."

Vesta's eyes roamed over the painting. The story Marco told was incredible but she had a sense that it was true. At that moment a shock of recognition stabbed her in the belly then raced to her head. She realized the young woman in the painting wore a turban. Just like Valentina. And even though the skin tone was much lighter than the First Blood's, Vesta could see the resemblance. She stared at it without breathing. The title of the painting, The Fortune Teller, must refer to what Valentina did during those times in the early Baroque.

"Valentina was a fortune teller when she met Caravaggio?"

"Yes. That was before she met my father and they were married."

The concept of being born as the same person with the same gifts for an endless number of times rocked through Vesta's thoughts even though it had become a reality to her weeks earlier. She shook her head and looked at the floor.

"Did you know him too?"

"No, he died while I was still an infant." Marco laughed. "He was always getting into altercations. Fighting, you know? Being arrested. He was sent out of many cities and told not to return."

"Did he know who Valentina really was?"

"He knew she held many mysteries and that cards were involved. Nothing more."

"His painting The Card Sharps, was that based on knowing her?"

"Quite possibly." Marco took Vesta's hand. "But we've gotten distracted. Let's move into my chamber."

Vesta glanced at her hand in Marco's. "Okay." She smiled and shook her head as if to dislodge the early Baroque and reenter the twentieth century. They continued to walk as she refocused on blocking Valentina from scanning her thoughts. A mental wall popped up on cue surrounding her with the instructions that no one would be allowed inside her mind. Her third eye began to whirl like a tiny top. Clues to what this family smuggled had to be contained in one of these rooms. She would try to access her InSight to get some help.

Marco swung open a heavy wooden door at the end of the hall. They walked in. Chalky moonlight flooded through the wavy glass windows along the back wall making the room resemble a black and white photograph from different era.

"These are my private chambers."

Masculine energy seeped from every corner. Club chairs covered in fine leather sat next to a massive fireplace. Across the room an antique wooden headboard with images of boars and deer carved into it framed a king-sized bed. A caramel-colored Italian silk damask duvet rested on top. Vesta inhaled a slow approving breath as her pulse quickened.

Marco slid his arm around her waist and drew her close to him.

"I have been looking forward to this moment all evening," he said.

Heat from her female furnace radiated throughout her body. She leaned in giving Marco a deep kiss. He groaned, soft and slow. Vesta knew they were headed for pleasure, but she also knew this was her only chance to search upstairs. She sighed.

"Ouch!" Vesta brought her hand up to her head.

"Vesta, what's wrong?"

"My head is hurting. I'm probably dehydrated from the air travel." She looked at Marco. "I have to remind myself to drink water. Do you mind getting some for me?"

"No. No. Of course I don't mind." Marco kissed her hand. "Is there anything else? A tablet to relieve the pain?"

"Oh, that would be good too." Vesta rubbed her head. "I'm sorry. Where's your bathroom? I'm going to splash some water on my face."

"Yes, let me show you."

Marco led Vesta across the bedroom into a limestone and marble room. Something that looked like an ossuary sat near a window overlooking an expanse of lawn and gardens.

"Is that your bathtub?"

Marco nodded.

"Were bones in there before?"

"What?"

"It looks like an ancient container for the dead."

"It has always been a place to bathe. It is Roman. Modified for modern standards."

"Your family really hasn't had to buy anything new for centuries probably, right?"

Marco smiled. "The sink is just over here."

"Thank you." Vesta gave Marco's arm a light squeeze. "This will help me feel better. And the water and aspirin."

"I will go get it now." Marco kissed her hand again and left the room. Vesta looked around.

Nothing in the room looked, or felt, intriguing. But what was she looking for? How would she know when she found it? Vesta knew she had to kick her High Priestess superpowers into action, yet she wasn't one hundred percent sure how to do that. She rubbed her head again, this time with the hope of activating her InSight.

"Come on. Flip the switch." She whispered to herself. Nothing happened.

Vesta walked out of Marco's chambers and into the long hallway. Heavy wooden doors, closed to peering eyes, stood like sentinels on either side. Moving past each, Vesta stretched out her psychic sensitivity, or at least she tried to. Why hadn't she accepted Amara's offer to train her on how to use her InSight? Even once would have been smart because she had no idea what she was doing at that moment. She couldn't stand Amara and her sanctimonious, all-knowing attitude. That's why she didn't. The thought of Amara sharing some secret ancient wisdom with her ignorant friend, no, better, her ignorant sister who cursed herself with a memory spell was more than Vesta could tolerate. Amara's superior demeanor cloaked in care and poise was a nauseating thought.

Vesta froze mid-step. The back of her neck tingled. Consumed by her thoughts, she hadn't noticed where she was. There, staring at her from its commanding place on the wall was The Fortune Teller. Vesta's heart began beating fast. She looked at the door next to the painting. This was the place she was looking for, she was sure. Her hand trembled as she stepped forward and grabbed the knob. It was unlocked.

Pushing open the door Vesta crossed the threshold and

gasped. The room looked unlike any other she had seen in the villa. No medieval tapestries or Baroque paintings, no marble busts or French fauteuils. Instead, the limestone floor was bare except for what looked like a real leopard skin laid in front of a daybed covered in deep blue fabric. Vesta noticed the bed's legs were painted a shiny gold and sat in stark contrast to the cobalt cushion on top of it. As she looked closer, she realized the legs weren't painted but were made of actual gold. Strewn across the walls were Egyptian hieroglyphs and images of half-human, half-animal figures. Vesta recognized a few; Horus with the head of a falcon, jackal-headed Anubis and Isis with her imposing sun disc headdress. A huge sarcophagus with the image of a woman rested in an upright stance against a wall with a large wooden chest sitting beside it. Both appeared to be authentic and ancient. A kneeling woman with her arms outstretched in opposite directions, wings attached, adorned the front of the chest. Other symbols Vesta didn't understand littered the top and sides. On a wide table near the daybed a shallow metal bowl held a live flame. It flickered as Vest approached. Sitting next to the bowl, a glass ball the size of someone's head rested on a golden stand bearing the sculpted legs and talons of a giant bird.

The air was perfumed by some exotic fragrance; frankincense perhaps. Its intoxicating scent made Vesta light-headed. Her third eye began throbbing. She swayed slightly feeling a bit off balance and decided to sit down on the daybed. The sensation of someone touching her caused her to jerk her head to one side, but she saw no one there. The feeling of being touched continued. First on her arms, then on her back moving at last to a stroking of her cheek. Slow and caressing strokes making her more relaxed with each moment. Then the voices began, soft in a language she didn't recognize. They murmured to her. Soothing sounds that, even though she didn't understand what they were saying, she knew they were trying to comfort her, to assure her that she was protected and cherished.

A breeze swept with gentle motion through the room. The flame in the shallow metal bowl flickered and drew Vesta's attention to the table. There was no apparent source of the flame. No candle or oil in the bowl just the small bright flame, its image reflected in the glass ball that sat beside it. Vesta's gaze moved toward the flame in the ball, staring into its depths. The fire grew large in the glass swallowing it whole. An image emerged from the fire. It was her. Vesta felt a shock race up her spine. She was staring at an image of herself. It began talking.

"I killed them. There was no other choice. They were going to kill me."

Psychic paralysis seized her. The voice, her voice, was in her head but it was also coming from the glass ball, and it echoed off of the walls. Her eyes couldn't move, they could only stare at the ball.

"They lied to me. They used me. The spell was because of what they did to me."

Her image faded and in its place a vision of a room came into focus. Lying on the floor were several bodies. She moved closer to them recognizing Amara and Jared, their blank eyes staring at nothing. Next to them were Sandor and Cyrus, also dead. And slumped over in a chair was Liam lifeless and ghostly white. Vesta choked for breath as she witnessed the scene. Someone was standing beside her. She turned to see. It was Valentina. A thin smile slashed across her face.

"You are one of us. And now you know. All the power is yours. Nothing can stop you. You will help us and we will help you."

Valentina extended her long bony brown arm. Her hand touched Vesta's. A frigid spark lit up her body, her mind exploded into a thousand images. Dancing in front of a bonfire at night, a medieval throne room with people bowing, flames leaping onto her feet and catching her dress on fire.

Vesta screamed, then a sound of rushing in her ears, the feeling of hands grabbing her. Everything turned black and silent.

CHAPTER 15

The image of a falcon holding a hockey stick came into focus as Vesta opened her eyes. She stared at it for a moment. Why would a bird have a hockey stick tucked under its wing? And it looked like it was sitting in a Spanish paella pan. Vesta frowned. Where was she? She widened her gaze. The dozens of strange images scrawled across the ceiling drew her back to reality. A chill flooded her body and she held her breath.

"Are you alright? I've called for the medics." Marco knelt beside her.

Vesta raised her head and sat up.

"No, don't move. You're not well."

The spot between her eyebrows hurt. It ached. Vesta rubbed it with her fingers. "I don't need any medics." Her eyes wandered around the room and landed on the glass ball sitting on the table beside her. She shot up from the daybed. A swirling sensation in her head caused her to wobble. Marco rushed to his feet and grabbed her.

"You must sit. I think you fainted."

Vesta pointed to the glass ball. "It was that thing." She

shook her head. "I need to get out of here." Her balance was uneven at first but she gathered her wits and stood up. By the time she reached the door her steps became surer. Crossing the threshold into the hallway felt like she was moving from one dimension to another. Vesta blinked her eyes several times. She exhaled and felt the fog and nausea lift. Marco followed her.

"I have your water and aspirin. I was looking for you."

Vesta turned to him. "What is that place? I wandered in there while I was waiting for you."

"This is my mother's private chamber," Marco said as he closed the door. "No one enters it but her. I thought it was locked."

Vesta massaged her forehead.

"Are you alright? Did you have vision?"

"I need a driver to take me back to my hotel right now."

"Why don't you rest in my chambers for a little while? I can make you very comfortable in there."

Vesta shot a look at Marco that would have dropped most men at twenty paces. "No. I'm leaving."

Marco followed Vesta as she walked down the stairs at an uneven pace and out the front door of the villa. A group of men stood clustered around the stone landing outside. Their bodies stiffened as Marco walked out. He issued orders in Italian. Vesta guessed it was for a driver. Two of the men hurried down the ancient stone steps toward the driveway.

"Would you like for me to accompany you back to Rome? I can make sure that you have everything you need once you arrive."

"No. I do not want you to come with me."

Voices, in English, caused Vesta to look toward the front door. Amara rushed out followed by Jared.

"Here she is," Amara said.

Sweat broke out on Vesta's face. The vision she'd seen in the glass ball flashed in her mind.

"Are you okay?" Amara walked toward her.

"Yes." Vesta put both of her hands out to stop Amara's approach. "Stay there. I'm leaving."

Cyrus and Sandor emerged through the door. Liam was close on their heels but froze when he saw Vesta's face.

"What's happened?" Cyrus asked.

"Vesta is leaving," Marco said.

She knew the expression on her face conveyed that something was terribly wrong but she didn't care. She pointed to the trionfi. "I don't need anyone's assistance. I'll be fine. Leave me alone." Vesta turned toward the steps leading to the driveway and willed herself not to wobble as she walked down. Marco approached to take her arm.

"I'm fine Marco. Don't touch me. Just get the car ready."

The trionfi spoke in rapid hushed voices amongst themselves. All except Liam who leaned against the stone wall for support. His face had become as pale as the limestone.

Vesta reached the car whose back door stood open for her. She got inside and told the driver where to go. She leaned her head against the back seat and stared out the window. The car pulled away from the house and its massive exterior staircase. The villa came into Vesta's view as they circled the drive to leave. Her gaze was caught by a figure standing in a window on the second floor. It was tiny and thin with a turban piled high on its head. The bright crescent moonlight illuminated Valentina so well that Vesta could see even the viper's smile that sliced across her wicked face. Nausea washed over her again like a baptism of vomit.

The long drive back to J.K. Place Roma aggravated the situation. The car's motion of winding through the hills then speeding along the highway made Vesta feel weak and sweaty. A sense of imprisonment bore down on her. She wanted to run and scream then beat something hard with her fists. One thing she didn't want was to see that scene from the glass ball again. She pushed hard, then harder on her mind to shove the image out. The palms of her hands were wet. Her heart was skipping beats every few minutes. An ache that would register nine on the Richter scale pounded in her head.

Balancing on her last shred of composure, Vesta almost cried when they crossed the Tiber River, passed the Palazzo Borghese and saw the hotel come into view. Once the driver opened her door she shoved a handful of euro at him and hurried inside. Vesta bolted into her room expecting it to offer safety and relief. Instead a lack of circulating air all evening left it stuffy and hot. She peeled her clothes off her body and pitched her shoes into a corner. Standing naked in the room made her feel like prey ready to be devoured. She shivered in the heat. Pulling a Sybarite sundress from her suitcase and a pair of flat sandals, she dressed and ran out of the hotel.

Vesta didn't know Rome as well as she would have liked. Her only focus was to get to a place where she felt comfortable. Where that was, she had no clue. Waving off a doorman who wanted to hail a cab, Vesta set out on foot in the opposite direction from the river. She wandered with no destination in mind. Thoughts rattled around in her head. No logic superseded her spinning fear. She knew she had to gain control of the runaway train.

Ahead of her was a piazza filled with outdoor restaurants and people engaged in animated conversation. Vesta found a table on the periphery and sat down. She ordered a glass of red wine and drank it to calm her nerves. Many minutes passed before she noticed she was sitting across from the Pantheon. On a normal trip to Rome she might pop into the two thousand year old temple, now church, to admire the rotunda with its oculus. That night she didn't care if it fell down in front of her.

"That wasn't real," she murmured to herself. "It was a trick. The evil bitch got into my head again." Vesta rolled her glass back and forth in her hand. "There's no way I could do that, right?" She gulped the remainder of her wine, dropped some euro on the table and left.

Vesta headed down one of the narrow streets that lead to another narrow street. She wanted to be lost where no one could find her. She argued with herself as she walked. What she saw in the glass ball couldn't be a glimpse of the future. She had never killed anything in her life. Nothing could bring her to do that. Even though she wasn't fond of Amara, Jared, Sandor or Cyrus, she would never think of killing them. Then there was Liam. A sharp pain flared in her heart. Liam. He was her closest friend and he betrayed her. But betrayal wasn't grounds for murder.

Vesta turned a corner onto the wide traffic intersection at the column of Trajan and Piazza Venezia. During daylight hours these roads were filled with cars and people. At this hour only an occasional vehicle passed. Vesta paused looking up at Trajan at the top of his pillar of accomplishment. One of his battle victories carved in stone for the world to see. He did some heinous things in the name of his country for what he thought was right.

What was right for her? What if the trionfi were using her and lying to her? And what about the spell? Did they cause her to cast the spell on herself? Maybe what she saw in the glass ball was another InSight moment like the one when she touched the Fabergé egg, or when she saw the Castillo del Papa Luna in Peniscola, Spain? That vision turned out to be real. Vesta's head ached but she walked on.

The night was thick and quiet. She knew she was on the Via dei Fori Imperiali heading toward the Colosseum. She had sped past the Roman ruins many times in taxis as she made her way through the city on business over the years, never taking the time to visit the ancient parts. Now as she walked she felt a growing comfort with each step. She had no idea why. She didn't speak Italian. She didn't know much about Italian history, except in fashion, but Vesta felt a sense of ease as she approached an overlook at the Palatine Hill, the most ancient part of Rome. The crowds were gone, only the crumbled remains of two-thousand-year-old temples and palaces lay deep below modern street level.

Vesta inhaled a slow deep breath. She felt a sense of peace here. Her thoughts seemed less jumbled and jagged. Even though it was quite dark, the crescent moon dipping beneath the horizon an hour or so earlier, her eyes adjusted to the darkness and wandered along the stone roads laid out in orderly fashion revealing the remnants of a glorious civilization. Legendary emperors and philosophers, warriors and artists walked those streets carving out the beginnings of the modern world. She gazed at the remaining pieces of buildings, fragments of arches and columns. The architecture held an astonishing beauty for her, especially one small section of wall in particular where three columns stood in front of it. Vesta's mind quieted as she gazed at it.

A breeze rushed through a grove of stone pines growing nearby. She could hear the gentle sound as it caught the tips of her short hair in a gentle dance. It soothed the fever in her brain. She closed her eyes and breathed easily into the moment.

"It's not here, what you seek."

The voice shattered her tranquility and startled Vesta to the core. She jumped as she spun around, any remaining vapor of calm destroyed. How unbelievable that she let herself be lulled into such a vulnerable position that someone could walk up and surprise her. More incredibly, she couldn't believe what she saw standing before her – a stout woman dressed in solid black with a small turban wrapped tightly around her head. The only points of color on her body were two bright green eyes.

"Madame Kali!" Vesta wasn't sure if she should duck for cover or run. The last time she saw the Egyptian tarot card reader she warned Vesta about causing a tragedy. She had barked the words out like a curse. Then the old woman slipped into Vesta's mind for a look around. It had been the most bizarre experience in Vesta's life until the one at Villa Spada that evening. Vesta fumbled for words.

"I went to Chartres. I did what you told me to. There was nothing there. And my uncle was killed but I didn't cause it. And please don't get into my head. I'm having a really bad day." She blurted out disjointed thoughts that didn't make sense even to her.

Madame Kali shifted her gaze from Vesta to the Palantine Hill. "You have created many problems." She looked back at Vesta. "That you must fix."

Vesta began shaking her head. "I don't know what to do about anything right now."

A snort issued from Madame Kali's mouth. "I know that. That is why I have to show you."

"Show me what?"

"How stupid you are."

Vesta reared her head back. She was confused and distraught to an extreme extent but she wasn't going to stand by while someone who had previously kicked down her psychic door and proceeded to do a home invasion of her soul began insulting her.

"You need to get away from me right now." Vesta walked past Madame Kali back toward the Piazza Venezia. A taxi was certain to pass that way sooner or later. The old woman caught up with her. Her gait was fast and smooth for someone who had to be in her seventies.

"Did you think you could outsmart the First Blood?"

Vesta walked faster. "Are you working with Valentina?"

Madame Kali spat on the sidewalk. "Evil lives in that woman. I take no alliance with her."

"So how do you know about tonight? You are talking about what I saw, aren't you?"

"Aye, I saw too."

"How?"

"This is what you have to learn."

"Was that real? What I saw. Is that going to happen?"

"Only you know the answer."

"How do I stop it from happening?"

"Learn what you forgot."

"That's what you want to teach me? How to be the High Priestess?"

Madame Kali stopped walking. "Aye," she said.

Vesta exhaled and her eyes misted over. "Do I have a choice?"

"No."

Vesta put her hands up to her head. "I'm so overwhelmed and confused. My life is going to change forever, isn't it?"

The old woman cackled. "Such ignorance." She waved her hand toward the side of the road. "Look your Highness."

Vesta looked in the direction Madame Kali pointed. In a clearing stood a small temple surrounded by a wrought iron fence, shadows glinting around it. She squinted to see a large opening on the east side. Figures glided through the door even though it was closed, young women who danced down the steps and waved at Vesta while they formed a circle prancing together.

"Who are those women, and why are they waving at me?"

"They are the virgins of the temple."

"Virgins?" Vesta asked as the women began to fade from her sight. "What's happening? They're becoming invisible."

"They are from another time. Only here to show you honor."

"I don't understand."

"Stupid woman. This place is for you. And where you stood over there. That was for you." Madame Kali muttered something in a language Vesta didn't understand. Then she shook her finger at Vesta. "You will waste no more time. Come with me."

"Stop!" Vesta screamed. "Please. Tell me what's going on."

The old woman drew her lips together like she was going to spit again. Vesta took a step back.

"They are temples dedicated to you from ancient times."

Vesta sucked in her breath and held it. She looked toward the Palantine Hill then at the temple in front of her.

"I had temples?"

Madame Kali scowled. "You are not worthy to even look on these places at this moment. We leave now." She raised her arm and a hundred yards away headlights came on.

Vesta heard a car engine start. A black Mercedes pulled up on the street beside them.

"Get in," Madame Kali said.

"Where are we going?"

"Back to the old school."

CHAPTER 16

Two reasons stood out to Vesta for why she was wearing sunglasses inside the plane at such an early hour. The first was because she hadn't slept the night before. Not even for a moment. The second sat beside her.

Madame Kali's grim expression greeted everyone as they boarded the flight and walked past the first-class section. The total black ensemble of the tightly wound turban, long-sleeved plain shirt and long shapeless skirt with the lime green eyes studded on her dark brown face like Mrs. Potato Head added to the spectacle. Vesta looked out the window trying to ignore the stares of the other passengers. She wanted a drink, anything with vodka, but since it was early morning the flight attendants were only handing out coffee and juice. Pulling up the collar of her Oscar de la Renta trench coat Vesta leaned her head against the seat back and closed her eyes.

"You cannot drink alcohol anymore." The rasping voice with its mangled accent hissed in Vesta's ear.

"Get out of my head." Vesta spoke with slow punctuated words. She opened her eyes and looked at Madame Kali. "The first thing you're going to teach me when we get to Chartres is how to block you from reading my thoughts."

The old woman let out the hollow cackle Vesta had heard the night before. "Ignorant of everything but still making demands." She shook her head as she examined another passenger head-to-toe who walked past her.

Vesta sunk as far back into her seat as she could go, closed her eyes and wished she could become invisible.

After landing in Paris and taking the train from Montparnasse to Chartres, Vesta settled into a chair in the Henry IV suite at Le Parvis for a few minutes to call Jenny. Madame Kali was ensconced in Chambre Bleue an entire floor away. Spending hours with the woman, most of the time in silence even though Vesta knew she probably read her thoughts throughout the trip, was exhausting. A sharp rap on the door as soon as she hung up from her phone call startled her. The knob turned and Madame Kali walked in.

"Time to go," she said.

"How did you know it was unlocked?"

The old woman looked up at the ceiling for a moment then shook her head.

"We just got here. You haven't told me anything about where this school is. Can't you instruct me here in the hotel?"

"Your questions are a waste of time. We must go." Madame Kali walked from the room. Vesta got up and followed her out of the second floor exit door down to the street level.

"Is the school far or is it close to the cathedral?"

No answer came. Vesta followed the tarot card reader across the cobblestone street of the rue du Cheval Blanc to the eight-hundred-year-old cathedral. They walked up to the Port Royal entrance. Once again, as had happened when she visited months earlier, she sensed eyes watching her and felt something like a cobweb touching her skin. Brushing off her arms she followed Madame Kali as they entered the cathedral.

The late afternoon sunlight had departed the magnificent stained glass windows. Only candlelight from pilgrim's votives and single bare bulbs dangling at the ends of long cords along the aisles illuminated the interior. The cavernous space was silent. Vesta walked behind Madame Kali as she led her down the long nave. Rows of chairs sat on top of the labyrinth as they usually did six days out of the week. The center of it lay exposed in the middle of the aisle. It felt odd to Vesta to bisect the sacred symbol. She stepped lightly across it.

A lone figure sat in a chair close to the transept. He turned as they approached. Vesta gasped recognizing him immediately. It was Peter.

She was face-to-face with this man she didn't know, had spoken to only once, here at the cathedral in the center of the labyrinth, but the inexplicable instant connection she felt for him that day sent her searching in vain for him before she left Chartres the first time. In Paris she saw him at the Musée d'Orsay and again at Liam's concert but he purposefully eluded her. She hadn't thought about him since Paris. Even on the flight she had been so consumed by the horrifying events at Villa Spada that she hadn't thought about searching for Peter. And now here he was in front of her.

"Peter," she said.

The thin man with the mop of shaggy brown hair wore the same black turtleneck sweater and black pants as last time she saw him there. He smiled. "Vesta."

"She's yours now." Madame Kali waved her hand as if turning loose of something repellent.

"What?" Vesta flicked her head toward Madame Kali. "You said you were going to teach me."

"No. You assumed. I brought you here, that is all. The rest is up to him." Madame Kali turned and began walking away. Over her shoulder she called out. "Learn what you're supposed to this time or we will all suffer the consequences your Highness."

Vesta looked back at Peter who gave her a sympathetic smile. "Will you sit with me?" He returned to this seat. She sat down next to him with a billowing exhale.

"Confused?" Peter asked.

Vesta stared at him for a long moment. "I really don't know where to begin. Since I saw you here months ago my life has turned upside down. I'm guessing you know all about it."

Peter nodded.

"On top of that I get this vision at the Parrino's villa last night." Vesta shivered. "I think it was a trick by this woman but I can't shake the feeling that maybe I was seeing the future."

Vesta leaned over putting her head into her hands. "It was me talking about how I murdered these people I know." She looked up at Peter. "Maybe you know them too."

Peter again nodded. Vesta gave him a weak smile. "I'm beginning to figure out that all of you are connected."

"You are correct."

Vesta cocked her head. "Why didn't you tell me that when you first spoke to me?"

"You weren't ready to hear it."

"I came here because," Vesta waved her arm in the direction of Madame Kali's departure. "She told me to, to learn something to avert a tragedy. Did you know that?"

Peter nodded.

"Is she a trionfi member too?"

"No. She's one of the trusted ones though. Her line has been in close contact with our group for many generations."

"Why didn't you help me when I came here the first time?"

"I had to honor your wishes."

"You mean the spell I put on myself?"

"Yes."

"Couldn't you have at least warned me about Raz and what was about to happen?"

"No one was certain about the outcome except Raymond, and he kept it to himself."

"Uncle Raymond knew that he was going to be killed and he let it happen anyway."

"It was the way to get you back into the trionfi in this life."

The thought of her uncle sacrificing himself so that she could break the spell and reveal who she really was made Vesta's stomach churn.

"He died because of me."

Peter looked down in his lap.

"I came looking for you after we were in the labyrinth," Vesta said. "Did you know that?"

"Of course."

"Why didn't you help me then? I was ready. The episode I had in the center of the labyrinth began peeling away the layers." Vesta stared hard at Peter. "You could have helped me. Maybe Uncle Raymond would still be alive."

Peter shrugged his shoulders. "I felt that I couldn't help you at that point."

Vesta's gaze burrowed into Peter. "You didn't even try."

Peter looked up at Vesta and gave her a weak smile. "C'est la vie."

"That's all you have to say?" Vesta looked around the cathedral as if it would speak the answers she sought. "And what about now? Am I relying on you to teach me these great mysteries so that I don't murder my father and the rest of the trionfi?"

Peter was still for a moment then nodded. "Yes."

Vesta snorted. "Look, I have a life. Apparently, a couple of them right now. One is on hold while I get up to speed on this

High Priestess gig. I'm not crazy about doing this but it seems like I have no choice." Vesta shook her head. "I can't let that vision become a reality. Can you help me?"

"I can teach you."

Vesta exhaled. "Okay. Where's this school the old bat was talking about?"

"You're sitting in it."

Peter stood up. His tall, slender frame clad in all black almost disappeared into the gathering darkness of the cathedral. He stretched out his arms.

"A thousand years ago a mystery school existed here. It was famous throughout the world."

"What is a mystery school?"

"Chartres focused on the quadrivium. Mathematics, geometry, music and astronomy as taught by ancient Greek scholars like Socrates and Pythagoras was the curriculum. These subjects of science were also recognized for their mystical qualities."

Peter stopped talking and leaned in toward Vesta. "They were mysteries because they weren't taught to everyone." Then he straightened up and began to laugh. "The most amusing part is that while the esteemed teachers and carefully selected students were here learning, we were too."

"We?" Vesta said. "You mean you and I?"

Peter nodded. "Yes."

"We would go through the normal studies but then the bishop would give us free rein for our extra work." Peter stood up and began walking down the aisle toward the transept. Vesta followed.

"You see, the bishops of Chartres knew about us. The information was passed down throughout the centuries to certain groups. The Templars struck an agreement when they funded the building of this place. The trionfi would be allowed to study here whenever they wanted. During that epoch we came here each time we reincarnated to hone our gifts."

"How many times was that?"

"A lot over that three hundred years or so." Peter glanced around the transept as they approached it. "It was much better here after the original popularity of the place faded. That's when I really began to enjoy it."

Peter stopped walking and faced Vesta. "That's why I never left."

Vesta wrinkled her forehead. "What do you mean you never left?"

Peter began walking down the nave away from the altar. "I found the deepest parts of my being here. The energy of this place resonates with me on a cellular level." He winked at Vesta. "The architect created it out of love for me."

Peter twirled around, his arms outstretched. "Frozen music is the way some architectural experts describe the dimensions of this place. And it's true. It plays the song of my soul."

"Are you saying you're trapped here?"

Peter cocked his head, deep in thought for a moment. "I could leave if I wanted but that's not my nature right now." He moved closer to Vesta. "You haven't asked me an important question yet."

"What's that?"

Again Peter spun around lithe and agile like a dancer. "Who am I in the tarot deck?"

"Oh," Vesta said. "The Hanged Man. I figured it out a long time ago from that card you left on my sandal. It matched the image of you in the dream I had."

"That's a lovely way to communicate, isn't?" Peter drew one leg up crossing it over the other. "And do you know what strength I represent in the trionfi?"

Vesta raised her hands. "I'm sorry but I don't own a tarot deck and don't really know much about it."

"The Hanged Man in the tarot deck represents the patterns we repeat until we can release them and free ourselves for a more conscious life." Peter uncrossed his leg and began walking toward the labyrinth motioning for Vesta to follow. "The situation for me is I discover a limiting pattern in my life from walking the labyrinth and work through releasing it on my walk out of it." He tilted his head down watching his feet move as he spoke. "Only then I find more stuck energy patterns that must also be released. That cycle has repeated itself here for me life after life since the labyrinth was built in 1307."

"What? You've been here almost seven hundred years?" Vesta stared at him. "You are trapped."

Peter held up his hand. "No. I'm not. As I said, I can leave any time. I came to see you at the museum, and at Liam's concert. Remember?"

He gazed around the cathedral as it gathered more shadows from the day.

"You see, out of all the trionfi, I'm the one who is least attached to this material world. In one of my early lives, much earlier than the construction of this place, I became devoted to an ascended spiritual master. His teachings expanded my conscious mind and I reached the highest potential that the ancient elders had hoped for me when they gave me my gift."

He held up his right arm and pulled the sleeve of his sweater toward his elbow exposing his wrist. Vesta saw the symbol of a cross in thick black ink tattooed on it.

"My name was Simon in those days, but I was given the name Peter after the spiritual master chose me to carry on his work after he left his physical life."

A tear trickled down Peter's cheek. He quickly wiped it away. "As much as I've tried, I've never been able to attain that clarity again in my following lives." Peter fell silent for a moment and looked around the cathedral. "The level of true enlightenment that I had in that life has never returned to me. As a result, I've been a failure to the trionfi, not teaching the Others," He leaned close to Vesta. "I don't like to call them the hurtful name that some in the trionfi do."

Vesta wrinkled her nose. "What name?"

Peter winced before he spoke. "RanChans."

"Oh, that name."

He shrugged. "So, I stay here and walk, certain that someday I will find that incredible space within my mind, my heart, my soul where I am truly conscious of the pure essence of the Divine once again. And I can restart my teachings to the Others knowing that I come from a place of authenticity."

Peter stopped walking when he reached the center of the labyrinth. Vesta stood beside him. "You know, the architect of this magnificent cathedral designed the labyrinth for me. Well, for everyone else too, but especially for me. The intent was to help me regain that gnosis I had lost. Such a beautiful, loving gift."

Peter turned to Vesta with a piercing gaze. "Tomorrow you will begin dislodging your memories and your gifts. I'll show you how."

"Thank you Peter."

"Thank you Vesta."

She cocked her head. "For what?"

"For being willing to open yourself up to your true nature." He placed his hand on hers and gave it a small squeeze. "And for creating this magnificent place."

CHAPTER 17

Sleep came in knotted minutes for Vesta. When it did arrive it brought dreams of prison cells, sometimes with her in them, sometimes with Peter. In one tormented episode Madame Kali waved a key at a locked door while Vesta begged to be released. In other dreams she revisited the murder scene from the glass ball. Bodies strewn around a room while she and Valentina stood together looking over them. Cold sweat covered her like a glaze as she dreamed.

At last the morning sunlight tiptoed across the well-worn wooden floor of the room until it reached her bedside prodding her with warm caresses until she sat up. Rubbing her head which held too many thoughts, her brain ached and that irritated her. One thing was for certain, she couldn't ignore who she was any longer. She was the High Priestess of the trionfi. Questions had to be answered and she must regain control of her life as well as master her gift of InSight. It was time for her to dig deep within and pull out the determination that catapulted her to the top of Sybarite. She was ready to accept the job.

After a shower and café crème downstairs in the Le Parvis restaurant while she left a message with explicit tasks for Jenny in New York, Vesta walked across the street to the cathedral. This time as she walked past the saints, philosophers and monarchs carved into the pillars of the west portal she smiled at them. "I'm back," she whispered.

She pulled open the simple wooden doors and began walking down the center aisle of the giant cathedral looking at the labyrinth lying under her feet. Most of it still obscured under rows of chairs on either side. Peter's words echoed in her head from the night before saying that she created it for him. Pausing at the crenulated center lying uncovered in the aisle, she knew that if that was true, it meant the woman in the black cape who appeared to her in the time lapse vision, or whatever it was, at that very spot was actually her.

Vesta blinked hard. The encounter occurred four months earlier but she recalled every detail. From the center of the labyrinth she saw time running backwards. The cathedral and all its surroundings grew younger, all the way back to before the cathedral stood on that spot. A woman walked toward her in a black cape with the pale blue dress of the High Priestess, a white cross emblazoned on her chest underneath. The spot between her eyes began to glow as if a hot poker had been stuck in it.

"That was me," she said out loud.

Her previous self spoke of the necessity to be disguised as a man to carry out her plans for building the cathedral. And the last thing she said to Vesta before the time fold unraveled was the explicit direction to "allow it." What that meant, she now realized, was to allow her true identity to be revealed and accept who she was and had been for ages.

The hint of a smile crept across her face. She knew she was a bad ass in this life but she must have been one for many lives before. Hiding the fact that she was a woman to bring her architectural dream into reality took some vision and guts. Especially in medieval France.

Vesta nodded to herself. Even though major pieces were still missing of her previous lives, a picture was beginning to form. Despite wiping out her memory of who she really was, she maintained her resolute steadfast nature of accomplishing the goals she set in this life. Accomplishing her next goal would be no different.

Stepping out of the labyrinth center she walked toward the apse. Morning light streamed through the stained glass windows soaring above her head. It was a moment to behold. Vesta paused and stared transfixed at the rich rainbow hues.

"It's mesmerizing, isn't it?" Peter had approached in silence without her noticing and stood beside her.

"The colors from the stained glass seem... alive."

Peter beamed a radiant smile. "They are. Alive with the energy of God." Peter opened his arms. "Welcome to the first day of the rest of your life."

Vesta returned his smile.

A shuffling sound on the other end of the cathedral alerted them that parishioners had begun dragging rows of chairs off the labyrinth to fully expose it.

"It's Tuesday," Vesta said. "They're opening the labyrinth today?"

"They are."

"Why?"

"Special request." Peter smiled.

"You did this for me?"

"When I found out you were coming, I pulled a few strings. We truly need your InSight and it was agreed this was the best way to bring it back to you."

"You and the other trionfi?"

Peter nodded. "Are you ready to begin?"

"I am," Vesta said. "But first, were you serious yesterday when you told me I created this place?"

"Yes."

"So, you're saying I was the architect of Chartres Cathedral?"

"Absolutely."

"I drew up the design of this cathedral and the labyrinth?"

"Yes."

"The bishop let a woman waltz in here and," Vesta began.

"He didn't know you were a woman."

Vesta nodded her head.

"You were disguised as a man."

Peter took her by the hand as they walked toward the labyrinth.

"It wasn't the first time you did it either. The time before, that was really something, it had tongues wagging and heads spinning for centuries. And it's a story to be saved for another day. We have priorities to attend to now."

"I had this vision the last time I was here. The High Priestess of the tarot appeared to me. She said that she was the architect of the cathedral. That was me, right? I was talking to myself through this vision."

"Yes, that was a transactional memory you created."

"You're saying my subconscious made that happen."

"It was your super-conscious mind prodding you. It overrode your spell by coming in the form of your InSight. But you had to stop short of revealing your true identity to yourself. The structure of the spell prevented it."

"I know I've resisted embracing who I really am." Vesta gazed around the cathedral. "But I'm ready now. This place feels like home to me." She leaned in close to Peter. "I know I'm home."

As they made their way to the labyrinth, they walked past the stained-glass window of the seraphim whose wings held more than a dozen blue eyes on them. The image terrified her when she saw it for the first time months earlier. Now it reminded her of the horrifying vision she experienced at Villa Spada. She clutched Peter's hand tight.

"I'm afraid of what I saw in that glass ball coming true. I want to master my gift so I can make sure it never really happens."

"Don't worry. The First Blood was planting her own goals in your mind. They weren't yours."

Vesta shook her head and continued. "I'm a fast learner and a high achiever." A quick laugh escaped her lips. "But this." She waved her arm in a wide arc. "It might take me a minute or two to get up to speed this time. Creating something like this is beyond what even I could imagine."

Peter gave her hand a quick squeeze. "Vesta," he said gently. "You have no idea how amazing you really are."

Several people had already queued up for their walk in the labyrinth. Vesta and Peter stepped in line as they waited for the last rows of chairs to be moved.

"So what am I supposed to be doing?" Vesta asked.

"Walk. That's all right now."

"Alright. Then what?"

"Walk again." Peter smiled. "We'll take a break for lunch though."

Vesta leaned in close to him. "How many times am I supposed to walk this?"

"As many as it takes."

"It's barely nine o'clock and you're saying I'm going to be walking this labyrinth over and over until noon?"

"We have lunch later than you Americans."

"Four hours?"

"You're getting the crash course."

Vesta looked around the cathedral. "Is there something I should be thinking about or doing while I walk?"

"No."

"This is mildly frustrating. I'm not used to operating like this."

"You will be after today." Peter smiled again.

Their turn came to enter the labyrinth. Peter bowed his head to Vesta. "Entre nous, madame."

Vesta stepped between the black painted lines on the ancient stone. The undulating surface pocked with tiny craters from eight hundred years of shoes and chairs being scraped across it. Comfort accompanied each step, like familiar terrain leading home. Her pace slowed as she began to think about the juxtaposition of who she was at that moment in her present life, the CEO and chairman of the board of Sybarite, and who she was when she laid out the architectural plans for the cathedral disguised as a man. Vesta felt gob smacked by the notion of living so many lives in such a powerful way.

"Can we talk as we walk?" She spoke over her shoulder to Peter.

"If you want to," he replied in a low voice.

"This church is almost a thousand years old, right?"

"Parts are even older, but basically yes."

"That's over a dozen lifetimes from then until now."

"Sixteen and a half roughly if you count sixty years for a life average."

Vesta gave Peter a quizzical look. He shrugged. "I told you, this was a school devoted to mathematics. Some of it stuck."

"So how can you possibly keep up with all those lives? Remembering what you did in each one?"

"Think of it this way. You live three hundred sixty-five days in a year, give or take a leap year. Do you remember every day of that year? No. But you do recall the special days. A birthday or anniversary, or when something special happens." Peter shrugged again. "It's the same thing."

It made sense. She fell silent and kept walking. Fifteen

minutes passed before they reached the center of the labyrinth. Vesta waited for the woman already in the center to leave. She watched her breathing deep and raising her arms above her head then murmuring to herself, a prayer perhaps. After a few minutes she moved back onto the path to exit. Vesta stepped into the center. Peter joined her.

"Now what do we do?"

"Nothing."

Vesta clapped her arms against her sides. "I feel like I should be doing something in here. Did you see that woman in front of me? What was she doing?"

"Trying too hard."

Vesta let out an exasperated sound. "Fine. Then I'm going to walk out."

"Good."

Vesta left the labyrinth center and unwound her path. When she and Peter reached the end he turned to her.

"Now, continue this until I come for you."

"Where are you going?"

"I'll be around."

Vesta looked toward the entrance line. It had more than doubled in size since they entered. She turned back to Peter to say something but he had vanished. She looked in every direction but he was nowhere to be seen. Vesta released a long exhale and walked to the end of the line to wait for her turn again.

Questions popped into her mind like little weeds in a springtime garden. She decided to grab hold of one and logically wrestle an answer out of it. What was the purpose of walking the labyrinth repeatedly? She assumed it was to regain her gift of InSight, but how many circuits around the labyrinth would that require? As many as it takes was the answer blossoming from the center of her third eye. Vesta rubbed the spot and registered a mild protest but stayed focused.

Did the vision in the glass ball of her and Valentina mean that they would become allies? Vesta shivered. It couldn't mean that. She hated Valentina and wanted to ruin her life. She would never allow that vision to become a reality. Peter said it was Valentina's desire transposed into her mind. He was probably right.

Had she given up on trying to find Raz? More than a month had passed since he'd fled to Russia and only a few brief calls had come from the private detective on the case. He said they were working with their contacts in Moscow but so far had no hard leads. Vesta felt a stab of guilt for not making that a bigger priority in her life. When she learned how to control her InSight she would use it to find Raz. She sensed him on the periphery of her awareness just out of reach. The next step was to bring it into focus.

The queue thinned in front of her so that she was next to enter the labyrinth. Take three steps turn to the left, ten steps and make a U-turn, ten more steps before turning left again. She had already memorized the number of steps around the huge circle. As she watched her feet move one in front of the other between the black lines her mind wandered in aimless directions. No clear thought manifested.

Arriving at the center a quarter of an hour later, no more enlightened than the dim bulbs along the dark aisles of the cathedral, Vesta stared at the little lumps of metal embedded in the stone. Legend had it that a plaque had once lain on top of the lumps. It represented the myth of Theseus and the Minotaur. A bit misrepresented, Vesta thought, because those two played out their bloody battle in a maze, not a labyrinth. The former meant to confuse, the latter to enlighten. Vesta sighed. This wasn't what she should be thinking about. She stepped out of the center and walked back to the starting point.

Time ceased to be relevant. Vesta stopped counting how

many times she had walked the labyrinth after her third circuit. Instead she put her mind into the same place she used to when she would follow Enid through the woods on the slopes of Crested Butte as a girl. She had no interest in the herbs and berries her mother would point out but it was her duty to help gather them, so she did. It was a mindless task so she would let her thoughts go idle as her body went about the routine.

At what point she couldn't say for sure, but Vesta stopped being aware of others around her. The twists and turns of the labyrinth became ingrained in what she did and who she was. Her steps were automatic. If she had to wait in line for her turn to walk again her mind remained detached from her actions. Where her mind was, she couldn't say. Random images of her childhood vegetable garden, her mother's huge old armoire holding all her herbal remedies and the pond by their cabin seeped from her memory. She registered no emotional reaction to them, merely observed them and let them slip away.

Her fingers tingled like she had run them across a wool sweater in winter then reached for doorknob. Not an unpleasant sensation but one she noticed was increasing. She saw her feet still moving in front of her, moving along the path but she didn't actually feel the treading any longer. It was as if a cushion of air spread out between her feet and the ancient stones with each step. She made a mental note of this without any emotion attached to it. Without pause she stepped into the center of the labyrinth.

A cascade of golden energy drenched Vesta from above, her head jerked back gasping for air. Deep breaths began to flow in and out of her body. Instincts at the core of her being told her to relax, it wasn't an assault, instead it was ecstasy. She closed her eyes and let the sensation envelop her. Hungry, gorging in a feeding frenzy she pulled more of it in and breathed deeper. Several minutes passed before a balance settled into her.

Sublime vibrancy radiated from her head and within her heart. The equilibrium resonated in every cell of her body. She shimmered like a mirage as she stood in the center of the labyrinth. Somewhere on the periphery of her awareness she knew that those who were walking in the cathedral had stopped to stare at her. She didn't care. Nothing mattered but how she felt at that moment.

Through the pale golden haze that surrounded her, Vesta sensed an image taking shape. Lines grew sharp, colors became more vivid until the face of Peter fully formed in her mind.

"Vesta, may I take your hand?"

"Yes," she murmured.

He touched her fingers but she felt it on her forehead between her eyebrows. It was gentle yet firm as it tugged on her to follow. Vesta opened her eyes. The expanse of the labyrinth came into view and Peter was leading her out of the center.

"I just had the most incredible feeling come over me," she said as she followed behind him.

"I know."

"You knew? Why did you interrupt it?"

"It was time." Peter looked back at Vesta. "Are you hungry?"

From a logical perspective Vesta knew she was walking on the stones as they departed the labyrinth, but her feet felt like they were walking on cushions of air again. The residual afterglow of her experience in the center lasted until she took the first step outside of the black painted lines. Only then could she feel the slight undulating surface of the ancient floor.

Peter led her across the street to Le Café Serpente. Seated at a corner table Vesta gazed around the restaurant like she'd never seen one before.

"This is a beautiful place."

"It is lovely, isn't it?"

A young woman arrived at their table asking what they would like to eat.

"Oh, nothing for me. Merci," Vesta said.

"You must eat," Peter said.

"The usual for you Monsieur Peter?" The woman asked.

"Oui, Deux, sil vous plait." Peter looked at Vesta. "Would you like some wine?"

"No. I'm fine." Vesta said, her eyes shining like glass.

"Et du l'eau," Peter said.

"Merci Monsieur."

The woman left the table and Peter smiled at Vesta.

"Are you wondering what happened?"

Vesta nodded. "Yeah."

"You had a very productive morning."

"I've never felt like that before. This energy, or something, came down through the top of my head and into my entire body. It wasn't an electrical shock or anything like that though. It felt amazing. And the color all around me was this soft gold. That's all I could see."

"Do you recall anything else?"

"No, you interrupted me just after it began."

Peter watched Vesta for a moment. "You were standing there for over half an hour."

Vesta's mouth dropped open. "I was not."

"You were." Peter smiled making the wrinkles around his eyes curl up.

"With all those people watching me?"

Peter nodded. "It's okay. That's why they come here. To see miracles happen."

"Is that what it was?"

"No, but they thought it was."

Leaning across the table Vesta whispered to Peter.

"So what did happen?"

Peter spread his arms out wide, a gesture Vesta had now come to be familiar with from him. "Are you ready for some heavy info?"

"Yes."

"You had a mystical experience. Speaking from a hermetically philosophical point of view."

"I felt like I was getting some sort of information, now that you mention it, but I can't recall what it was."

"That's because you were receiving it vertically, and you aren't accustomed to it in such high doses yet. Some of the older ones call it the descent of revelation."

"Why can't I remember it?"

"You will next time. This was a shock to your system. You got a heavy blast of it."

"It felt great." Vesta rubbed her head. "Even though now I do have a bit of a headache coming on."

"Normal. The water will help. What you experienced was gnosis. Becoming conscious of mystic knowledge."

"Gnosis? Does that mean ancient science?"

Peter laughed. "Actually it's the opposite. Gnosis reflects what is above in the highest vibratory realms. Science is the interpretation of what we observe and seek to explain below, here on Earth."

Two mushroom omelets arrived at their table along with a large bottle of sparkling water. Vesta realized she was starving and dove into the meal.

"It's grand to have you back," Peter said. "Now we start to work."

CHAPTER 18

After lunch Peter instructed Vesta to return to her room at Le Parvis. He told her to have a long nap then shower and meet him at the cathedral at seven-thirty that evening. Further details included to wear comfortable clothing and not to consume any food or alcohol after she awoke.

Her experience in the labyrinth allowed her to realize the gift the Elders had given her was more powerful than what she could have ever imagined. If she was the only one who possessed it then she had to rediscover it, refine it and put it to use. Somehow, she would balance her life at Sybarite with her duties to the trionfi.

Vesta followed Peter's directions walking into the cathedral at the precise time even though access to non-clergy was supposed to end at seven o'clock each day unless there was a special event. One of the priests of the church locked the door behind her after she entered and disappeared from view into the solid silence. Darkness filled most of the space, yet she could feel the gigantic structure hovering above her, beside her, protecting her. It felt separate but distinctly enmeshed with her.

A ring of votive candles circled the labyrinth providing the only illumination in the cathedral. The soft golden light created a magical glow that was other-worldly and breathtaking. Peter approached from a dark corner.

"Did you rest well?"

"I did."

"Great. Come with me. The diocese has given the labyrinth to us for the night."

Vesta followed Peter. As they walked toward the circle of light a man wearing a turban, dressed head to toe in white with a long flowing white beard came into view. She let out a quick gasp.

Peter laughed. "He's not God. Don't worry."

Peter had either read Vesta's thought or made an astute assumption because that was exactly who she thought he was at first sight. The man's twinkling blue eyes and kind smile gave him a certain divine-looking quality.

"This is Siri Bahadur Khalsa," Peter said.

"And Siri, this Vesta Beauvais."

"Nice to meet you Vesta."

A gentle wave of loving energy washed over her coming to rest at her third eye. She sighed at the exquisite feeling. "It's nice to meet you too."

"Amara flew Siri to Chartres today to help you."

"Really? Why?"

"He lives in Austin, which is in Texas."

"I know it's in Texas."

"Siri teaches kundalini there. Amara says he's the best there is. He will help you open up to your gift of InSight."

Siri Bahadur smiled. "Shall we begin?"

Vesta nodded. "Sure."

"I'm going to take a seat and get out of the way," Peter said before vanishing beyond the wall of darkness.

"I understand you're familiar with kundalini yoga," Siri Bahadur said.

"Well, barely. I did it once with Amara at her place in Tofino."

"At least you have some of the basics down. That's good. Why don't we begin by you walking the labyrinth to the center."

"Okay." Vesta took a few steps in before she realized Siri Bahadur was still standing at the entrance. "Aren't you coming?"

"No. This is just for you. I will be sitting here. The practice begins when you reach the center. Don't hurry. This part is as important as the rest."

Moving her gaze back to the thick black lines painted on the ancient stone floor, Vesta began her walk. No epiphanies or astounding thoughts came to her as she circumvented the space. When she arrived at the center she stepped in and turned around to face Siri Bahadur who was seated on the floor just outside of the entrance.

He smiled at her. "Come to a seated position in the very center."

"Okay, but I have to tell you that I can't sit in that pretzel pose, lotus pose as you call it, for very long. My legs go to sleep."

"That's fine. Stretch them out when you need to."

Vesta sat down and crossed her legs. Siri Bahadur asked her to close her eyes and explained how to align her body so that the kundalini energy would flow through it. Once her back was straight and her head floated in the perfect position above her torso he began the practice the way Amara had.

"Ong namo guru dev namo," The words glided out in resonate tones from his throat. Vesta felt the urge to say the words with him but decided against it. She loathed embarrassing herself and that seemed like a good way to do it since she wasn't sure of exactly how to say the chant. After he finished the invocation he told her to keep her eyes closed and began a guided meditation.

Awareness of the base of her spine came first visualizing breath originating from that spot. Vesta struggled with the concept at first but stayed focused and slowly began to feel her breath coming in and then leaving that part of her body. After several minutes a comfortable flow settled in. Concentration on breaths coming in and going out left no room for other thoughts until the image of a snake coiled at the bottom of her spine pried its way into her mind's eye. She watched it unwind as it spiraled up each vertebra in her body. With a tilt of its head when it reached the top, it gazed eye to eye with her. Vesta gasped as she recognized the face of the serpent as the one she saw in her dream months earlier.

In it the giant snake had risen from dark water as Vesta stood on a dock at night. It rose to stare at her with its large scaled head a combination of human and serpent. Gemstones the color of the chakras, red, orange, yellow, green, light blue, indigo and purple, were dotted above the eyes where its brows should have been. The creature was beautiful and yet terrifying to behold. Then it spoke to her.

"You can't hide from me forever." Were the words it chose as the obsidian eyes rimmed with long eyelashes stared at her. Its full human lips painted red curled at the corners in a smile. Vesta wasn't sure if it was a threat or a promise, but now it stared at her once again, square in the eyes.

Part of her wanted to scream, but the other part knew there was nothing to fear. She watched as the serpent flew through the top of her head only to arc and dive into her again with its full force racing in a spiral down her spine. Vesta felt herself gasp for air. Her breathing became rapid and shallow and somewhere in the periphery of her awareness she could hear Siri Bahadur saying this was the breath of fire and to stay with it. Her body became an automated system of short breaths as her mind opened up and saw a daylight scene far away from the ancient cathedral in France.

A large boat was docked at a tropical location. Even though she knew she was sitting in the center of the labyrinth she felt like she was also standing on the dock next to the boat. Should she be alarmed that her awareness had split into two pieces? Was this the way her gift of InSight was supposed to work? An awareness settled inside of her, this was exactly how it was supposed to work. Vesta told her fearful thoughts to sit down and shut up so she could get a closer look at the scene. She relaxed and felt her body rise up.

As her heels lifted off the dock, she could see the name of the boat. Regina Spada was written in cursive letters on the side. Vesta's mind hunted for the translation. She knew spada was the word for sword in Italian. And regina meant queen. Her body stiffened. The name of the boat was the Queen of Swords. It belonged to Valentina.

Vesta's breathing became erratic and she fought to bring it under control. Focusing she regained her breath of fire and studied the scene more closely memorizing every detail. Men were unloading wooden boxes from the boat onto the dock. From there they were loading them into a van parked on the street a hundred yards away from the pier. The scene reminded her of the vision she saw at the house in Napa Valley. Where was the boat docked? She knew she could control her movements if she tried and willed herself to float up higher.

Many boats came into sight as she rose above a marina. Turning her head she looked across a landscape of suburban houses and streets crowded with restaurants and shops. Beyond those sat a white lighthouse in the distance. Close by was a two-story house lined with tall windows, each one surrounded by pea green shutters. She recognized the house as the one Ernest

Hemingway had once owned. She had visited it when she was in Key West on business several years earlier. She remembered the white lighthouse being a block away from it. That meant Valentina's boat was in, or was going to be in, Key West, Florida. And something was being smuggled in those boxes. She could catch Valentina, or at least her workers, if she acted quickly.

Her breath became unstable again and she gasped for air. The image was lost in her mind and she opened her eyes.

"Control your breathing," Siri Bahadur said. "Think only of your breath now."

Vesta struggled to focus on the air coming in and going out of her lungs. She wanted to recapture the vision but it had vanished. "I saw," she began then stopped. Acting hysterically wouldn't bring the vision back and wouldn't help her in any way. With a long exhale she centered her thoughts on her breath. A minute passed before her rhythmic breathing signaled that she regained control.

Peter walked from the cavernous shadow of the cathedral and knelt by Siri Bahadur.

"I saw the jeweled serpent from a dream I had months ago," Vesta said. "It uncoiled itself from the base of my spine and shot through the top of my head. It returned inside me. That image kept repeating until I saw this boat, the Regina Spada. Somehow I willed myself to float up in the scene. I recognized where the boat was, or is, or will be docked. It's in Key West, Florida."

Vesta shook her head and rubbed the spot between her eyebrows.

"Men were unloading these wooden boxes. The same ones I saw in a vision a few weeks ago. I know who the boat belongs to and I know they're smuggling something."

She uncrossed her legs and stood up. "And I'm going to stop them."

"Hold on," Peter said. "Let's take this one step at a time." He looked at Siri Bahadur. "The serpent, I have an idea what that was, but I think you're the expert here on that. Can you explain it?"

Siri Bahadur nodded. "It was your kundalini rising."

"I don't know what that means. But I do know I need to stop the evil witch who owns that boat."

"Vesta, please calm down and listen," Peter said.

"The serpent is a common symbol for what is activated in kundalini yoga. The meditation that I guided you through was specific to calling up that energy. According to your dream it sounds like it was prodding you to release it." Siri Bahadur smiled. "And my guess is that the meditation worked very well for you."

Vesta blew out a sharp exhale. "I'll say it did." She stretched her arms above her head. "It felt great."

"You can access this energy any time you want by going into this meditation," Siri Bahadur said. "With your natural abilities it should become easier each time, if not instant."

Vesta nodded.

"Now for the vision," Peter said. "You tapped into your InSight. Since you weren't guiding it the strongest one came through."

Peter stood up and began walking in the labyrinth toward her. "You can control what you want to see. Say you want to check in on a meeting of the NATO allies, for example." He stopped walking and stared hard at her. "You can do that."

"Really?"

"That's just to illustrate a point, but you can see anything if you choose to." He began walking again. "But you will have InSight into things you don't know are happening. Like just now. There is significant energy that surrounds such actions. Especially when the intention is to cause harm."

Peter spread out his arms. "Love and goodness are long soft

frequencies of energy. Kind of like waves that gently lap on the shore of a placid lake. You can feel it here in Chartres Cathedral. Remember when I told you that experts sometimes refer to the design of this place as frozen music?"

Vesta nodded.

"Didn't you think that analogy was odd? I mean how can a solid structure represent frozen music?"

"I don't know," she said with a tone of disinterest.

"It's important that you do know." Peter replied leveling his gaze at her.

"Alright."

"It's because of the perfect scale and proportion of this place. You created it. You should know this."

"Okay."

"Look, this magnificent cathedral is one gigantic perfect note struck to the glory of God that has resonated for almost a thousand years." Peter closed his eyes as a smile spread across his face. "That's why people are so drawn here. Why they feel so close to the Divine here. Our universe is set up on these logical principles of proportion and scale. Whether its music, architecture, the structure of the human body and those of all living creatures, it's all this sacred geometry."

Vesta nodded. "I get it. It makes sense to me."

"So when this harmony falls out of alignment sensitive people feel it." He pointed to her. "That's where you come in because your gift is this super sensitivity to what is and what has the potential to be."

"What I saw isn't etched in stone?"

"No. It's only the most likely outcome." He began walking in the labyrinth again. "A million things, major or minor, can happen to change what you saw. But left untouched, that is probably what will happen."

"Am I always seeing the future?"

"Absolutely not. You can see the past and the present too, but you have to learn how to control your InSight. Right now you're like what the Americans call a monkey with a gun."

"Oh thanks."

"It's true. But that's where I come in, along with Siri Bahadur's enormous expertise."

Vesta looked over to the kundalini yoga master who remained silent and still sitting on the floor. "Peter, was it okay to just spill all those details about me to him?"

Siri Bahadur smiled as his light blue eyes twinkled. "I've heard much stranger stories than yours in this lifetime."

Vesta raised her eyebrows.

"Don't worry about Siri. He has helped us all at one time or another get our mojo in check. He doesn't spread secrets, only love."

"That's great. Thanks for helping me Siri but I need to get going. I must catch a flight from Paris to Key West tomorrow." Vesta began walking out of the labyrinth.

"I think that's unwise," Peter said. "You're not prepared yet."

"Siri said I could access this gift of mine anytime I want. Weren't you listening?"

"I was but that's only the start of it. You don't have a clue about how to control it."

"Peter, you don't know me very well. At least not in this life. I'm a quick learner and tend to learn as I go. I'm not going to let Valentina smuggle whatever is in those boxes into the U.S. Plus, that's what my InSight picked up on so I know it's important. You said so yourself." Vesta picked up her pace as she walked through the labyrinth.

"I know where the boat is and I'm going to alert the local authorities when I get there. I can stop it and destroy that other hideous vision I had of teaming up with her."

"What about her mind reading you?"

Vesta paused in her hurried walk. She had forgotten for the moment about that nasty trick. "Send me an email about how to block someone from reading my thoughts."

"An email?" Peter laughed. "I have no clue how to do that. I don't even own a computer."

"Well give Amara a call and ask her to do it," Vesta said with slight sarcasm. "She's good at telling other people what to do."

Peter came face to face with Vesta as she was walking out of the labyrinth. He held up his hand.

"Please listen, you are all we have now that Raymond is gone for a while," his eyes locking onto hers. "If we lose you while Rasputin is still tearing through the world making trouble then it's going to be much harder for us to catch him."

Maintaining eye contact Vesta set her jaw firm. "I under-stand. And I will focus on what he is up to as soon as I deal with Valentina. You said yourself that without choosing what I want to focus on my visions pull out the most pressing issues. Remember? Well obviously this is something that needs to be handled." She gently lowered his hand with a steady movement.

Peter sighed. "You've always been so sure of yourself."

"I guess some things never change." Vesta gave Peter a quick kiss on the cheek and patted Siri Bahadur on the shoulder as she made her way out of Chartres Cathedral.

CHAPTER 19

The flight from Paris to Miami gave Vesta time to lay out the rest of the week at Sybarite. According to her plan, she would spend the night in Miami then fly home to New York on Thursday with the intention of working all weekend. That would more than bring her up to speed on everything.

After landing, she hired a private car service to drive her to Key West. From her InSight at the cathedral she had a general idea about where the marina was located and where the Regina Spada was docked. From there she would contact the local FBI office to alert them about the smugglers. Some sort of federal customs agency had to be there, too.

The plan sounded solid and would allow her to accomplish several things. She could test out the accuracy of her vision. Was it the present or the future she saw? If the boat hadn't docked yet she would tell the FBI it was coming. But how would she explain that she knew it was coming? She couldn't tell them it was through a vision.

"I will tell them that Marco confided in me," she whispered to herself as the car sped across the longest the bay bridge she had ever seen. The story would be that Marco wanted to make everything in their family business legal. Even though she knew he would never betray his mother, she could use Marco to make him look like a hero to the authorities. Vesta felt her third eye begin to gently spin and considered that validation of her plan.

What would she tell the authorities they were smuggling? Each time the vision came she could see only wooden boxes the size of a case of wine being unloaded. A logical assumption would be wine although the truth was, she had no idea. There was no reason why they would smuggle wine when they were already licensed importers of it. When she had the first vision it was because she had touched an original Fabergé egg made for the Russian royal family at the end of the nineteenth century. Her logical reasoning pointed to antiques that would be sold on the black market. Maybe they had acquired a large cache of antique coins from an archeological site in Italy that wouldn't be allowed out of the country so they hid them in the wine boxes.

Vesta shook her head. Her imagination could take her in many directions but the point was to get the customs officials to open the boxes and look inside. It didn't matter what she told them was in there. Once they opened a box they would see the illegal contents and arrest the crew that would lead to the arrest of Valentina. A smile settled on her face. The venomous witch with her old gifts was no match for her. She would prove that soon enough.

After the car dropped her in Key West, she checked into her room at the Casa Marina and changed into the most casual clothing she had in her luggage. While it looked more appropriate for Florence than Florida, Vesta chose a black Gucci button down shirt, black brushed-cotton pants and a pair of Ferragamo ballet flats. Wanting to look as much like a tourist as possible she purchased a wide brimmed straw hat from a boutique in the lobby. Donning her favorite Ferragamo sunglasses, huge black frames with the darkest lenses, Vesta got a map of the town from the concierge and headed out.

Recalling details from her vision she made her way toward the A & B Marina. As she walked past the house that Ernest Hemingway once owned, she thought about the dozens of six-toed cats supposedly descended from his own cat and who now had free run of the place. Tourists were cued by the front door and down the sidewalk waiting for their tour. When she had visited the house years earlier it had been closed to the public for a formal cocktail party that was part of a resort wear show. And while the lingering odor of cat piss was present, even with scented candles in every room, she didn't mind. Hemingway had been the first person to inspire her to travel when she read his book A Moveable Feast. Checked out from the Crested Butte library the book was an annual favorite to read during the summer from her middle school years on until she left for college.

Two blocks beyond she passed the white lighthouse from her vision. Her heart beat faster as she approached the marina. Other times in her life when she acted on intuition rather than a carefully thought out plan it had paid off. Her intuition had never let her down. This time, working with the supercharged intuition of her InSight, she knew if she followed it but also applied logic as well in the early stages the chance of success would increase.

A nervous alertness buzzed between her eyebrows. She rubbed the spot as she turned a corner where a big red, white and blue sign announced the A & B Lobster House Restaurant. Beyond it sprawled a large marina filled with boats of all sizes. Standing on the sidewalk she looked longingly at the bar that she could see through the windows. She really wanted a cocktail to steady her nerves.

"Don't do it," she whispered. "It's not going to help."

Pursing her lips together she walked toward a gated and locked entry leading to the docks. Timing her pace to a couple with two children who exited the area as she approached gave her the needed entrance. Gray weathered wooden planks creaked underneath her feet walking down a long dock she recalled from her InSight. On the last branch of several docks shooting off into the bay she turned right. Fishing boats of various sizes sat idle, their long reels standing upright like sentinels beside heavy nets piled on the decks waiting patiently for the next deep-sea adventure. A ripe golden hue from the late afternoon sun tamed the bright white paint of the boats into a cool cream. Beyond them, at the end sat the biggest boat in the marina. Vesta recognized it before she read the name on the side. She inhaled a deep breath and felt the buzz between her eyes increase.

Her vision had been correct about the location of the boat but boxes weren't being unloaded. There was no movement at all onboard that she could see. Slipping her hand into her purse she fumbled around searching for her cell phone. She had already located the phone number for the FBI in Miami and the U.S. customs department in Key West. If they didn't respond, she would call the local police. But what would she tell them at this point? They would see no reason to rush over to board the boat as it sat there in the dock just like all the rest. Her insistence that contraband was on board would hardly be enough to motivate them.

Vesta shook head. She needed evidence. Had the boxes already been unloaded? Or were they still onboard? Glancing in all directions she didn't see movement anywhere except for the lazy bobbing of the boats in the water. An idea popped into her mind that she knew was risky even in the best of situations. Her logic said she should resist it but her determination to follow through with the mission pushed her forward.

Her third eye spun like a top as she moved toward the steps of the boat and began to board it. She could feel her heart beating so hard that she thought it might fracture a rib. Everything was silent on the boat as she paused at the top step looking around. She had come too far to give up. All she needed was a small piece of evidence. Placing one foot then the other onto the deck she let out an exhale. No sounds came from the crow's nest at the top or from the main cabin area. A quick search was all she would do, starting below deck.

Walking to a door in the center of the boat she tugged it open and stepped inside. Recessed lights close to the walls illuminated dark wood paneling throughout the interior. Three steps took her down into the galley that opened into a saloon area. Beyond that she could see sleeping quarters. As her eyes adjusted to the dim light she gasped because sitting on a deeply tufted banquette in the saloon was Valentina.

"Come in your Highness. I've been expecting you."

"I was just," Vesta began. "I was walking down the dock and happened to see..."

Valentina's lips slid apart like an ugly gaping wound exposing a glimpse of white teeth. "I know exactly why you're here."

Vesta corrected her posture to make sure she stood tall and straight. "Very well. I'm going to report your smuggling activity to the authorities. I've known about it for a while now through my visions."

Laughter sounding like an animal caught in a trap gurgled from Valentina. "Even with the help of Kali and Peter the Lost, you weren't capable enough to learn even the basics of your gift."

"I saw where this boat was docked. And I saw your stooges unloading boxes that certainly contain something illegal inside."

"Yes. Would you like to find out what it is?" Valentina's eyes glittered like polished emerald stones. "Sit your Highness. I will show you."

Every hair on the back of Vesta's neck stood up. The spot between her eyes was blazing hot. "No. I'm going for the police right now."

She turned and walked up the steps to the door. Before she could open it the door swung open. A hulking man dressed in a navy polo shirt and white pants blocked her exit.

"Senora Parrino has asked you to join her," he said with a thick Italian accent.

"Get out of my way."

"Please your Highness." He moved toward her.

"I said move!" Vesta sensed an electrical current of sorts racing up from her spine and shooting out of her eyes mentally shoving the man as he stumbled backwards a step.

"Enough!" Valentina yelled.

Vesta felt her knees go weak as the man stepped forward, grabbed her by the arm and pushed her down the stairs. He held shoving her to the table where Valentina sat.

"Sit your Highness," he said.

As she jerked her arm away from him Vesta stumbled onto the banquette seat directly across from Valentina. Robed in a silk caftan splashed with bright orange, red and pink topped by an orange turban balanced on her head, Valentina's dark brown skin glowed in sharp contrast. On the table in between them she recognized the Waite-Smith tarot deck sitting in a stack except for the High Priestess card which lay surrounded by the Tower, Death, the Moon, the Devil and the Queen of Swords cards.

She looked up at Valentina. "You were reading the cards and knew I was coming here."

Again the gaping wound smile sliced across Valentina's face. "I don't need these. They were only for amusement while I waited." She leaned forward. "I've known you were coming since the thought first came to your weak little mind."

Vesta knew her face must have registered an expression of shock because Valentina's eyes glimmered like jade and her grin widened.

"The Lost one was correct. Your unbridled and foolish self-confidence has led you astray more than once. Learning to close your thoughts to me should have been the first thing you accomplished."

Valentina dragged the cards lying face up into the stack. "This time your stupidity will cost you and the trionfi more than ever before."

The rashness of her decision to board the boat reverberated in her thoughts. Was Valentina right? Had she made stupid choices as the High Priestess before only to repeat the pattern again? Vesta blistered herself with condemnation. She should have learned how to permanently block Valentina from reading her mind in Chartres. Over confidence created the situation, now she must use intuition to get her out of it. Her jaw tightened as she looked across the table.

"I am telling you what you already know. The truth stings you like the serpent." The emerald eyes glittered.

"Get out of my head." Vesta spoke the words as a command that had worked before when Madame Kali took her uninvited tour. She had shut her psychic door then, maybe she could do it now.

Valentina leaned her head back making that sickening sound Vesta recognized as a laugh. "It's too late. For everything."

Behind her the sound of the door to the main deck opening caught her attention. Heavy thuds on the stairs followed. The large man in the navy shirt and white pants walked up to the table and set a wooden box down. Vesta recognized it as one of the boxes from her vision. He reached into his pants pocket and pulled out a screwdriver. With quick motions on each side he pried the lid off. Placing the tool back into his pocket he opened the box and stepped back from the table.

Valentina's mouth curled at the corners as she leaned forward and picked up a small plastic tube from the box.

"Each life brings its own small unique joys. The periods of riding into battle on horses were glorious times. I do miss them." She unscrewed the end of the tube and let a syringe slide out into the palm of her hand. "But in this age our brains work harder than our bodies."

She looked at Vesta and lifted her eyebrows. "I have no problem with that. It may not be as exciting but it can be much more effective."

"What is that?" Vesta's eyes widened. "Some kind of drug, isn't it?"

"It's not stolen treasure from a ruined civilization." Valentina examined the syringe as she held it up. "No. It is an escape for some. More powerful than any they've created before." Pulling the cap off the end to expose the needle, her eyes widened. "We have had mind altering substances as far back as the beginning. But they required more work than they do now. The laboratories create the ingredients in huge quantities now."

Valentina nodded to the man who pulled a long thin rubber cord from the other pocket of his pants. He stepped toward Vesta.

A cold sweat broke out on her face as she realized what was about to happen. She leapt up from the table in the direction of the door. The man clutched her by the neck and shoved her back onto the banquette. She gasped for air as she heard the door open again and another man clamored down the steps into the saloon. Dressed the same as the first but taller and thinner than the other, Valentina nodded at him. The large man pinned her arms to the table top while the thin man wrapped the rubber cord around her right forearm.

"Let me out of here right now! I'm warning you. Don't touch me!" Vesta blurted out the words even though she knew it would do no good.

Valentina stood up as Vesta struggled to free herself from the tight hold. Moving her arms even an inch was impossible. But she kicked out her legs under the table landing a hard smack on the thin man's shin.

"Peter knows I'm here. He will tell the others. They'll come for me."

As the needle pierced her arm, she heard Valentina say, "They will never find you."

CHAPTER 20

Vesta felt herself falling into a black abyss. Her body lay someplace else, maybe back in the banquette on the boat in Key West. She wasn't sure and didn't care. Brilliant light in a rainbow of colors infused her with energy. The first was bright red creating a feeling of comfort and protection within her. Next a rich shade of orange flooded through her causing a deep sense of confidence to settle in. Lemon yellow flowed in next bringing a sense of invincibility. Emerald green blossomed from some point in her mind to bathe her in an overwhelming feeling of pure love. That was eclipsed by the brightest blue she had ever seen washing over her causing a feeling of pure inspiration to create something, anything. As the indigo blue filled her awareness she felt her mind accelerate and at the same time open up. She saw everything at once, the past, the present and the future. Rather than being confused, she was illuminated. The expansion within her felt familiar and welcome. When the dark purple color overtook her senses, she saw and felt sparkles of white light around her, through her as though her essence was that of the stars. Bright, dynamic energy that had neither a beginning nor an end vibrated through her.

The necessity and essential purpose of everything in the universe came into clear focus.

Joy beyond what could ever be imagined suffused her mind. It was where she wanted to be, part of the forever pulsating with the subtle rhythm of the universe. Nothing else mattered. A twitch caught her attention. Something tugged on her awareness. A sucking sensation like she was being pulled through a tiny funnel increased rapidly. She tried to stop it but couldn't. Harder it yanked. The splendid purple light deepened until it became black. A sense of extreme confinement sent a panic through her as pain enveloped the body she was once again attached to. Clattering noisy voices and an intense headache assaulted her as the smell of coffee brought her fully present in her human form. She slid her eyes halfway open.

Dim lighting in the room allowed her sight to adjust quickly to what appeared to be a parlor. She surveyed the scene. Across from her sat a large sofa and two wingback chairs with end tables tucked in between. Floor to ceiling French doors covered one wall that lead to a garden area. Underneath her was a chaise lounge covered in Italian silk. She raised her head from the upholstered pillow and sat upright. A sharp throb echoed inside her head.

"She's awake," said a man with an Italian accent. "Go tell Madame."

Vesta looked in the direction of the voice. It belonged to the thin man dressed in the navy shirt and white pants.

"Don't move," he said walking over to her. "It's best if you don't move for a few minutes."

"Where am I?"

No response came from the thin man. A moment later his huge counterpart from the boat lumbered in. Vesta stared at them trying to decide what to do next. Her mouth was drier than she could ever remember and the humidity in the room was stifling.

"I need some water." She leaned her head against the pillow roll again begging the throbbing in her head to stop.

The large man nudged the thin one. "Get her some." The thin one left the room.

"I want to know where I am."

"You're in one of my homes." Valentina walked into her line of sight. The turban was gone and a long plait of black hair lay down her back. She wore a sleeveless turquoise jumpsuit laden with thick necklaces of orange coral. Her bony fingers were weighted down with golden rings that matched the heavy hoops of gold dangling from her ears.

"You drugged me." Vesta wanted to stand up but her knees felt too weak.

The thin man brought a glass of water to her. Pushing herself up to a sitting position as casually as she could muster, trying her best to disguise the pounding pain she felt, she took the glass and drank all of it without pause, water spreading through every cell of her body in a reinvigorating flow. An exhale escaped from her lips. She clenched her fist to get better control of herself.

"And you kidnapped me. This isn't going to go well for you."

"You didn't like our little cocktail?" Valentina walked closer to the chaise lounge hovering over Vesta. "Now we must discuss business."

"Business?" Vesta smirked. "We have nothing to discuss except you getting me back to my hotel right now."

"I had one of my men bring your luggage last night. They are in your room here."

"Last night?" Vesta looked down at her watch. The hands pointed to almost eleven-thirty. "Wait. I've been out for over twelve hours?"

Bright sunlight filtered through the lipstick palms as she cast a quick glance toward the garden area. Vesta tried to shake her head but it manifested more as a wobble. "Lady, you are in big trouble."

Valentina's eyes gleamed as a grin sliced across her face. "I think it's time I brought our other partner in to say hello."

Shoes shuffling across the floor accompanied a grunt as Rasputin walked around the corner into the room. Vesta's eyes flickered as her brain tried to make sense of what she was seeing.

"What are you doing here?" Her words sounded stupid, even to her, as she spoke.

Jagged laughter made his rotund belly jiggle. "Ah still in the dark I see. At least we can make good use of your powers."

Vesta searched with her eyes beside the chaise lounge. "Where's my purse?" Another lame question she regretted the moment she asked it.

"In your room," Valentina said. "But if you're looking for your cellular phone, then you must hunt in the deep water near Key West for that."

Vesta demanded that her body stand up. Her knees felt stronger and her balance was better. She grounded her feet, pushed from her calves with her knees steady and stood up straight. Her head wanted to bobble but she wouldn't let it. Instead she leveled her gaze at Rasputin. "You killed my uncle you miserable bastard."

"Lucky for you otherwise you would still wear the spell you cast on yourself." Raz belched out a malignant chuckle as he walked over to the sofa and sat down.

"Rasputin, we need to lay out our brilliant plan for our High Priestess since she's going to be our partner."

"Yes. Yes. You do that." He motioned at her with his hand while pulling a handkerchief from his pocket.

"First, would you like a drink?" The First Blood pasted a counterfeit smile on her face. "Something to cool you?" Her coca brown skin glistened in the humid air. "I would. Diego, bring the drink cart." She glanced toward the thin man who quickly left the room.

"I don't want anything from you." Vesta took a step toward the door. "I'm leaving now and you're not stopping me."

"Leave now and you will cause the rest of the trionfi to die."

Valentina's words shoved the scene from the Egyptian room back into her mind. She froze, not sure what to do next.

"And they will be dead forever."

She scanned her face trying to understand what she meant by forever, then looked at Raz who cackled with laughter again.

"You see," Valentina said walking over to an ornate wooden box sitting on a table. "While you were on your little trip we drew some blood from you." She pulled a clear glass vial from the box. "This is yours," she said waving it at her. "It was the missing piece to our plan." She placed it back into the box.

"Yes," Raz murmured as he patted sweat from his head.

"You see, your blood has certain properties that when mixed with our special recipe can deliver a lethal dose to all the others in the trionfi." The car wreck smile crept across her face. She beckoned to Diego who waited at the door. He pushed a polished silver drink cart into the room. "I'll have the usual," Valentina said to him. "And for you?" She nodded toward Vesta.

"Nothing. I told you. Are you saying you mixed my blood with that drug you gave me?"

Valentina ignored her question. "Rasputin what would you like?"

"Ice water," he said dabbing the handkerchief around his neck. "I hate this climate."

Diego handed Valentina a tall glass of Ricard Pastis. She

added some mineral water from a small pitcher and stirred it while she eyed Vesta.

"A toast to our future alliance." She raised the glass toward Vesta and took a sip.

"Answer me!" Vesta shouted causing the pain in her head to throb even more.

Valentina set her glass down on the cart. "Before your spell was broken your blood was worthless to us. However the chemical composition of it changed once you remembered who you were. That was why you turned white for a few minutes on the roof of Castel del Papa Luna. Do you recall?"

Vesta stared at her.

"I know you do." Valentina continued. "In my life before this one we came close to creating the right mixture with the help of the ingenious scientists in the Third Reich."

Without being aware of it, Vesta's jaw dropped open.

"I miss those days. Everyone dressed for dinner. Of course, we brought the wine from our estate. Germans still have no appreciation for the reds." Valentina took a sip of her cocktail.

"Now," she continued. "We have your blood full of the natural virus you produce that is toxic to the trionfi. And if you don't join me and Rasputin in our business venture, I will make certain that every one of the people you know in that magical little group gets an injection."

Vesta blinked hard to recall every word Valentina had just spoken.

"You said you could kill them forever." Vesta frowned. "Do you mean so they won't reincarnate?"

"That's precisely what I mean."

"But that was a gift from," Vesta waved her hand. "From the Elders, or whatever you call them. How can you take it away?"

"With your blood. Weren't you listening," Raz said.

"You possess a certain natural virus strain in your blood that is deadly to the trionfi," Valentina said. "It aids your InSight. Once the curse you placed upon yourself was broken, your blood chemistry altered allowing for your InSight to return to its full power and its toxicity in full measure. Raymond had it too, but yours is much more powerful. And we had to be sure it's lethal."

Vesta looked down at both arms noticing purple dots on each from needle sticks.

"Why do you want to kill them forever?" Another pointless question, she chastised herself.

"Because they interfere too much," Raz said.

"I can't imagine the state of the world if you two were free to do whatever you chose." Vesta pointed at Raz. "You were turning all those young girls into sex slaves."

Raz waved his hand. "Amusements for friends."

Anger boiled her blood. "You sick asshole." Her hand clenched into a fist. "This is what you were injecting them with, right? And now you continue smuggling these dangerous drugs. What kind of monsters are you?"

"We merely provide a product that many desire," he said. "I'm told it makes you feel good, happy, right?" He laughed again patting his forehead with the handkerchief.

"Why do you want me involved in this?"

Valentina stepped closer to Vesta. "Your InSight. You can warn us when authorities get too close. By seeing the future you will help us avoid any problems."

"And help you distribute illegal drugs that will end up killing people and destroying lives."

Raz shrugged. "They are going to destroy their lives anyway. It's always the same story."

Vesta's thoughts turned toward the ghastly vision she had in Italy. She would never let it become a reality.

"Ah but what you saw in my looking glass will come to pass," Valentina said with her jade-colored eyes staring at Vesta.

"Get out of my head."

"Your highness you will be rewarded with whatever you desire," Raz said. "Money. Houses. Artwork. Anything."

"I have those things already. But that's not the point, I will never contribute to murder."

"The egg by Fabergé that caught your attention is only one of several I acquired, all original, priceless," Raz said. "That one of course was a gift from me to Madame Parrino. But there are others you could have."

"I don't want an egg. And I'm not going to help you. As soon as I get to Key West or whatever city is closest to this place, I'm going to the police."

"You would sacrifice your friends for this?"

"I'm going to tell them what your plan is. You won't get near them."

Valentina smirked. "Do you think it would be me or Rasputin who would be giving these injections?"

She walked back to the drink cart and stirred more water into her glass. "We will make it a coordinated event where they all die in one day."

After a pause she lowered her gaze at Vesta. "Except for the Fool. He would be the last. And I think it should be at one of his concerts during a performance."

She shrugged. "He steps into the shadows for a moment to take a sip of water and someone is waiting to pop the needle in. Voila. He is dead a minute later on stage in front of thousands. What a spectacle!"

Vesta rushed toward Valentina. A wave of nausea swept over her.

"You should know that one of my many gifts is that I have my own protection in place at all times. As it is, I will have to take the time to show you how to bring your gifts into their full power. You are weak and no worry for me at this moment." She waved Vesta away. "Go to your room now. Lunch will be served at one o'clock. Join us then to discuss our future."

"You're an evil bitch and the others are going to find me."

"Doubtful as I of course have blocked them from my thoughts and have protected this home from their detection. Your InSight won't work here."

She looked at Diego standing by the door. "Show Madame Beauvais to her room."

Vesta wanted to protest but she decided she needed time to think. And she was glad to put her legs back into action. She followed the thin man across an entryway covered in black and white marble in a harlequin pattern and down a long hallway stopping at the third door on the left. The walk took some effort, each step focused on keeping her legs steady and her throat felt parched again. He opened the door for her and she stepped inside.

"Would you bring me some water please?"

"Yeah, sure," he said.

Vesta closed the door and walked to a pair of French doors on the opposite side of the room. Palm trees stood lush and abundant in her view. Along the manicured lawn beside a walkway red hibiscus dotted the landscape. Beyond the lawn was an ocean as turquoise as the jumpsuit Valentina wore. There was no lock on the door leading outside. An escape would be simple. There must be a catch, Valentina would never let escape be easy. A knock at her door distracted her thoughts.

"Come in."

Vesta turned to see not the thin man returning with her water but Marco walk through the door. She lifted her chin.

"I told Diego I would bring this to you." He held up a bottle of Evian.

"So you're part of this plan too. I'm not surprised." Turning back to look outside she twisted the doorknob and pulled the door open. The sea breeze caught her hair. It felt refreshing and the slight taste of salt in the air welcome.

"Are you here to seduce me into complying with your mother's wishes?" She spoke to him over her shoulder.

Marco looked down at the tile floor. His black hair in big soft curls fell toward his face. The Calvin Klein t-shirt and blue jeans fit him well showing just enough of his toned body underneath without being garish.

"Look, I didn't know she had this planned." He gazed up at her. "You probably don't believe me, but it's the truth."

Vesta squinted as she turned to face him. "How can you be part of this?" She waved her arm around the room. "Sex slaves and drug smugglers?"

"I'm not part of the sex thing. That's all Rasputin. Even my mother thinks it's deplorable."

"I don't believe that. And even if it was true she's still smuggling drugs. Ones she created it sounds like. Getting people addicted to them. Ruining lives. Killing them. What kind of person does that?"

Marco looked down at the floor again.

"And are your father and brother involved in this too?"

"Francesco is too old and frail to be involved in anything really. He is here and knows what's going on but nothing more. Giovanni tries to stay on the periphery of matters like this because of his political motivations but he knows."

"And they're okay with all of this? Do you all know that Valentina has threatened to kill the other trionfi if I don't align with her? And not just kill them but inject them with that drug ending their reincarnations."

Pursing his lips, he looked up at her again.

"And you're just standing around to let her ruin all these lives?"

Vesta walked toward Marco and took the bottle from his hand. "If I don't cooperate with her, she kills my friends." She exhaled. "Even my father. If I do what she wants then she kills even more with that drug. Or at the very least destroys their lives with addiction."

She reached her hand out touching Marco's arm. "You have to help me."

"It's impossible. This is my mother's nature. Being First Blood, she was bred not to have many sentimental emotions. Their survival depended on not showing weakness."

"Yeah, that whole First Blood thing I'm still fuzzy on. So, the Elders created them as destructive demons?"

"That wasn't their intent. But unfortunately, the Elders didn't foresee correctly how it would all turn out."

"And I was part of the next generation? Is that how it worked?"

Marco nodded.

"Does that mean you've watched her destroy lives and kill people time after time?"

"As I said, it's her nature."

"What about you? Is that your nature too?"

"It is not. Her eggs don't carry the dominant genes of First Blood like they did hundreds of years ago. That's why she chose the sperm she did for me this time, to enhance my abilities for future lives. Unfortunately, the trionfi member she chose did not provide her with the results she expected."

"You mean your father Francesco? He's the King of Swords."

"No. I'm referring to my biological father, Jared Schultz."

CHAPTER 21

Vesta stared at Marco unable to form words for a moment. "Jared is your father?"

Marco looked away from her but nodded. Vesta frowned. "That can't be. You said you were thirty."

"I am."

"But Jared is only forty-one."

"He's forty-two actually but I understand your confusion."

Vesta felt a rush of heat to her face and her breathing became shallow as she made a quick calculation in her head. Jared would have been twelve when Marco was conceived. "Did she rape him?"

Marco shook his head. "No. She was able to convince his mother that he needed to give a specimen when he reached puberty for what she convinced her were routine tests. Her assistant collected the sample and gave it to my mother who was then inseminated."

Vesta stared at him.

"The procedure was fairly new at the time but she knew about it from the experiments her German friends were conducting during the previous war."

"Does Jared know?"

"Yes."

"And Francesco?"

"He knows too. After Giovanni was born my mother told Francesco that she wanted a stronger son. She could tell even at his young age that Giovanni was not what she had hoped for." Marco looked toward the tropical landscape outside. "So, she made me."

"And Francesco was okay with that?"

"Yes, because he wanted an impressive son too, to represent the family name."

Vesta raised her eyebrows. "Well that's some real heart-warming stuff for a son to know."

Marco shrugged. "I represent my ancient family well."

"But you're not the brutal killer that she wanted."

He stared at Vesta for a moment then shook his head. "Maybe it's the sperm of Rasputin she should try in the next life."

"Oh my god, that's a disgusting thought."

Vesta opened the bottle of water and drank all of it. She sighed and sat down on the bed.

"So you'll help me get away from this place?"

"There's no escape. We're on a private island miles from Key West. You're free to explore. There are no locks as you can see but the boats are prevented from leaving except with a special key that only my mother possesses. Her bodyguards patrol the grounds."

"You seem completely resigned to what she's doing."

Marco shrugged again. "I have no choice. There's no way to stop her. She doesn't even care about the consequences of killing other members of the trionfi."

Vesta stood up. "What consequences?"

"One of the Elder's laws states that you can't kill one of your own kind. There will be serious repercussions if someone does."

"What repercussions?" She stepped closer to Marco.

"I honestly don't know. I've never been told and haven't read about it in our family history. They implemented the law after the First Blood slaughtered their own almost to extinction."

"That's right. Valentina is the last of the First Blood, right?"

"As far as we know."

"So, she killed her own kind?"

Marco nodded. "My mother lives for battle."

"And you're just going to stand by and watch her rip apart lives, mine included?"

"You don't have the awareness of your past lives like the rest of us. That is because of the spell you cast. But we have lived through so many that we know some turn out better than others."

"In other words, chalk this one up to you just looking the other way and move on to the next life. Better luck next time?" Vesta cocked her head at Marco. "Is that it?"

"If you cooperate with my mother you will live in luxury the remainder of this life. Even though you may not agree with what she is doing, very little would be required of you. Just alert her of what you see coming."

"You mean sit in a palace somewhere knowing the misery I'm supporting but ignore it?"

Vesta pulled the door to her room open wide. "You may be able to do that Marco, but I can't. I won't."

A grimace flashed across his face. "And so your friends die. Forever."

Vesta shook her head. "You sniveling bastard. Get out!"

Marco left and she slammed the door with a bang. Hate for him, and a new word that she needed to invent beyond the word hate toward his mother and Raz gnawed inside every pore of her body. There had to be a way to stop their murderous plan. She looked around the room as if the answer lay in a corner. Still feeling a bit wobbly and definitely stale in her wrinkled, sweat-stained clothes she walked into the bathroom connected to the bedroom. An old-fashioned claw-footed tub stood beside a wall. Maybe a bath would help her think. It would certainly help her look and feel better. But she wrestled with the idea of indulging in one of her favorite activities when she knew she needed to be taking action.

"What is my plan?" She paced the bathroom several times scanning her thoughts. "I have no plan." Her hand clenched into a fist. "Get off this island," she murmured. How? With Valentina surely monitoring all her thoughts it would be impossible. First, she had to do what both Liam and Peter told her to do, and the best way to accomplish that was to relax and focus. A bath would help. Was that just an excuse? No, she decided. It was necessary.

Guilt struggled with logic as she slid into the warm water, a sigh floating past her lips. She closed her eyes and leaned her head against the cool white porcelain of the tub. Recalling the mental expansiveness she felt during her drug-fueled trip she let her mind wander wherever it wanted. The seven colors representing the chakras rolled into view. They pulsated with energy forming into clusters. The mint green orb grew in size until it eclipsed the others, filling the screen of her mind's eye. Vesta felt herself relax, the hate within her turn loose.

The image of a little girl about six years old faded into focus slowly blotting out the green light. Perched on a large rock with an evergreen forest behind her, she smiled at Vesta. Her pale blue eyes sparkled in the sunlight causing the curly white blonde hair on her head look like a halo. Amused, Vesta returned the smile. Something seemed familiar about the girl although she couldn't name what exactly.

"You must block entry into your thoughts by visualizing a wall around your mind. Build it brick by brick staying absolutely focused on what you want to do. Then say your own words of protection to keep others out. Say them slowly and with determination. Do it now."

Vesta furrowed her eyebrows above her closed lids. "Such grown up words for someone so young," she said. The girl smiled again and the image faded. "Don't leave." She stretched out her hand which wasn't a physical hand, she understood, but an extension of her mind, longing for the girl to return yet she had disappeared from any awareness.

As she rolled her head from side to side against the tub, she wondered what her mind would look like. Could she somehow step back and regard her own consciousness? Observe the observer? Puffy white clouds with lightning bolts sparking inside came into view. Around the clouds lay scattered hundreds of dark gray bricks. She saw herself picking them up, heavy and solid, one by one, placing them around the cloud bank. Her breath moving into a deep rhythmic pattern as she focused on the task taking her time to make sure they fit tightly, securely. After the circumference was completely walled in, she covered the top and the bottom of the mass as well, being certain not even a wisp of cloud remained outside. The little girl hadn't mentioned such precision but it seemed vital. Methodically she inspected the wall, that was actually more like a sphere, making certain no crack existed between the bricks. She stepped back appraising the whole and nodded with approval. Choosing her words with care, she began to speak.

"I call upon all my power as the High Priestess of the trionfi to seal this wall so that no one may enter my thoughts ever again. Any attempts will fail and I will be aware of who is trying to gain entry."

She examined the wall a few moments longer before physical sleep wrapped its gentle arms around her carrying her safely into a happy dream about walking hand in hand with Enid on the side of their mountain on a bright summer afternoon.

Vesta awoke when her head dipped deeply to the left causing tepid water to lap against her face. Opening her eyes Vesta realized she had fallen asleep in the bathtub. And by the temperature of the water it had been quite a while earlier. She climbed out and dried herself off realizing the headache was gone and she felt like her normal self again. Her Patek Phillpe watch laying on the dressing table by the sink said it was twelve-fifty. Lunch was being served in ten minutes and even though she wasn't hungry, she needed to engage Valentina and Raz in conversation to figure out a plan of escape.

She pulled her luggage open and chose a Prada ivory silk devoré floral maxi dress. The light blue flowers were the same shade as the dress of the High Priestess on the Waite-Smith tarot cards. It was the closest she could come to matching it but it felt right. She slipped on a pair of Ferragamo sandals and gave her hair a quick comb.

Walking down the hall she could smell garlic cooking and realized that she was starving after all. She hadn't eaten since the sandwich in the car ride from Miami the day before. While she didn't trust the Parrinos, she also didn't believe they would try to poison her. They wanted her help. Eating seemed like a prudent thing to do while she figured out a plan to escape. Following the enticing aroma, she found the dining room toward the back of the house. A row of floor to ceiling windows looked out over a swath of green grass with the startlingly blue ocean beyond. Inside Valentina, Raz, Marco, Francesco and Giovanni were seated at a large oval dining table. A middle-aged woman dressed in a navy polo shirt and white skirt was pouring wine into glasses.

"Vesta," Francesco said from the head of the table. "I'm glad you could join us."

Giovanni stood up and pulled out the chair next to him. "Please," he said.

Vesta sat down. "Thank you. Lunch smells wonderful."

"It is linguine with clam sauce. My mother's recipe from the old world," Francesco said. "And a nice pompano."

The woman walked to Vesta's side. "Would you like some white wine?"

"No thank you."

"It's from our Italian vineyards," Marco said. "Very light and dry."

Vesta shook her head. "I'll pass. Just water."

The woman filled Vesta's water glass and served the meal. As the group began eating Vesta felt a slight twitch in her thoughts and the name Valentina began echoing inside. She was confused for a moment but looked up to see Valentina staring at her with a cold gaze. As she returned to eating she realized that Valentina had tried to read her thoughts but failed and that she had been alerted to who made the attempt. Her protection was working. Vesta smiled to herself.

The group ate in silence. When Francesco finished he placed his napkin on the table.

"I know you have things to discuss." He looked at Valentina, then Vesta. "I will leave you to them," he said.

Giovanni stood up and stepped to his father's side helping him from his chair. The pair walked out of the dining room.

Raz stopped eating and picked up his glass of wine, her waved it toward Vesta. "Have you decided to accept our offer?"

She set her fork down looking directly at Raz. "No. I will not accept it. But I will let Jared, Amara, Liam, Sandor and Cyrus know what you're planning to do. I have a feeling they can handle your pathetic little scheme."

"What about Enid?" Valentina asked.

"My mother is dead."

"Hardly." The gaping wound smile opened up on her face. "Who do you think that blonde girl was in your vision who told you how to block your thoughts? How are you going to warn her?"

Vesta could feel the blood drain from her face. Her body went numb as she stared at Valentina. "My mother is alive? Again?"

Raz chuckled. "Get us more wine," he said to Marco. "This will be a good show."

Marco left the table.

"Of course she is. And I know where. But you don't."

Marco returned with a bottle and refilled Rasputin's glass.

"You wouldn't hurt her. She's just a child."

"She already knows who she is and used the gift to contact you."

Vesta felt panic race through her.

"Now that you've learned how to block your thoughts I must resort to asking you. Are you willing to have your mother killed because you wouldn't cooperate with us?" Valentina looked at Raz. "We might even be able to arrange a video memento of the event."

Raz nodded. "Certainly."

"You are a monster! How can anyone be so evil?"

Valentina leaned her head back and laughed. The sound could have cracked glass on the windows.

"And you, Marco. You sit there and do nothing. You're only half of this malignant thing." She pointed at Valentina. "The other half is a decent man."

"My son was bred to be superior to others and restore the strength of my line. He is handsome and virile giving pleasure to many women, even the old ones, as you know."

Vesta knew Valentina's remark was supposed to dig deep into her ego but the sting was dull. All she felt was disgust.

"You stole Jared's DNA trying to create a superhuman just like your Nazi friends but it didn't work. He's not the demon you hoped for."

"Yes, maybe Jared was too young to give the potency I desired." She looked at her son. "Marco is a good son nevertheless. He obeys my instructions. Jared Schultz was a disappointment."

"Jared is the Emperor in the cards because he is strong and fair and honest."

"He's arrogant and has never tried to be a part of my life," Marco said.

"He's still your blood father. That counts for something," Vesta said.

Marco's cheeks were blushed. "Look at how you treat your father. You despise him."

"It's because he abandoned me and Enid."

"What's the difference? You condemn me while you do the same thing."

Vesta paused. Marco made a valid argument as much as she hadn't wanted to admit it. Now that she knew the reason behind Cyrus's absence from her childhood, she must be more accepting of him. The awareness laid bare her foolish, destructive behavior, and she felt ashamed.

"You're right." She shook her head. The anger she had felt for decades toward her father began to fade like a dark cloud lifting from her soul allowing her to see clearly who he was for the first time. A sprite of fast-moving energy raced up her spine then dove back down, recirculating at a lightning pace, reinvigorating her.

"He is a meddler who deserves to die," Raz said.

Vesta's eyes flashed at him. "You're going to go down hard you bastard. Wait and see."

Raz cackled. "How many times have they tried over the centuries?" He waved his glass toward Valentina who nodded. "In much more brutal ways than they do now. If you want to kill someone go ask a Russian how to do it." He put his lips to the glass. "That is why I keep the name Rasputin. Good luck charm." He laughed again and drank his glass dry.

"We weren't given these gifts to create misery. My uncle said that the Elders chose each one of us to help people. Even you, Valentina. Your First Blood was created to give humankind an advantage at survival. What does it say about us that we turn it into something horrifying?"

"You don't know anything about me or my kind." Her words sounded like a warning.

"She has always been a fool," Raz said.

Valentina stood up. "I've wasted enough time on this matter. If you don't agree right now to join me and Rasputin in our business, I will slaughter every one of your trionfi and make certain they never return again. And I shall start with your precious Empress sister. Then your mother. And I will leave the dead corpse of Peter the Lost in the center of your crumbling labyrinth in France after that."

Vesta gasped before she could stop it as Valentina's words formed a horrifying image in her mind. She wanted to believe that no one could be capable of committing such heartless, demonic actions but now she knew better. She knew Valentina would if she didn't help her. Vesta's hands began to shake with fear.

"That drug, it will kill people."

"Not necessarily," Raz said. "You had a good trip around the moon. You didn't die."

"But if I help, you will be unstoppable. There will be

millions of people addicted to it. It could change the course of history on this planet."

Valentina began to laugh. Vesta wanted to cover her ears to block the shrill sound. People would die no matter which choice she made. And if she made no choice? Valentina would kill the trionfi and still spread the drugs around the world.

"Please don't do this," Vesta knew she had lost. A tear rolled down her cheek. She wiped it away and straightened her posture.

"What is your answer?"

Giovanni walked into the room and whispered into Marco's ear.

"You're certain?" Marco said.

Valentina jerked her head toward her son. Marco stared at her for a moment before speaking. "One of our boats has been boarded by customs."

"Where?" Valentina growled.

"In the Key West marina."

"Merda." Valentina said as she pushed herself from the table and stood up. "You will give your answer to me when I return." She pointed at Vesta before she turned and walked out of the room. "Or they will all die."

Marco and Giovanni followed their mother. Raz began to laugh, his huge flaccid belly jiggling up and down. "Finally, some entertainment."

"Where's a phone?" Vesta stood up. Raz ignored her as he reached for the wine bottle.

Vesta left the dining room and walked through the house. In the parlor she found a telephone. The large man still wearing the navy shirt followed her.

"You can't call anyone," he said.

"I need to let my assistant know I won't be in the office in the morning. If I don't, she will send out people looking for me."

"No one can find you here." He picked up the phone from the table and unplugged it. A dull smile flickered on his lips. "Useless to try." He lumbered out of the room with the telephone in the crook of his arm.

Vesta's jaw tightened and she fought the urge to scream. She had made up the reason for the phone, it was the first thing that popped into her mind, but she really did need to check in at Sybarite. Not showing up, not calling simply wasn't an option. Jenny would know something was wrong but she wouldn't call the police right away. No one knew where she was. The thought of jeopardizing her job added more panic. She had to get off the island. Vesta's eyes darted around the room. Nothing within view looked helpful. She rushed to the garden room door and swung it open.

Outside the sea breeze had settled underneath a vibrant blue sky. Walking beyond the garden Vesta realized that the island wasn't large. The house sat on one end anchored by a pool and tennis court clustered near the garden. Walking out to the edge beyond the palms and hibiscus, a wide lawn stretched for several hundred yards then transitioned into sand and rock all the way to the opposite end of the island about a half mile away. No one followed her so she continued to walk along a paved wide pathway that lead to a point.

As she neared the end of the island a dark gray surface shimmering in the heat came into view. She recognized the giant symbol painted in the center, a red heart with three swords slashed through it. The same symbol on the boat and above the mantle in the Napa Valley house.

She looked around at the enormous expanse of asphalt. "Helipad," she said to herself.

From her vantage point, she could see other small islands floating in the distance like dead flies on the bright blue ocean. Nothing was even remotely close to the island she stood on. She was ridiculously isolated. Shouting for help wouldn't do any good. Neither would waving her arms. And there were no boats visible in any direction.

But there was a boat house somewhere on the island. The thin man in the navy shirt mentioned it. She turned her back to the helipad and spotted a large dock on the other side of the house. Her pulse doubled in pace as she ran toward it. A thick chain-link fence stretched from the wooden planks of the dock to the rafters and spanned the length of the covered open-air building. The only entrance appeared to be through a gate which was secured with a giant padlock. Beyond the fence the boat she boarded in Key West, the Regina Spada, lay docked next to four other boats. Vesta picked up the heavy lock and turned it over in her hands for a solid minute searching for a way to pick it. She blew out a deep exhale letting it drop. Getting past the fence wouldn't be easy.

"She's at the dock."

Vesta jerked her head toward the voice as she saw the large man in the navy shirt speak into a walkie-talkie. He approached her with quick steps. She considered running but realized it would ultimately be pointless as there was no safe place on the island where she could escape.

"Madame wants you back at the house now." He reached out to take her by the arm. "And it looks like a storm is coming so hurry."

Vesta took a step back from him. "Don't touch me. I will go."

As she walked toward the house, she was stunned by how much the weather had changed in the few minutes since she had been in the boathouse. Dark clouds had gathered in the sky but they felt oddly close as though they were just above her head. The wind began to whirl around her as thunder rumbled from all directions.

The approaching storm outside of her echoed the gathering

storm inside. Valentina would demand an answer as soon as she returned to the house. The idea of helping her and Raz distribute drugs around the world was unacceptable. But if she didn't agree to it then the drug laced with her own blood would kill the trionfi. Vesta shivered from the adrenaline rushing through her. There had to be another option. On the periphery of her intuitive sense something began to seep in that she couldn't quite grasp. Something vital to the situation that she was so close to understanding yet remained concealed an inch beyond her psychic reach. Her third eye lit up like a lantern as validation to her thought but provided her no clues beyond that. And she was out of time.

CHAPTER 22

Vesta followed the large man into the parlor as a loud crack of thunder bellowed from the sky. He nudged Vesta into the room and stationed himself in front of the garden room door. Valentina sat in one of the wingback chairs while Raz perched on the sofa looking pleased. The thin man called Diego stood in the doorway leading to the hall. Marco stood close by his mother.

"Did your drug ring get busted?" Vesta asked trying her best to act calm as she surveyed the room.

Valentina smirked. "One of the boats that cannot be traced to us was boarded but there was nothing to find." She waved her hand. "Perhaps a feeble attempt by one of the others trying to locate you."

Vesta's heart beat faster.

"Don't feel encouraged. They will never find you here. My protection spell won't allow them to see where you are. And now that you've closed your thoughts," Valentina smiled. "They never will."

"Let's get on with it. I wish to leave the heat of this wretched place," Raz said.

"Yes, time to hear your decision." Valentina stood up. "Will you agree to be our partner or will you send your friends, father and mother to their death?"

"There has to be another option," Vesta spoke with rapid words. "Listen, there has to be another option."

"There are no other options. You must make your choice immediately or I will make it for you."

"I need just a little more time to think about it." Vesta's eyes raced around the room looking for something, anything to help.

"No! You waste my time. And I'll show you what happens when someone wastes my time." Valentina's emerald eyes flashed.

"Diego," she motioned with her hand. The thin man walked to the side of her chair and knelt down. As she whispered in his ear his eyes cut a sharp glance across the room toward the garden door. She handed him a syringe that she pulled from a pocket in her silk jumpsuit. Diego stood up.

Valentina turned her attention to the large man in the navy polo shirt who stared back at her. Vesta saw her eyes widen as her pupils narrowed. At the same moment, a crackling sensation fired up between her own eyebrows while a low hum started to vibrate in her ears. The First Blood's gaze froze in that position for a count of four, maybe five, seconds before she snapped her fingers. Vesta felt the crackling in her third eye stop and the vibration dissipate. The man's head lurched forward slightly hanging at an odd angle while he started to shuffle from the garden door across the room.

"Sit down there," she said pointing at the sofa.

Raz made a disgruntled sound as he wiggled in heavy plops to the far end away from the large man as he sunk down onto a cushion.

Even though she had never seen anything like it before anywhere but the movies, and never imagined it to be possible in real life, she realized Valentina had cast something like a spell on the man who now moved as if he were sleep walking, or in a trance. He was clearly following her instructions. "What are you doing?" Vesta asked.

Diego walked over to the large man and pulled the cap off of the syringe.

"I told you others would suffer if you did not cooperate with me."

"Don't do that! You can't do that!" Vesta screamed. "He works for you. He's loyal to you."

The large man looked down at his arm as Diego placed the needle against it. His face registered no response when the thin man plunged the needle and the contents of the syringe into him. Vesta recoiled at the sight.

"You drugged him just to show me how cruel you are?"

"No." The smile that sliced across Valentina's face looked like a gaping wound. "Half that amount would have drugged him."

A gurgling noise rattled from the large man followed by gasps as he slammed against the back of the sofa in a violent spasm. He clutched at his throat as his feet kicked against the low table in front of him.

"Help him!" Vesta screamed. "Don't let him die!" Sweat sprang from her body coating her in a thin glaze. Her heart beat like it was bursting out of her chest. She watched the large man in the navy polo shirt jerk and sway for a moment longer then collapse in a heap falling toward Raz.

Clucking under his breath Raz pushed at the man's head. "Get that thing away from me."

Diego reached over pulling the lifeless body into an upright position, leaving the open eyes to stare blankly into the room.

"Oh my God! You're a monster!" Vesta screamed at Valentina. "Both of you." She looked at Raz. "All of you!" She swung her head toward Marco who registered no emotion.

"I told you what would happen." Valentina picked up a crystal glass sitting beside her and took a sip of clear liquid that Vesta guessed was water. "You did not believe me?"

Deep thumping sounds Vesta thought might be her own heartbeat, hammered in her ears. An urgent message from her brain to collect her thoughts, but she couldn't. The horrifying scene she had just witnessed was more than she could emotionally process.

"Will you become partners with me and Rasputin using your InSight to keep our business safe? Or will you send your friends and father," Valentina nodded. "And mother to their final deaths in a manner exactly like this?"

Raz chuckled. "That would be a delight to see this time around."

Between Vesta's eyebrows a blaze spread out from her third eye that felt like it scorched her skin. She clutched her forehead. "What do you mean, this time?"

Raz threw his head back letting a full-throated laugh gurgle out. "No one has told you?" He leaned forward to perch on the edge of the sofa as though he were a child about to open a birthday gift.

"Told me what?"

"How Enid died the time before this one."

"Yes, tell her Rasputin," Valentina purred as she licked her lips.

"You convinced your mother to run into the field and hide," he said, eyes lighting up.

Every muscle in Vesta's body stiffened as the words Raz spoke caused an image to form in her mind.

"Stupid idea. As usual from you," she heard him say as the room in the Florida Keys dissolved from her view. In its place a bright blue sky shone above a field of golden wheat waving waist-high around her. Enid, dressed in a drab gray blouse and long skirt, her white wispy hair tucked under a black cap, stood close by. A thundering sound cracked through the air.

"Mama, get down!" Vesta heard herself yell. "Lie on the ground!"

"Are you sure? Maybe we can make it to the oaks," Enid called out.

The rumbling noise grew louder, punctuated by metal shrieking and scraping in fits and bursts. Vesta could feel her heart beating at a wild pace.

"They will see us. Get down!"

Enid flattened out amongst the tall stalks of wheat, Vesta throwing herself beside her mother on the dry ground. The roar deafening as the earth shook. Above them the blue sky became blotted out by blackness. Vesta grabbed Enid's hand and held on tight. Piercing through the monotonous roar of the Nazi Panzer tank, bullets zipped through the air all around them. She turned loose of Enid's hand to muffle the sickening sound raging in her ears. They waited, lying still for endless minutes in the wheat field until the shrieks and roars of the terrible machine rolled far into the distance. Vesta lifted her head and whispered. "Now let's run for the oaks Mama."

She pulled herself up to a sitting position and grabbed Enid's hand again. "Mama! They're gone. Let's go."

A chill shot through her from the base of her spine through the top of her head. The hand she grabbed no longer carried the spark of life. She knew it within that split second but cried out anyway. "Mama! Get up!"

No response came from Enid.

"Let's run for the oaks like you said," Vesta begged.

Tears began to flow down her cheeks and she felt like she was drowning on the inside. "No!" She screamed as the bright blue sky and golden wheat began to fade from her sight.

Vesta wiped the tears from her cheeks as the room in Key

West Florida seeped back into view. She looked at Raz who grinned, eyes still gleaming.

"Yes, you were responsible for Enid's death. She trusted you but your poor judgement once again caused someone to die."

"Where," Vesta stumbled through her words. "Where was that place that I saw? With the wheat field."

"It was somewhere in Poland," Valentina said. "You two were trying to help those wretched people escape my Third Reich. But you were only fools who got yourselves killed."

"And then you put the curse upon yourself to forget who you are in this life, so great was your guilt of killing your mother."

Vesta knew Raz spoke the truth. It resonated throughout her mind and body that was the reason why she cast the spell. Now she understood why none of the other trionfi wanted to tell her. She looked down at the floor, speechless, still feeling the pain of what she saw.

Valentina broke the silence. "Time sixty seconds on your watch starting now." She looked at Marco. "Now you must make your choice." She pointed at Vesta. "There will be no further discussion."

Vesta jerked her head up. "Wait! You have to give me more time. There has to be another way."

"No," Valentina said as Raz began to chuckle again.

Marco stared at his watch. Vesta's breathing became shallow. Inside her mind she begged her InSight to give her the third option. She knew another one existed. She felt it in the way she had felt other things that came into being. Why couldn't she see it?

She glanced at Valentina knowing her final seconds of prolonging the situation were at hand. Ditching her intuitive sense, she began thinking of logical ways to negotiate. Nothing came to mind. She either capitulated to her demands or the trionfi would die. Either way people were going to die.

"Ten seconds," Marco said.

A cold sweat broke out on Vesta's forehead. She could hear thunder rattling outside to the point it almost shook the house.

"Time's up," he said as lightning flashed beyond the garden room doors.

"What will it be, your Highness?" The First Blood spoke with a calm, measured tone.

"If I agree," she stumbled for words. "Will you destroy the drug that has my blood in it?"

The hideous gaping wound slid across Valentina's face baring a little row of white teeth. "No."

"Why not? You won't have any use for it if I agree to help."

"I would never consider destroying something so precious. What is your choice? Name it now."

"I, I will," Vesta's voice trembled and she wanted to vomit. "I will agree to join you. But you have to swear that you won't hurt any of the other trionfi."

A satisfied look settled on Valentina's face. "I will do better than that. You and I will write out a blood vow that consecrates our deal."

Vesta stared in numb silence watching Valentina, wondering how the life she so carefully designed and struggled to get turned into an utter nightmare.

Raz cackled as he leaned forward on the sofa. "Ah, the mighty priestess at last has fallen."

Valentina snapped her fingers and Diego walked over to a small table in the corner by the hallway and picked up a silver tray. On it was a rolled up piece of parchment paper, two small bowls, an old-fashioned ink pen, a stack of white napkins and a knife. He set the tray on the largest table in the room.

"Marco," his mother said. "Roll out the paper and hold it for us. You are the witness."

He walked to the table and spread out the single sheet of

thick paper. Vesta could see writing in black ink scrawled across it. Valentina walked to the table and motioned for Vesta. The wind howled outside and shook the French doors. Lightning struck close by again and bright light flashed inside the room.

"Read it," she said to her.

With hands shaking so badly that she could barely pick up the paper, Vesta lifted the parchment and began to read. It stated that Vesta Beauvais, by her own choice, entered into this agreement with Valentina Parrino and Rasputin Dragomirov. It spelled out her responsibilities of providing InSight to both of the other parties regarding the successful transportation and distribution of the products they manufactured. The agreement would be in effect for the remainder of her current life.

Vesta looked up at Valentina. "Why do I have to sign it in blood?"

"Because it is unbreakable at that point. It is something the Elders created." She cocked her head to the side. "For other reasons, it is true. But it serves our purpose well today."

"What happens if I do break it?"

"The others will die for the last time by my hand, and so will you."

Vesta wanted to vomit. She wanted to run away, throw herself into the wicked weather outside, do anything other than what she was about to do. Casting a quick glance toward Marco she noticed he looked uneasy too, but he averted his gaze from her toward the storm.

Valentina picked up the knife and slid the sharp blade across her left palm. Vesta winced at the pain that must be present but noticed the expression on Valentina's face was almost ecstasy as a deep slice opened across her skin. Blood swelled to the surface. She held her hand over one of the small bowls as fat, thick drops fell into it.

"See how easy it is?" Valentina picked up the metal-tipped

pen and dipped it in the bowl. She moved the pen over to the parchment paper. In large letters she scrawled her name across the page.

"Now it's your turn," she said handing the knife to her.

The room was quiet to the point that she could hear Marco breathing as though he was lying beside her again after having spoken soft, playful words into her ear. Her hands shook and her palms were glistening with sweat. She wasn't sure she could hold the knife. "My hands," she began to say.

"You are useless except for your InSight." Valentina grabbed Vesta's left hand and sliced the knife across it.

Pain shot through her, a throbbing started in her hand and began moving up her arm. Valentina jerked Vesta's hand above the second small bowl. She watched her blood dribble in making a shallow puddle as white light streaked past her and the silence in the room was obliterated by a loud cracking sound. All eyes turned in the direction of the garden.

Through the garden room doors, they could see palm trees, philodendron and hibiscus snarled by the wind. Giant leaves ripped off their stems and flew away in a mad dance. Valentina's distracted attention caused her grip on Vesta to loosen. She jerked her hand away. Blood dripped in heavy drops on her dress staining some of the high priestess blue flowers a deep purple.

Voices shouted from the garden. Diego ran toward it, threw the doors open and disappeared outside. More loud cracking sounds that Vesta recognized not as thunder but as gunshots rang out. Raz scrambled up from the sofa and toddled the opposite way out of the room. Valentina leapt to a corner by the desk and reached inside what Vesta at first thought was an umbrella stand but quickly realized it wasn't. From it she pulled out a long scabbard. A thin, polished blade emerged from its sheath and

Valentina with eyes glowing a strange reddish-green ran with it into the garden.

Marco moved toward Vesta. She pushed him away. He grabbed one of the napkins off the tray, took her hand and wrapped the napkin around it.

"Hold it above your heart," he said.

Vesta grasped the napkin wrapping it tighter around her hand to stop some of the pain as she glanced at Marco who stood calmly beside her. Why didn't he run outside with Valentina? She began to walk toward the garden.

"No, don't go out there. You'll be safer here," he said.

"I want to see what's going on. And why aren't you out there helping your mother?"

More shouting erupted from the garden but words were impossible to decipher over the roaring wind. Thunder shrieked above them as Sandor ran into the room with Valentina's sword in his hand.

"Are you alright?" He bolted toward her. Marco walked to a chair and sat down.

Vesta had never seen Sandor's eyes so wild or his cool demeanor so rattled. And despite the tense situation they were in at the moment, seeing him wearing green fatigues and combat boots, looking like a life-size GI Joe doll, made her almost burst out laughing.

"Are you hurt?" He reached for her bloody hand.

"Just a cut. I'm fine," she said trying to sound calm, realizing in that second that fortune had shifted back in her favor, and that this was the third option she could feel instinctively but couldn't see coming.

"What's going on?" She asked hearing more shouting outside.

"A rescue, of course. Are there more goons here in the

house?" Sandor glanced over at the dead man propped on the sofa. "Other than him?"

Vesta shook her head. "I don't think so. How did you know I was here?"

"You told Peter to call Amara, so he did."

"I meant here on this island." Vesta looked down at her hand to inspect her wound.

Sandor picked up the sheath lying on the floor and placed the sword back into it. Another crash of thunder shook the windows as lightning immediately echoed in response sending a flash of white light through the room. The garden room doors banged hard against the walls inside several times breaking glass in most of the panes. The piece of parchment paper holding Valentina's signature blew off the table. Vesta jerked her head up to see Amara walk into the room dressed in the same green fatigues as Sandor, her long blonde hair pulled back into a ponytail. She waved at Vesta.

"Give me a minute," she said breathing heavily. The wooden frames of the doors shuddered on their hinges.

In a quick motion Amara sat down on the chaise lounge, closed her eyes and brought her legs into a lotus pose. She became very still. Vesta watched as a pale golden glow emerged around her body. It hovered close to her and intensified in color to a bright yellow then turned into a soft green light before fading away.

"What's happening to her?"

"She's calling off the storm," Sandor said.

Vesta furrowed her eyebrows and stared at him. He pointed his index finger up.

"Listen," he said.

The rumbling thunder and rush of wind began to slow. Everything fell silent outside a minute later. Amara opened her eyes and smiled. "I could really use some water," she said.

"I'll get it," Marco stood up and left the room just as Jared walked in from the garden.

Cyrus followed close behind pulling Valentina into the room by her arm. She saw that the First Blood was wearing handcuffs. And she gasped when she noticed that Cyrus had a large blood-stain on the left sleeve of his fatigue shirt.

"You were shot!"

"Flesh wound, that's all." He tugged Valentina's arm. "She got only one glancing blow in before Sandor disarmed her."

Vesta whirled around to look at Sandor. "You disarmed her?"

He cocked his head and grinned.

Marco walked back into the room with a glass of water for Amara. He handed it to her.

"My son was not involved in this. You must set him free," Valentina said.

"Well he was involved," Jared replied. "But not in the way you're thinking."

"He did what was in the best interest of everyone in the world," Amara said. "And he's well on his way to redeeming himself as a member of the trionfi."

Marco lifted his chin and looked directly at Valentina. "You see mother, I do possess my own strength of mind. You were just unaware of it."

"What are you saying? You are responsible for them being here? You overrode my protective shield?" She shook her head. "That's impossible. Only thoughts shared by a direct blood line member could penetrate the shield. And she," Valentina pointed at Vesta. "blocked her thoughts like a fortress. Even the Empress over there wouldn't have been able to get through that. And certainly not you." Valentina glared at Cyrus.

Marco raised his eyebrows and looked at Jared, who smiled in return and nodded his head. The Page of Swords looked back at his mother.

"I could not watch you go any further with killing and the spreading of this drug."

Valentina's eyes flashed bright green tinged with streaks of red. "You betrayed me! And with this man who is nothing to you but a donor of his sperm. I will kill you for this," Valentina shouted.

"You underestimated the half of him that is Jared," Amara said with a smile.

"I don't think Marco should be too worried," Cyrus said. "You're going into custody with the Feds who have a half dozen charges all ready for you. The manufacturing and distribution of illegal drugs across international borders is only the beginning. There's also kidnapping and several weapons charges they'll throw in."

"You should have stayed in your lane with your price jacking of those basically worthless old Roman coins you were pilfering," Sandor said. "We weren't going to bust you for that."

Vesta nodded. "So, they were smuggling antiques too."

Valentina wiggled in her handcuffs. "You may have slowed me down temporarily but Rasputin will make sure my end of the bargain will be successful."

"You mean injecting all of us with that drug you souped up with Vesta's blood?" Sandor said. "Yeah, that won't happen. Marco told Jared where your lab was too in their little Vulcan mind meld. The Feds are there right now. And as far as Rasputin goes, we caught his fat ass running for the boat dock. He's going back into custody with Scotland Yard. He won't be released this time."

"Why did you do this Marco?" Valentina stared at her son. "You had everything, and now you have nothing."

Marco looked past the people in the room out into the fresh sunshine of the garden. "When Vesta admitted that she had been wrong about her father."

Cyrus glanced at Vesta. She could feel herself blushing.

"I realized I had been wrong about a couple of major things and that it was never too late to make amends." He looked at Valentina again. "You were disappointed in Giovanni when he didn't exhibit the murderous spirit you have. So you tricked Jared's mother into his DNA to create me. Then when I didn't have the lust for killing, you settled for me being just another servant."

Marco shook his head. "You never once tried to understand what I cared about. Nothing matters to you except who you can destroy next. And while I followed with your schemes for a long time, I realized that you were stepping over a line I did not want to cross. Today I own who I truly am."

"You are a worthless son. And you will pay for what you've done."

Marco shrugged. "Maybe I will. We'll see."

"The helicopter is ready to go," Cyrus said. "I've heard enough from Tina here."

Valentina cut a razor-sharp glance at him. "You know I hate that name," she hissed.

"Yes, I do. Let's go." Cyrus led her out of the room.

"The helicopter, was that the thumping noise I heard?" Vesta looked around the room for an answer.

"Yes," Amara said. "I created the storm so hopefully no one would hear the helicopter landing."

Vesta looked down at her left hand. She removed the napkin and looked at the wound. Blood had stopped oozing from the gash but it was a nasty cut. Amara stood up from the chaise lounge and approached her.

"Let me see that." She took Vesta's hand in her own and closed her eyes. Moving her other hand above the knife wound in a slow circular motion she began saying strange words that sounded more like dove coos. A peculiar itching sensation prickled Vesta's hand. As she watched the wound began to close and pink skin lay where the slash in her hand had been.

"How did you do that?"

Amara patted Vesta's healed hand and turned it loose.

"It's one of my gifts. Major wounds are more challenging but this was easy."

Marco stepped beside Vesta. "I heard you could do this but never believed it," he said to Amara. "That is amazing."

Amara smiled. "Thanks for your help."

"I'm no hero. And now with my mother gone, at least for a while, I can run the family business as I want. In a legal fashion. My father is too infirm to do any more and my brother needs to keep his distance from it."

Jared cleared his throat. "Marco, I want to thank you too."

Marco took a step back. "I neither want nor need anything from you. You're not my father. At best we can hope to be friends one day. But for now, I respect you for the position you hold in our group. That is enough."

Jared nodded.

"I will get the key to the boathouse from my mother's safe. You are free to take any boat back to Key West." Marco left the room.

Vesta put her hand up to her head. "Oh my God what a day. I have to call Jenny at the office before it gets any later." She motioned toward Sandor. "Do you have a cell phone?"

"Here you go," he fished one out of his pants' pocket and handed it to her. "Now we need to get that blood off your party dress."

Vesta smiled at the welcome comic relief. "Party dress? At least I'm not outfitted head to toe in drab green." Vesta glanced at Amara. "No offense."

Amara lifted her hand and smiled. "None taken."

Vesta turned back to Sandor. "I need a photo of you dressed this. I never have a camera when I need one." She looked at Jared waving the cell phone. "Why can't you make these things take photos too since we're always carrying them around with us?"

She turned and walked out of the room, across the black and white harlequin-patterned entry floor, and down the long hallway to her room. She changed out of the Prada dress but left the bloodstains on it. The way she looked at it, her blood on the dress represented her initiation back into the trionfi. She had earned the right to be the High Priestess once more.

Marco returned with the key and the group walked down to the boathouse. Jared chose the Regina Spada for the trip to Key West. When they arrived Vesta, Sandor, Amara and Jared disembarked leaving Marco on the boat. They watched him pull out from the dock and cruise from the harbor into open water and his new life. Amara pulled out her phone and walked away from the group.

"Will he face charges too?" Vesta asked.

"No," Jared said. "Nor Francesco or Giovanni. While they knew that Valentina was plotting with Rasputin, they all only recently learned about her getting involved in the drug trade. And Marco was the one who alerted me. I'm sure he will testify against her."

"They'll all have a new life without Valentina breathing down their necks," Sandor said.

"What about his next life?" Vesta asked. "I mean, Marco returns as the Page of Swords again, right." She shook her head. "I can only imagine what Valentina will do to him to get revenge."

"He won't have me as a father next time," Jared said. "Francesco will be unless Valentina chooses someone else.

Marco won't be the same person again. And he won't remember this life at all. The minor arcana members never do. Their previous lives are recorded in a family history that is shared when they reach the age of ten."

A sad smile crept across Vesta's face. "So, he's only going to be this person once."

Jared nodded. Vesta turned around to look out across the water. Marco's boat had disappeared into the horizon.

"I hope he makes the best of it."

"Well," Amara said in a happy tone as she rejoined the group. "I have reserved a room at Casa Marina. I think we should change out of our battle gear and go for a lovely dinner somewhere."

"That sounds fine," Jared said. "We would like to share some information with you, Vesta. And we could use your help on a couple of other projects we have working. Maybe we could discuss those things briefly during dinner."

"Sure. I have a room at that hotel too," Vesta said.

"Did you get one for me?" Sandor asked looking at Amara.

"I'm sorry, I didn't."

Sandor let a sly smile slide across his face as he pulled a red rose from the inside of his drab green fatigue shirt and handed it to Vesta. "Do you think I can share yours just for tonight?"

She laughed as she admired the rose, still perfect in its shape after all it must have been through. "Maybe," she said. "Let's see how dinner goes."

THE END

Read the next book in the series, The Red King, as Vesta steps into her power as the High Priestess of the tarot. But she's in a race against time to save a sacred guardian—or risk the destruction of humanity. Thrust into a perilous world of alchemy, ancient rites, and shadowy forces, Vesta must uncover the truth, and time is running out.

Get free bonus chapters, and be the first to know about new releases. Join Victoria's newsletter, victoriabelue.com.

ABOUT THE AUTHOR

Victoria Belue is the author of The Tarot Legacies series, which includes six books: The Hand Dealt, The Wild Card, The Red King, The Seven Pentacles Prophecy, The Everlasting Day, and The Time Rip Chronicle. She is also the author of The Fairforest Witches series.

In her previous life, she was an award-winning writer and producer for network television while spending weekends reading tarot cards for friends and clients. On a plane ride to Hawaii, the first story in the series popped into her mind fully formed.

She stacked the deck focusing her attention on The Tarot Legacies, while still reading cards. The wheel of fortune has turned in her favor since.

If she's not at home writing her next book in the series, you can probably find her walking in the ancient Medieval labyrinth at Chartres Cathedral in France. It's a magical vortex amid stunning 13th-century stained glass windows and high Gothic arches. Plus there's a crypt underneath hiding many secrets.

Victoria shares her discoveries about this cathedral and other legendary places in her series and on Facebook and Instagram.

Remember, magic is part of our world every day if you know where to look.